CastLe HaNGNaiL

CASTLE HANGNAIL

BY
Ursula Vernon

DIAL BOOKS for YOUNG READERS
an imprint of Penguin Group (USA) LLC

DIAL BOOKS FOR YOUNG READERS
Published by the Penguin Group
Penguin Group (USA) LLC
375 Hudson Street
New York, New York 10014

USA/Canada/UK/Ireland/Australia/New Zealand/India/South Africa/China
PENGUIN.COM
A Penguin Random House Company

Library of Congress Cataloging-in-Publication Data
Vernon, Ursula.
Castle Hangnail / Ursula Vernon.   pages cm
Summary: When little, twelve-year-old Molly arrives at Castle Hangnail to fill the
vacancy for a wicked witch, the minions who dwell there have no choice but to give
her the job; at first it seems she will be able to keep the castle open, but Molly has
quite a few secrets that could cause trouble.
ISBN 978-0-8037-4129-4 (hardback)
[1. Witches—Fiction. 2. Magic—Fiction. 3. Haunted houses—Fiction.
4. Humorous stories.] I. Title.
PZ7.V5985Cc 2015   [Fic]—dc23   2014017106

Printed in the United States of America
1   3   5   7   9   10   8   6   4   2

Designed by Jennifer Kelly
Text set in Horley Old Style MT Std

For Kevin, my favorite minion

It was a marvelously
dark and dour twilight at the castle.

Clouds the color of bruises lay across the hills.
Rooks and ravens flapped into the battlements
and were met by bats leaving for the evening.
True, there were only three ravens,
but there were plenty of bats, so
the overall impression
was of a small cloud of
winged smoke hanging over
the highest tower.
The castle guardian was pleased.

Sadly, Castle Hangnail was not surrounded by jagged mountains, which would have been ideal, but you couldn't have everything. The grassy hills around the castle were doing their best impression of a blasted moor. The guardian tried not to notice the dandelions growing on the hillside. They were much too cheerful. He would go and have a word with the gardener tomorrow.

It was a *good* Evil castle, he thought fiercely. Anyone would be proud to have it! Even with the dandelions and the aging ravens and the unreliable plumbing. Castle Hangnail had *history*. Dark and terrible deeds had been done there. Probably.

He shuffled an empty teacup out of the way. Someone had left it on an end table near the door, and he hid it behind a stuffed crocodile.

The ravens had assured him that the new Master or Mistress of the castle would arrive tonight.

He hung about the main door, waiting. Would it be an Evil Wizard? A Dark Sorceress? A Loathsome Hag?

He hoped it wasn't the Hag. A certain degree of dust and cobwebs were expected in an Evil castle, but a really dedicated Loathsome Hag would have slime dripping off the walls and dead mice at the dinner table. It got to the point where you were embarrassed to have people over.

But an Evil Wizard, now . . . well, there was a lot to

 2

be said for an Evil Wizard. Or a Witch. A Wicked Witch would be just fine. Perhaps she'd even have a cat.

The guardian was fond of cats.

Really, though, he wasn't picky. Any proper Master would do. Necromancer. Cursed Beastlord. Even an ordinary Mad Scientist.

"It's been so long . . ." he said out loud. "I was afraid no one would answer the letters."

"You're telling me," said Edward, clanking. "And all those nasty letters from the Board! I was starting to worry that I'd have to go down to the crypt and see if I could find our old Master, the ancient Vampire Lord, but I wasn't sure I'd be able to get back up again, with my joints."

"I'll get you some oil for them tomorrow," said the guardian absently.

"Oil won't help. I've rusted solid all through the knees." The magical suit of armor sighed. "Well, it wouldn't have mattered. We'd need blood to bring him back, and I don't think you've got much in you."

"I've got plenty of blood," said the guardian, peering out the peephole. "I keep it down in the cellar, where it's nice and cool. We gave away at least a dozen bottles of O negative during the blood drive last Christmas."

A blood drive was not the sort of thing you could imagine an Evil Sorceress allowing, mind you, but you had to move with the times. That was one of the problems with raising the old Vampire Lord. He was very old-fashioned. He'd have been flitting around the town, biting people's necks, before you could say "stake." It was easier just to leave him quietly dead.

"Did the ravens say anything?" asked Edward.

The guardian shrugged. "They're ravens. They mostly see the tops of people's heads. They said the Master-or-Mistress was walking."

"Hmm." Edward thought about that.

There was nothing inherently *wrong* with walking to your new castle, of course. The last Witch had walked. The Evil Sorceress before her had ridden in on the back of a Dark Phoenix, though, and the Wizards all had dragons. There was nothing like a dragon to really make an entrance.

"Perhaps the new Master just wants to take in the scenery," said the guardian.

"That's probably it."

He hoped the scenery would be satisfactory. By darkness it should be all right. By daylight, the land around Castle Hangnail insisted on being picturesque, and Miss Handlebram down the road had a white picket fence, but perhaps the new Master wouldn't notice.

And the castle had crypts! Proper crypts, not just a wine cellar with a coffin shoved in the back. Plus a moat. Well, a mini-moat. Surely that would make up for the picket fence.

The guardian looked through the peephole again.

"Getting on full dark soon," said Edward as he leaned back.

"Perhaps they'll come at moonrise," said the guardian. "Moonrise is perfectly respectable."

It was actually a few minutes before moonrise when the *someone* lifted the door knocker and banged it down, hard.

The guardian *wanted* to throw the door open. He wanted to cheer and throw confetti. The Master—or Mistress—had arrived!

But he had been a castle guardian for centuries, and he knew what was expected.

He waited for five long seconds, then allowed the door to creak open. The hinges squealed like a dying rabbit.

He looked out.

He looked up.

He looked left.

He looked right.

Finally he looked down.

Ravens mostly see the tops of people's heads. It does not occur to them that some people are shorter than others, because when you fly, *everyone* is shorter than you are.

A small, determined face looked up at him. It belonged to a girl wearing black clothes, a black coat, and a silver necklace with a vulture on it.

She looked to be about twelve years old.

"My name is Molly," said the girl. "I'm here to be your Wicked Witch."

CHAPTER 2

What the guardian saw was a plump girl with a round face, a stubborn chin, and frizzy brown hair. She was wearing black boots with metal caps on the end. They were very serious boots. Molly had laced them with purple shoelaces. They looked as if they could kick a hole in a stone wall and have fun doing it.

What Molly saw was a very old man in layers of gray rags. Parts of him looked to have been dead for quite some time.

He was not naturally a hunchback, but he was making up for it by walking bent over and keeping his shoulders drawn up around his ears. He had scars and sutures and one white, clouded eye.

Because he was hunched over and she had on very tall boots, she only had to look up a little to see into his eyes.

"*You're* the Wicked Witch?" said the guardian.

"Yes?" said Molly. She fingered her vulture necklace nervously.

"Are . . . are you sure?"

"Oh, quite sure."

The last Sorceress had been nearly six feet tall, with hair the color of bleached bone and eyes like chips of flint. Molly had brown eyes, and the only way she would ever be six feet tall would be if she stood on a stepladder.

"A *Wicked* Witch?"

"Extremely Wicked," said Molly. "It would curl your hair, how Wicked I am."

(This was purely academic, as the guardian had not had much hair for at least a century.)

"A Wicked *Witch*, though," said the guardian.

"Very Witchy." Molly tilted her head. "I've got loads of silver jewelry. And I like snakes. And toads. I had a pet toad back home."

"A familiar?" asked the guardian hopefully.

". . . sure," said Molly. "A familiar. Definitely."

"I don't suppose he's here now?"

"Well, no," said Molly. "He had a family and a nice pond in the backyard and I didn't want to make him unhappy. Mom promised to feed him mealworms every other day, though."

"One moment," said the guardian, shutting the door.

The guardian had a problem, and not just Edward hissing, "Is it a Sorceress? I want to see!" behind him.

He'd never seen a Mistress this young before. If she was the real Mistress, he was definitely wrong to keep her waiting, and he really shouldn't shut the door in her face, but if she *wasn't* the Mistress—if she was an imposter, say—then when the *real* Mistress arrived, there was going to be a *very* unpleasant scene. It would probably involve screaming and fireballs and some of the torture devices in the spare bedroom.

On the other hand, there were the boots. The boots had to count for something.

"It's not a Loathsome Hag, is it?" whispered Edward, who had been hiding behind the door.

"No, no . . ." The guardian waved him into silence. "It's a Wicked Witch. I think."

"Yay, a Witch!"

"Hush! There might be a problem!"

The guardian poked his head out the door again. Molly was still standing there, gazing up at the tower with vague nearsighted interest.

"You *can* do magic, right?" Magic was a requirement in a new Master, unless you were a Mad Scientist, and Molly didn't look like the sort to hook lightning rods up to cadavers while wild theremins wailed in the background.

"Absolutely," said Molly. "I've got a book of potions. And I can turn invisible if I hold my breath."

The guardian rubbed the back of his neck.

"You seem a little . . . young."

"I'm smart for my age. I can read at a tenth-grade level."

The guardian found his gaze drawn back down to the boots again. They were very Wicked boots, but were they Wicked *enough*?

"Could you do something . . . I don't know, unpleasant?"

Molly shifted her backpack from one shoulder to the other. "If you don't let me in and show me to the bathroom, I'll do something very unpleasant right here on the doorstep."

The guardian shuddered and opened the door all the way. The candles streamed in the sudden breeze.

She stomped past him. She was probably merely walking, but the boots turned it into a stomp by the time they reached the floor. The guardian pointed her in the direction of the bathroom, which was off the main foyer and down a short hallway.

They heard the door shut, and the rattle and gurgle of ancient pipes.

"Seems a bit . . . young," said Edward.

"Yes," said the guardian. He had been a member of the Minion's Guild in good standing for many years—had even won "Minion of the Year" six times—but he could not remember a Master as young as Molly.

"Good boots, though."

"Oh, very."

"Do you think the Board . . . ?"

"We don't have to tell them how old she is," said the

12

guardian firmly. "It's just a check box—Witch, Wicked, yes/no, in residence in castle, yes/no."

There was another gurgle as the Wicked Witch washed her hands and then the door opened again.

"The black guest towels are a nice touch," she said.

"We can have them monogrammed," said the guardian. "If you're staying."

Molly shifted uncertainly inside her boots. "You need a Wicked Witch, right?"

"Well . . . yes . . ."

"I'll be a good Wicked Witch. I mean a bad—well, I'll be good *at* it. Being Wicked, I mean."

Edward and the guardian exchanged glances. This is difficult to do when one party has helmet slits instead of eyes, but the guardian had known him for a long time.

"It's just . . ." the guardian began.

He stopped. He started again. "There was a letter, you understand, that was sent to potential Masters—"

"I've got it right here," said Molly, interrupting. She thrust a hand into her coat pocket and pulled out a black envelope with a bloodred seal.

"Oh!" said the guardian, relaxing. Edward gave a relieved rattle. "Those are ours. We sent them out when the old Mistress . . . left. If you got one—well, if you got one, I suppose it must be fine. They're magic. They wouldn't have gone to you if you weren't eligible."

He reached out a withered hand for the letter. Molly gave it over. Her hand went to her vulture necklace again.

The guardian flipped it over. "It's one of ours, yes . . . hmm. Says it's addressed to Eudaimonia—"

"That's me," said Molly hurriedly. "Only I go by Molly. It's—err—a nickname."

"I expect you got tired of people not being able to spell Eudaimonia," said Edward.

Molly took a step back in surprise. "You can talk!" she said.

"Very much so." Edward took his sword hilt in both hands and knelt, ponderously. The guardian winced, knowing how much the armor's knees bothered him. Edward bowed his head. "I, Lord Edward von Hallenbrock, swear allegiance to you, Mistress of the castle! I shall be your blade in Wickedness and your shield in adversity."

The guardian knew that Molly was a *Wicked* Witch, but he did hope she would be kind to Edward. The suit of armor was very sensitive. One of the Sorceresses had laughed at him, and he had been depressed for months.

But Molly bowed to Edward—a bow, not a curtsy—

and said, "Thank you, Lord von Hallenbrock. I didn't know that the castle would have such"—she sought a word—"such *stalwart* defenders. I'm pleased to meet you."

Stalwart had been a nice touch. Edward beamed.

Both Molly and the guardian had to take an arm to get him upright again. "It's my knees," he said cheerfully. "Don't mind me."

"And I didn't catch *your* name," said Molly, when Edward was up on his armor stand again.

"Oh," said the guardian. "I haven't got one. Not as such."

"Well, I can't just call you hey, you!"

"The last Sorceress used to call me Lackey. And the Cursed Beastlord called me Wretch."

". . . I don't think I'd feel right about that," said Molly.

"Then you'll have to give me a name," said the guardian.

Molly thought about this for a moment. "What exactly is it you *do*?"

"Whatever my Mistress desires."

"He does everything," said Edward helpfully. "He makes sure the cook has supplies and the maid puts up the right sort of cobwebs and that the pipes don't freeze in winter. He's in charge of the castle while the Master's away."

"If it pleases you, of course," put in the guardian hurriedly. "I wouldn't want you to think that we minions were getting above ourselves." (*Getting above yourself* is considered very rude among minions.)

"I see."

"And he's been here for ages," said Edward. "Longer than I have. Back when the first Vampire Lord built the castle."

Molly screwed up her face. "How about . . . Major-domo? It's like a butler, only . . . better."

"I like that," said Edward. "Major Domo! Sounds almost military."

"It was on our vocabulary test last week," said Molly.

The guardian's eyes widened.

"In—err—Witch school," she added hurriedly. "For very Wicked Witches. In training."

Everyone relaxed slightly. There was the feeling of a difficult social hurdle navigated.

"Please forgive me, Mistress Molly," said Majordomo. "The ravens were . . . not very specific about what you looked like."

"I love ravens," said Molly, clasping her hands together. "They're such intelligent birds."

"Ye-e-e-es," said Majordomo slowly. "Yes, they're very intelligent. For *birds*."

"I love owls too," said Molly. "But I'm afraid they're not as intelligent, even if people believe in wise old owls."

"It's the eyeballs," said Majordomo. "It leaves very little room in their skulls for brains. You can't make a proper messenger out of an owl, they keep getting distracted by mice."

"My absolute favorites are turkey vultures, though," said Molly. "They're very intelligent. And social. And they throw up on predators!"

This was starting to veer into Loathsome Hag territory, thought Majordomo, but at least it was properly unpleasant.

"I'm afraid we don't have any vultures. We've still got a barn owl somewhere, I think. Cook can tell you all about it."

They left the foyer—Molly waved to Edward—and entered the Grand Hall. Two enormous staircases came spinning and slithering down from the heights of the castle. One was in complete ruin, but the other looked solid. Carved gargoyles crouched on the banisters and peeked out between the railings. The truth was that they hadn't had the money to fix the ruined staircase since it had fallen down last year, but this didn't seem like the proper time to mention it.

"Awesome!" said Molly.

Majordomo tried to remember if any of the previous Masters had called anything in the castle "awesome" before.

He ushered her around the back of the staircase, to the

17

dining hall. It was an enormous room, the far end lost in shadow, with great banks of candles flickering on the sideboard. The single chair at the head of the table was upholstered in black velvet and was carved into fantastical shapes.

"Ooooh . . ." said Molly, suitably impressed.

Majordomo sniffed. He knew that a proper Mistress should sweep in haughtily and accept such things as the bare minimum due to her station—but still, it *was* nice to have someone appreciate the work involved. The candles alone would have cost a fortune if not for the Clockwork Bees in the basement.

"So how did you come to be a Wicked Witch?" he asked, leading her past the table, toward the kitchen. Cook would be sitting up waiting to meet the new Mistress, and Majordomo knew better than to offend her. Masters might come and go, but Cook was forever.

"Uh. Right." Molly rubbed the silver vulture's beak thoughtfully. "It was perfectly logical. I'm a twin, you know."

"Oh, *twins!*" said Majordomo. He was on solid mythological territory now. "Do you have a special language that you use to communicate?"

"Yes," said Molly. "It's called English. And no, I don't know what she's thinking all the time. I don't know where people get these ideas."

Majordomo sighed. It appeared that Mistress Molly was not cut from the same cloth as the previous inhabitants.

This was worrisome. If she couldn't be a proper Master to Castle Hangnail—well, that was a problem. A castle *needed* a Master. They'd gotten on without one for this long, but every time he filed an extension with the Board of Magic, Majordomo had the sense of teetering on the edge of a cliff. If they couldn't get a new Master soon, the Board would decide Castle Hangnail was more trouble than it was worth.

Still, there were the boots.

"Anyway," said Molly, hurrying on, "she's the good twin. I'm the Evil twin. So I had to go into Wickedness. I would have been a Sorceress, but I couldn't figure out how to do the eye makeup."

"Are you *sure* she's the good twin?" asked Majordomo. Perhaps the letter had gone to the right household, but the wrong person had picked it up.

"Well, Sarah sings in the church choir. And she visits old people at the Shady Hills Rest Home. I used to go with her, but I got Old Man Parson to tell me about when he used to hunt trolls and he was acting it out and accidentally hit Miss Pennywidth with a bedpan. I wasn't invited back. Sarah still goes, though. And her favorite color is pink."

Majordomo was forced to admit that this sounded like good-twin behavior.

"I like black," said Molly. "And silver. And purple's good too." She rubbed the vulture again.

He pushed the door to the kitchen open.

The kitchen was bright and cheerful and had red-and-yellow checked tile on the walls. It was not the sort of place you expected to find in a dark and dreary castle, but Cook liked it.

Generations of Evil Masters had bowed before the whims of Cook. While a Vampire or a Beastlord might rule the rest of the building, in the kitchen, Cook's word was law.

The guardian realized that he was holding his breath.

On the far side of the kitchen, between the fireplace and an enormous slab of a table, Cook rose to her feet.

She came forward. Firelight played across massive shoulders, dagger-like horns, and deep-set, burning eyes. Her hooves struck the floor like thunder. The cleaver in her hand was the size of a battle-ax.

"Whoa!" said Molly. "You're a *Minotaur!*"

Molly lay back in her bed—a real four-poster bed! With dark red bed-curtains and dark gray sheets!—and let out a long breath.

She'd gotten away with it. The hardest part was over. She'd presented herself at the castle and no one had stopped her.

Majordomo clearly suspected that she wasn't really a Wicked Witch, but he hadn't flat-out refused to let her in. Lord Edward, the enchanted armor, was a dear. (Molly was particularly proud of the word *stalwart*, which is a word that you often see written but which hardly anyone ever says aloud.)

And Cook—

Well. Cook was *amazing*.

Molly had read all the books on magical creatures in the library twice. She knew the difference between a Wyrm and a Wyvern. She could tell a Hippogriff from a Griffin at fifty yards. She had once—she was almost sure—seen a Unicorn in the woods, even though her sister said it had been a deer.

But a Minotaur! Eight feet tall, with a bull's head—cow's head, in Cook's case, although there wasn't much difference.

Different than I expected, she thought. *I thought it would be a human with a bull's head, but Cook was shaggy all over, and she had hooves and her fingers were sort of stubby and hoof-like too.*

I wonder what else the books got wrong?

Cook had a thick, guttural voice and a white apron with roses embroidered on it.

"Is Minotaur," she said. "Is problem?"

"No! Not at all. I think it's *wonderful,*" said Molly.

"Good. Good." She turned her head from side to side, eyeing Molly thoughtfully. Her eyes looked like a cow's eyes, but with razor-sharp intelligence behind them. "You. Is child?"

Molly, thinking *very* quickly, said, "Yes. Is problem?"

Cook's face split into a broad bovine grin. She slapped one hoof-like hand down on the table. "Good! Be sitting. Bring you food."

"The Mistress should eat in the dining hall," said Majordomo.

"Is here. Food is *also* here." Cook went to the stove (which was black iron and the size of a small house) and pulled a tray from atop it.

Before Molly had a chance to worry what sort of food a Minotaur would cook, Cook set the tray before her. It had little pastries with jam and big meat pies oozing with gravy and medium-sized tarts with apples and pears sliced up and covered in syrup.

"Keep warm on stove," said Cook.

Molly dove into the pastries. It had been a very long walk from the village and she'd been living on sandwiches and a thermos of cold tea. "These are delicious!" she said, around a mouthful of pastry.

"Is learning to cook from first husband," said Cook. "Then is cooking *him*. Lousy husband. Second husband is chef, much better."

23

Molly paused halfway through her meat pie. "You cooked your husband?" She looked at the meat pie. It was delicious.

Probably nobody I know, anyway. She kept eating.

"*First* husband," said Cook. "Long time ago. Second husband is dying of natural causes. Third husband is running off with encyclopedia saleswoman, is leaving only encyclopedia, volume *Q* behind." Cook snorted. "Not being fond of letter *Q*. Not allowing *Q*s in this house. Not be making quiche in *this* kitchen, understand?"

"Seems fair," said Molly. "I suppose quinces are out too?"

"No quinces. And is not liking queens. Is not being Dark Queen?"

"Nope." Molly brushed crumbs off her shirt. It was her best shirt. It had black lace and everything. Unfortunately crumbs stuck to it, and lint and cat hair. *Especially* cat hair.

"I'm a Wicked Witch," she said, abandoning the crumbs.

Majordomo made an imperceptible sound at that.

Molly sighed, replaying the scene in her mind. No, Majordomo wasn't convinced. Having Cook on her side was good, but she was pretty sure that Majordomo was the one in charge.

But he'd let her inside. That was a start.

She wiggled from side to side. The mattress was thick and yielding and there was a bit of a divot in the middle.

If she slid herself into it and snuggled down, it was like being engulfed in a warm, cozy marshmallow.

I'll show him. He'll see I'm the best Wicked Witch around. I'll be great at being bad.

She was a little worried about that part, honestly. There were lots of people that probably deserved to have something Wicked happen to them, but actually *hurting* people . . . well, that was different.

I'll just have to find people who deserve it.

Once, some boys at her school had seen a bat hanging in the corner of the coat room and had knocked it down to the floor with a schoolbook. It had flopped sadly along the floor, half stunned and very frightened.

Molly had been so furious that she forgot that the boys were bigger than she was. She'd stormed into the middle of them and shoved Todd, the biggest one—who had been about to *step* on the poor bat's *wing!*—and told him that if he didn't leave the bat alone, she'd turn him into an earwig and feed him to the toads.

And it had *worked.* Just for a minute, they backed away, looking confused. And that had been long enough for the teacher to come and see what was happening, and for Molly to scoop the poor bewildered bat into her lunch box and take it home.

If she could have turned Todd into a earwig, she would have.

I probably wouldn't have fed him to a toad. Maybe I would have shown him a toad, though. Just to scare him. Maybe then he'd realize what it's like to be a little tiny creature that people pick on.

The bat had been fine. She'd let it go that evening and it swooped around her head, making chattering noises, and then flew off into the night.

That had been the moment when she realized that magic wasn't just a fun thing she could do—it *mattered*. Not very many people could do real magic, but she could. She could smite people—not nice people, obviously, but the sort of people who were mean to innocent bats.

And that's why I'm a Wicked Witch, and not an Evil Sorceress. Evil is bad. Wicked is just a little bad.

Well, that and the eye makeup.

She pulled the covers up to her chin.

She loved her bedroom. She loved everything she'd seen in Castle Hangnail so far, but her bedroom was the best.

There was a window seat with bookcases built all around it. She had always wanted a window seat. The books were bound in black leather, with skulls on the binding. The walls were deep, warm gray, and the wainscoting was made of dark, gleaming wood. A tapestry hung on the back of the door, showing three ravens in front of a crescent moon.

It was what she'd always wanted her room at home to look like, but Sarah would never go along with it. It's very hard to make a suitably dark and gloomy retreat when one side of the room is full of stuffed animals and pink pillows.

Sarah couldn't do magic and didn't think it was fair that Molly could. And she had always squealed when Molly brought home bones. "That's so disgusting!"

"It's neat," said Molly defensively. "Look, it's not rotten or anything, it's just a deer skull. It's been picked clean. I found it in the woods."

"I won't sleep in the same room with that thing!" shrieked Sarah, and went off to tell their mother.

Here even the candelabras were made of bones, holding candles in their skeletal hands. It had taken her ten minutes to go around and blow out all the candles.

Perfect.

She could do it. She could be Wicked enough. And they'd let her stay at Castle Hangnail.

And if she was very lucky, nobody would ever find out that the invitation hadn't been addressed to her after all.

CHAPTER 4

"She's no Evil Sorceress, that's for sure," said Major-domo.

The other two people at the table nodded. One said "Hmmmm" in a thoughtful fashion.

The thoughtful one was only a person if you were feeling particularly generous with the term. He was a doll made out of burlap, with heavy pins stuck in his head like hair. His name was Pins.

When you show people dolls full of pins, they tend to think of voodoo. Voodoo is a very interesting religion and is not, as some people believe, all zombies and pins stuck in people. Nevertheless, Pins was not a voodoo doll. Nobody was quite sure *what* Pins was. He had shown up a few decades earlier and taken over doing the laundry and tailoring in Castle Hangnail.

He stood about eighteen inches tall and had a seam for a mouth and holes for eyes. You could see his white stuffing through the eyeholes.

Pins lived in a small room over the laundry with a talking goldfish. The goldfish was intensely neurotic and convinced that she was always sickening for something. Pins took very tender care of the fish and was currently knitting her a very small waterproof scarf.

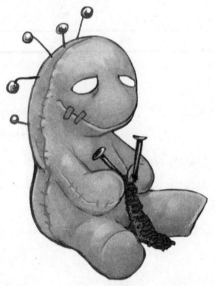

"Does she not *look* like an Evil Sorceress?" asked Pins. "She's a Wicked Witch, isn't she? Or is it more than that?"

Majordomo thought about this for a while.

If anyone else had asked him this question, he would have defended Molly without question. One simply did not bad-mouth the Master to outsiders. It wasn't done.

But they were all minions here, and minions are traditionally all in this together.

"She *definitely* doesn't look it. Although," he added, with the air of one being fair at any cost, "she does have very Witchy boots."

"Good shoes are the foundation for any wardrobe," said Pins, knitting another row on the scarf. "If it's just a matter of sewing, I'll have her looking properly Wicked in no time." Pins was very proud of his tailoring, because after all, nobody knows fabric like someone who's made out of it.

"I suppose," said Majordomo dubiously. He had great respect for Pins's sewing, but Molly was rather small and round and frizzy. He didn't think any amount of costuming could turn her into a tall, elegant Sorceress with ice dripping off her fingertips.

"Is she not magic enough?" asked the other person at the table.

Then she went "Fsssssssssss . . . ." like a train coming into the station. The other two ignored this, because that was just how Serenissima talked.

Serenissima's father had been a djinn, a spirit of immortal fire. Her mother had been a shopkeeper in the capital. This sort of thing goes on all the time, and nobody pays much attention, except for the fact that one of her mother's distant ancestors had been a mermaid.

Mermaid blood can lie dormant for generations. Serenissima's mother had been fond of the seaside and taking long baths, but those were the only signs. But when the mermaid blood met the djinn blood, they fought as only fire and water can fight and produced a creature of immortal . . . steam.

It's from the word *djinn* that we get *genie,* but you couldn't have put Serenissima in a bottle. It would have exploded from the pressure. She lived in a teakettle instead. She dripped scalding water wherever she went, and clouds of steam rolled off her constantly. She could turn a room into a sauna just by sitting quietly in the corner.

She couldn't very well work in a shop with these handicaps, so when she was fourteen years old, she had answered an ad in the paper to come and do maidwork at

Castle Hangnail and had been there ever since. She had even been granted her associate minion degree last year and was considering graduate minion studies.

The huge rooms were too large to turn into saunas and wherever Serenissima walked, the stones would be scoured and the carpets steam-cleaned. She could clean most of the castle merely by taking a brisk walk around it, and she spent the rest of her time in her teakettle on the stove in the kitchen, writing epic poetry about boilers.

"I don't know," said Majordomo, in answer to the question. "She says she can turn invisible if she holds her breath, which isn't bad."

"Not really enough to make a career on, though," said Serenissima.

Majordomo sighed. "Well, she said she was in Witch school. I suppose they teach them witchery there."

"They must, mustn't they?" said Serenissima. "Witch Economics and . . . oh, Toadology or some such. She's bound to know all sorts of spells."

"I suppose." Majordomo rubbed his finger over the wood-grain of the table.

There was a long silence.

"Will the Board of Magic think it's enough?" asked Pins finally.

Majordomo hunched his shoulders up even higher than usual. "They will if she completes the Tasks." He stared down at the table. "They gave us an extension again. When I said that there was a new Master coming."

"They said this was the last extension, though," said Pins. The Board of Magic, it should be said, is not like a government that rules over magic. Magic is ungovernable. There's no king or queen, no president or prime minister.

But the various people who use magic had found, over the years, that it's useful to have an organization that takes care of practical matters, like making sure fairy roads are kept up and standing stones don't get overgrown with ivy and that somebody's pet octopus doesn't have an accident in the laboratory and grow eighty feet tall and start devouring tour buses.

This is the Board of Magic.

One of the things that the Board of Magic does is oversee old magical castles. If they have a proper Master, everything's fine. But if their Master isn't up to the Board's standards . . . well, then the problems arise. Magic is a lot like water, and if there isn't a fit Master in charge, it'll puddle up everywhere, the basement will flood, and weird things will start laying eggs in it.

Castle Hangnail had filed eleven extensions so far, and the Board was running out of patience. If they didn't get a Master soon, the castle would be decommissioned.

Which meant "de-magicked and sold."

Which meant all of the minions would be out of work

and out of their home. Some of the younger ones—Pins, maybe, or Serenissima—might be able to find new jobs, but it would be hard for Majordomo to find another castle. And even if he did, he probably wouldn't be in charge of it.

It was one thing to take orders from the Master. It was quite another to take orders from a butler or a housekeeper. He shuddered at the thought.

"The Board will accept her," said Majordomo. "I don't have to write down how old she is, or that she's fresh out of school. They'll just see 'Wicked Witch' and sign off on it, once she's completed the Tasks."

"Unless they send someone out to have a look," said Serenissima.

Majordomo shuddered again.

"Board or no Board, she'll have to do something to earn money," said Pins. "Cook's been selling eggs to Miss Handlebram, and Angus is doing odd jobs at the farm over the hill, but you can't keep the whole castle up on egg money."

"We do all right," said Serenissima. "Every woman in the village brings you her silk and velvet to wash. They won't go anywhere else."

Burlap can't blush, but Pins dropped a stitch on his scarf. "It's nothing," he mumbled.

"We do all right," Majordomo echoed. Then he

sighed. "We do all right for a half-dozen people in a castle without a Master. But what if she's wanting to throw masked balls or have a chariot pulled by cockatrices or some such?"

All three of them stared at the table.

Masters were prone to extravagance, and the castle was supposed to provide it. But there just wasn't very much money in Castle Hangnail. They didn't have a cellar full of gold or a gallery full of paintings by great artists.

Between all the minions, they made enough to pay everybody a small wage and buy soap and sugar and tea and anything they couldn't make themselves. But a masked ball would stretch them very thin, and they certainly could not have afforded even a very small cockatrice.

"Ungo the Mad could turn lead into gold," said Pins. "That was useful."

"I don't think Wicked Witches can do that," said Serenissima. "The old Sorceress used to zap bandits and take their money, though."

"Not as many bandits as there used to be," said Pins. "She was zapping bank robbers toward the end, and look where that got her."

All three shuddered. Their most recent Master, the old Sorceress, had been very old and a bit senile toward the end, and had zapped an innocent television repairman. The authorities had to get involved. She was reportedly in a home now and thought she was a rosebush, which was better for her but had left the minions in a pickle.

"We've always managed before," said Majordomo firmly. "We'll manage this time. I'll just explain that we haven't had a Master in a while and things have been a bit . . . tight. I'm sure she'll understand."

"The old Sorceress wouldn't have understood," Serenissima said finally.

"She'd have you encased in ice just for suggesting that she limit herself to one cockatrice for evenings and weekends," said Pins. "Some Masters *like* to be extravagant. And nobody'll bring the washing up if they're afraid they'll be turned into silverfish."

Unspoken between them was the knowledge that if Molly did not understand, if things went badly, they might find themselves in deep trouble. And if that happened, there were worse things than angry Sorceresses. If Molly left or wasn't found to be a fit Master, the Board would take steps.

None of those steps would be good for Castle Hangnail.

"We'll manage," said Majordomo, with confidence he didn't feel. "We don't have any other choice."

Molly took the news that there would be no masked balls quite well.

Rather *too* well, so far as Majordomo was concerned.

"Oh?" she said vaguely. "That's a shame. Were you planning on having one?"

"Well, no," said Majordomo. "But if *you* wanted one, you understand. Or a chariot pulled by cockatrices."

"Are they good at pulling chariots?" asked Molly. She applied herself to one of Cook's pastries. A pile of crumbs was building up around her plate.

"They're terrible at it," said Majordomo. "They have to wear smoked-glass goggles so they don't turn people to stone."

"Is not liking pulling," said Cook, sliding a poached egg onto Molly's plate. "Is half chicken, half snake. Chicken half is not liking pulling."

"Then it doesn't seem very nice to make them pull a chariot," said Molly. "This is a *great* egg."

Cook grunted. "Is from my chickens. Chickens is not pulling, but *is* laying."

"Can I see them?"

"Yes. *After* is eating."

Molly accepted this. Majordomo drank his tea and felt grave misgivings. The Master shouldn't be pleased with poached eggs and the prospect of meeting chickens. The Master should be storming around the battlements, defying the gods, screaming dark curses, raining lightning down on the village.

(Not anyone *specific* in the village, of course. He quite liked Miss Handlebram, who cared about her flowers the way some people care about their grandchildren. And it would be very awkward if lightning were to strike the mercantile, which was the only place in the village to buy tea.)

It was a matter of survival—minions serve Wicked Masters. Good Masters don't have minions, they have companions, and that was a totally different union with different rules. Majordomo did not think he could become a companion at his time of life. He'd been born a minion, raised a minion, had died a minion several times, and then been brought back to life with lightning rods, still a minion.

Molly hadn't cursed anyone or Brooded Darkly or vowed to violate the laws of god and man or *anything*.

Serenissima said that she'd gone into Molly's room to tidy up and found the bed already made.

"Are you *sure* you're a Wicked Witch?" he asked.

Molly rolled her eyes and said, "Fine." She took a deep breath . . .

. . . and held it . . .

It only took a few seconds. She went a little blurry around the edges, and then Majordomo could see the chair through Molly's body. A few heartbeats later, she had vanished completely.

The chair pushed back, apparently by itself. The cream cheese pastry on Majordomo's plate floated upward, around the table, and settled onto Molly's plate.

Majordomo was impressed despite himself. Invisibility was impressive magic.

Molly let out her breath in a whoosh and was instantly visible again. "Phew. I can hold my breath for almost a minute, but I start to get light-headed." She took a bite of the pastry. Around the cream cheese she added, "I didn't used to be able to make my clothes invisible too. That was awkward."

"That was my pastry," said Majordomo.

She swallowed and grinned at him. "That's how you know I'm a *Wicked* Witch."

Pastry-theft was not on the same level as lightning, but it would have to do for now. "When you're quite done," said Majordomo, "I'll give you a tour of the castle. You can meet the others who are here to serve you. Then it's time to talk about the Tasks."

Chapter 6

The more Molly saw of Castle Hangnail, the more she loved it.

She loved the bossy gray chickens in the courtyard and the bat colony in the tower. She loved the rookery and the elderly, good-natured ravens. She loved the dungeons with their appealingly nasty instruments and the windy battlements that looked over the hills and the dim, ratcheting hive of the Clockwork Bees.

"Invented by Ungo the Mad," said Majordomo wistfully. They stood together in the dark cellar. The hive was a huge, misshapen thing, wax hardening on three walls of the cellar. "I take the wax off whenever we make candles, but they make more."

The Bees themselves were oil-rubbed bronze, as big as Molly's thumb. They flew in and out of an enormous brass pipe that snaked back and forth across the ceiling.

"They go into the pipe every night to wind their little keys. It's all done with steam from the boiler."

He sighed. He missed Ungo.

"It's marvelous," said Molly. A Clockwork Bee landed on her wrist, and she lifted it up to eye level. It clicked a tiny bronze antenna at her. "Ungo must have been very talented."

"He made me the man I am today," said Majordomo. "At least my left arm, right hip, both knees, and my left nostril." He sighed again. "It's very hard to sew the nostrils. He was a fine hand with a needle. Pins says he couldn't have done it any better himself."

Molly could hear the sadness in his voice and she patted Majordomo on one hunched shoulder. She tried not to think about where his right arm, left hip, and right nostril might have come from. Majordomo was clearly a man of many parts. Some of them looked as if they'd come by way of grave-robbers.

41

For all that, it was very sweet the way that he was so obviously proud of the castle. He reminded her a bit of her pet toad from back home, who had been lumpy and grumpy and equally proud of his tiny pond. "I'm sure he'd be very proud of the way you've kept up the castle," she said.

Majordomo looked gratified and then immediately suspicious. Molly felt like sighing herself. She'd been trying to make him feel better, but she supposed that wasn't very Wicked of her. She tried to make her voice gruff, which is difficult when you're twelve and a girl. "Anyway, if Ungo the Mad were around today, I'd lock him in a tower and make him create terrible devices for me."

"Quite proper," said Majordomo, sounding more cheerful. "In fact, there's a few left over, if you can figure out how to work them. They're next on the tour . . ."

"What about the tower? The little short one off in the moat?"

"Oh," said Majordomo, without much enthusiasm. "*That* tower. The old Vampire Lord used to keep prisoners there, and then it got remodeled into an aviary, and then into a guest suite. But the causeway fell in a few years ago, and we haven't been able to get to it."

"That's a shame," said Molly, who would have rather liked a tower surrounded by water—even the sloppy greenish water of the moat. It sounded very mythical and romantic.

Molly met Serenissima, who was very nice, in a soggy kind of way, and Cook's son, Angus. Angus was broad and cheerful and good-natured and did not have an accent anything like his mother's.

She also saw Ungo's other devices, which were strange and cryptic and had buttons labeled THUNDER AMPLIFIER and STEAM THURIGIBLE and NEVER EVER PUSH THIS BUTTON. (It had clearly been pushed several times and was jammed in the ON position.)

She met Pins's goldfish, who was convinced that she had fin rot and ich and shingles.

"I don't think fish can get shingles," said Molly. "I think you have to be a mammal."

"I shall be the first," said the fish. "They shall write articles in veterinary journals about me." This prospect seemed to cheer her up. "I shall be remembered forever in the annals of medical history."

"Don't mind her," whispered Majordomo. "Being sick is her hobby. We tried to interest her in collecting stamps, but it's hard to get them in the bowl."

Pins himself said "Stand still!" and walked around Molly in a circle, frowning.

"Those are good boots," he said finally. "The rest is not so good, but I will fix it."

"Can you?" asked Molly hopefully. "I've never really looked all that—Witchy. Not like I *wanted* to. My mom always complained that I looked like I was going to a funeral, and she kept buying me pink shirts with rhinestones, even when I told her I wanted black lace."

Majordomo put his hand over his eyes in despair.

"No pink," said Pins firmly. "Pink has its place, but this is not it. I shall outfit you like a queen of the night!"

He surveyed Molly's small, hopeful face, and the regrettable frizz of her hair. "Well . . . a princess of the night anyway."

He took another step back. "A princess of moderately late in the afternoon, at any rate."

The doll picked up a measuring tape and went for her ankles.

It took twenty minutes. Molly giggled a few times when he poked a ticklish spot, then sobered up.

"Well?" she asked worriedly, when Pins had written her measurements down on a pad.

"I shall think on it," said Pins. "We will see what can be done."

Molly sighed. She had been hoping for something more enthusiastic. "Why yes, my lady, we can make you look like a terribly Wicked and also quite pretty Witch who is also interestingly pale and has fabulous hair!"

Well, it would have been nice.

The last stop on the tour was the library.

The library of Castle Hangnail was not famed throughout the world. It was actually rather small as old Gothic libraries go, no bigger than Molly's bedroom in the castle, and the book-lined shelves only went up for about twenty feet.

"It's not much," said Majordomo sadly. There are castle libraries that go up three and four stories, with spiral staircases and magical spirits bound to the card catalog. He had always secretly wanted one of those. "Ungo kept a great many volumes in his library, but when that exploded—well. I salvaged what I could."

Serenissima didn't clean in here, as steam is not healthy for books. Majordomo did the best he could with a dustpan, but what with one thing and another . . .

Well, at least there were cobwebs on the higher volumes. You couldn't argue with good cobwebs.

"It's *wonderful*," said Molly.

The library at her school was much smaller. It had low shelves that you could see over, and the books were all carefully spaced out, as if the teachers were afraid to let them get too close to each other.

Here the books were all crammed together in a leather-bound jumble. There were fat, dumpy volumes with titles like *An Investigation into the Reality of Were-Squid* and tall, thin volumes called *With Sword and Banjo Across the Great Desert* and *Fairy Gardens of the Northeast.* There were personal diaries and spellbooks with scorched bindings and a nearly complete set of the *Encyclopedia Thaumaturgica.* (Molly noted that volume Q was missing. Apparently Cook had gotten here already.)

There was an overstuffed armchair in one corner, lit by three candles. The candles were half melted to the top of a grinning skull. Generally Molly wouldn't have tried to read by candlelight, but these candles had two wicks each and were thicker around than Molly's thigh. The skull itself came up to the arm of the chair and had teeth the size of shovel blades.

"Hill giant," said Majordomo. "Tried to eat the hill out from under us. The Master—Vampire Lord Voltan—tried to get him to go away, but once they get fixated on a hill . . . well. It gives a lovely light, though."

Molly ran her fingertips over the *Encyclopedia Thaumaturgica,* pausing briefly at the missing Q.

"And now that you've seen the castle," said Major-domo heavily, "there is the matter of the Tasks."

Molly attempted to look as if she knew what he was talking about. "Of course. The Tasks."

The old minion reached into his breast pocket and pulled out an official-looking sheet of parchment. It bore an elaborate wax seal that read *BOARD OF MAGIC* in looping letters.

He handed it to Molly.

She unfolded the page. At the top it said "Form 11ZQ-A (Wicked Witch Version.)" The rest read rather like a business letter.

From the Board of Magic, to the new
Master of Castle Hangnail,

Welcome.

In order to be fully invested as the owner
of your new castle, the Board requires that
you perform the following Tasks within the
next six weeks.

1) Take possession of the castle and
surrounding grounds.

2) Secure and defend the castle.

3) Commit at least one (1) act of smiting
and three (3) acts of blighting.

4) Win the hearts and minds of the
townsfolk by any means necessary.

Failure to complete these Tasks in a timely
manner will result in forfeiture of said castle.

Sincerely,
The Board of Magic

Molly looked up at Majordomo. *Forfeiture* wasn't too hard for someone who read at a tenth-grade level—it meant she'd have to give the castle up—but she wasn't sure about some of the others.

"Win the hearts and minds of the townsfolk?"

"However you like," said Majordomo. "The old Vampire Lord liked to keep the hearts in jars in the basement, but he was rather old-fashioned. You could just grind them all underfoot and demand tribute if you like."

". . . Um," said Molly, who had never ground anyone underfoot in her life. (Blackmailing her sister the time Sarah had gotten a C on a geometry test probably didn't count.)

"All very standard," said Majordomo. "You'll have completed the first Task once we see a really good display of magic—something to prove your bona fides, you understand."

"Um," said Molly again, who had no idea what *bona fides* were. "A display of magic. Yes, of course." She folded the list of Tasks. "Indeed. Is there anything else you'd like to show me, Majordomo?"

"You've seen most of it," said Majordomo. "All Castle Hangnail has to offer. It's all yours now, I suppose."

He didn't sound too sure of this last bit. Molly hurried onward. "In that case, I'll want to spend some time here, reading about the history of the castle. If you could arrange to have my lunch brought up here, I'd appreciate it."

"Oh," said Majordomo. "Yes. Certainly, Mistress. I'll see to it."

He paused at the threshold and gave her a *look*.

Molly gave him a *look* right back.

You can say a lot with a look. In this case, Majordomo was saying "I am still not entirely convinced that you belong here, and I'm going to keep an eye on you until I figure out what you're up to."

And Molly's look, with the innocence that comes naturally to twelve-year-old girls who are often to blame for something, said "Who, *me?*"

Majordomo's eyebrows drew down, and his look said "Yes, *you.*"

And Molly widened her eyes and her look said "Well, good luck catching me, then!"

And she smiled brightly and shut the door in his face.

She waited until the footsteps had receded—Majordomo had a distinctive shuffling gait—and then turned back to the library.

This was more like it!

"Spellbook," she said under her breath. "Spellbook, spellbook . . . if I can just find a good spellbook . . ."

Molly ran her fingers across the books until she came to a title that sound promising—*The Education of a Sorcerer's Apprentice* by A. Nesbit. She pulled the book down, curled up in the armchair, and began to read.

It is all very well and good to be able to turn invisible when you hold your breath, but there is a great deal more to magic. Molly, who had not gone to a Witch's school—who had in fact gone to a perfectly ordinary, rather dingy school with most of the grades packed into one room—knew that if she was going to be allowed to stay in Castle Hangnail, she was going to have to be able to do more than turn invisible.

Magic is tricky stuff. Not everybody can be a Witch or a Wizard. You have to have a certain amount of inherent magic to be able to do a spell at all, and very few people have that much. Even among twins, like Molly and her sister, only one twin may have the gift.

But merely having magic isn't enough. Being a good cook won't help if you don't have ingredients and recipes to work with. Molly

had magic, but in order to use it for much of anything, she was going to need to find a spellbook.

Her mother would certainly not have allowed her to have a real spellbook in the house—not even one with a pink cover and rhinestones and a title like *Completely Unobjectionable Magic Spells to Help Very Nice Girls With Their Homework.*

She had told Majordomo the truth—she did have a book of potions. Unfortunately, it had been written by a very nice White Witch, and so it was full of potions for curing earaches and making vegetables grow. A distant relative had given it to her for Christmas one year, and Molly had hidden it immediately before her mother could get a good look at the cover.

Molly had used that book to win second prize for her giant zucchini at the fair three years running. But there was nothing terribly Wicked about zucchini.

The sad fact was that Molly knew almost no real magic. She knew a couple of the little spells that children teach each other on the playground—"Ladybug, Ladybug," say, which lets you talk to a ladybug, and "Ring Around the Rosie," which, when done properly, protects against the plague. (Ladybugs, sadly, are not very good conversationalists, so you rarely hear anything of interest, and there had been no plague in that country for a hundred years.)

She had once found a really wonderful spell in a library

book for turning someone into an earwig, but she hadn't written it down properly and she'd never been able to find the book again. She suspected that it had been mis-shelved in the children's section, and librarians look at you very oddly if you go up to them and say, "Excuse me, do you have any books on how to turn your enemies into earwigs?"

She knew a handful of other spells. She could start a fire with her thumbnail. She could get tangles out of the worst tangled hair. She could tell if her twin sister stepped into her side of the room. She could make her shadow come alive and dance with her (which is an exhausting spell, and she didn't enjoy doing it). She could turn a leaf into a teacup, and a teacup into a leaf.

These were the only *real* spells that she knew.

She had learned them from Eudaimonia.

CHAPTER

7

Molly eventually abandoned *The Education of a Sorcerer's Apprentice,* which was very dry and contained no actual spells, but a great many complaints about the quality of meals at the various boarding schools the author had attended.

If I can find a spellbook, though . . . something that can teach me real spells . . . I'll study it really hard. Even if it's boring. I'll learn them. I know I can learn them. Eudaimonia didn't think I could do the shadow spell, and I proved I could. I can learn these too.

And then I'll prove to Majordomo that I'm a proper Wicked Witch.

Let's take a minute to talk about spellbooks, since, in this day and age when magic is no longer taught in schools (or is, at best, an elective like Home Economics), very few people have the experience with spellbooks that they used to.

A spellbook is basically a cookbook for magic.

Cooking itself is the first cousin to magic, so it's not surprising that a spell resembles a recipe. In a good spellbook, the ingredients will be laid out, along with some indication of the time involved and how hard the spell will be. For example:

A Spell to Become Invisible

You will require:
A moonless night
A length of black silk thread
A pinch of fern seed
A triangle drawn in green chalk

This spell will last for three hours or until sunrise, whichever comes first.

And then the spell will, ideally, explain exactly what you do with the thread and the fern seed and the green chalk triangle, what magic words to say over it, and so forth.

In a very good spellbook for beginners, there will even be footnotes telling you how to acquire fern seed in the first place (this is quite difficult, as ferns prefer to reproduce by spores most of the time, and actual fern seed is itself invisible) and how to pronounce the more difficult words in the incantation.

This is all relatively straightforward, and if one has a bit of magical power (enough, say, to turn invisible when they hold their breath), they need only follow the spell and then enjoy their newfound three hours of invisibility.

The problem lies in finding a good spellbook to begin with.

Just as writing an easy-to-follow recipe requires an orderly sort of mind, so too does writing a good spell. Unfortunately, many Wizards and Witches and Sorcerers and so forth do not have orderly minds. Reading their spellbooks is rather like reading the recipe cards for a gifted but erratic cook—lots of scribbled notes to themselves and not much use to other people.

Invisbul Spell

    sprinkle fern seed—try spleenwort,

           A. platyneuron?

Tuesday night

    use thread from black scarf Mom sent me?

    Build wall of Octroi in ~~*hexagon*~~

                ~~*octagon*~~

                ~~*dodecahedron*~~

                pyramid

recite words from William's Spell of Unseeing.

    FIRST syllable, not second!!!

send Igor to store for green chalk

56

Molly began pulling volumes down from the shelves, looking for a useful spellbook. Unfortunately, she was getting a great many books written like the latter example, and very few of the first.

Majordomo came up with her lunch. Molly shoved the spellbooks under a copy of *A Compleat Historie of Castle Hangnaile* and looked wide-eyed and innocent at him until he went away again.

One book! One good book of spells that she could really use, all about Smiting and Blighting! A Wicked Witch who didn't Smite and/or Blight might as well just be a White Witch.

There's not anything *wrong* with being a White Witch, of course. It's just that once people figure out you're not going to turn them into a toad, that you will cure their earache and make their cow give extra milk, you become part of the service industry, like the pharmacist or the mailman. People show up at all hours expecting you to charm warts off their feet.

White Witches are much nicer people, but Wicked Witches have more fun. Molly pulled down another volume, saw that it was written backward and in Latin, and put it back. She knew two words of Latin—*carpe diem,* which means "seize the day"—and reading backward made her head hurt. She flopped down on the library stool and jammed her chin onto her hand. Surely somewhere there must be a book that could help her!

Her eyes traveled over the row of *Encyclopedia Thaumaturgica*, and paused at the gap, one book wide, for volume Q.

If Cook threw away volume Q, why is there a gap at all? Shouldn't P and R just be jammed up against each other?

She went over to the shelf and felt around in the gap.

A few inches back from the encyclopedias, nearly lost in the darkness at the back of the shelf, was a little book, not much bigger than Molly's hand.

The leather was gray and the pages were gray and the ink was silver. There was no title and no title page. The spells began on the very first page. Molly had to turn the volume to one side to make the light reflect off the silver ink so that she could read it.

It was written in a beautiful flowing hand, and except that every *s* looked like an *f* (which happens in very old books) it was remarkably easy to read.

To talk to any bird or beaft, take a hair or fcale or feather from the creature you wifh to fpeak with and wrap it in a dock leaf and tie it with a hair from your own head and fay over it the following wordf . . .

Molly read the spell three times over. There was not a list of ingredients, but it seemed very straightforward. She turned the page and there was a spell for "turning

fand into flying fifh eggf," which was perhaps not terribly useful, and on the opposite page, there was a spell to spy on your enemies.

She turned the pages faster. Some of them were odd and useless little spells—was there any point in making acorns sing? Or being able to turn stones into cheese?— but some of them looked very useful indeed. Molly could think of four or five situations where being able to turn a cow into a dragon would be extremely handy, although the spell only lasted for one minute, which did limit its utility.

"But will they *work?*" she whispered. "Or will I be able to cast them?" For there are very powerful spells that are very simple, but unless you happen to be the right sort of person, they will not work at all. (And a good thing too. You can raise the dead with five words and a hen's egg, but natural Necromancers are very rare. Fortunately they tend to be solemn, responsible people, which is why we are not all up to our elbows in zombies.)

There was only one way to find out. Molly slid the Little Gray Book into her sleeve and headed out to the gardens.

CHAPTER 8

The herb garden of Castle Hangnail had been untended for many years. Cook's garden was full of enormous lettuces and cabbages and tomatoes the size of softballs, but the only herbs were for seasoning. Bees buzzed happily on the flowers of the basil, interrupted by the occasional baritone droning of a Clockwork Bee.

If you walked through the courtyard that held Cook's garden, though, there was a little stone archway leading to a second garden. This one was smaller and completely wild. Twisted green stems grew over the stones, and the branches of strange trees rested against the sky.

Molly knew a fair bit about plants. Her mother had a garden at home, and Molly had to learn to identify various herbs in order to make the potions in her potion book. She knew many of the plants in this garden, but others were foreign. Many were medicinal. Some were poisonous.

As she walked the overgrown paths, she muttered the names of plants to herself—"Rosemary . . . that's skull-cap . . . valerian . . . oh dear, the mint has really taken over in this bed, hasn't it? I'll have to get in with the shears . . . Is that goldenseal? I thought it only grew in the mountains . . ."

Someone had clearly lavished care on the herb garden many years ago. Molly suspected that it had been another Wicked Witch.

However Wicked that Witch might have been, she had clearly loved the garden. Plants can tell when you love them, and if you don't love them, it takes a great deal of expensive fertilizer or powerful magic to make up the difference.

Molly was not looking for anything rare and special, however, but for a dock leaf. Dock is a very common weed. No weeds dared to enter Cook's garden, but perhaps here, wedging its root into the gap between two stones . . .

"Aha!" She pounced on the broad green dock leaf. It had wavy edges and a thick white vein down the middle.

"May I help you, Mistress?" asked Majordomo from the archway.

"Nope!" said Molly. "Found what I was after." Dirt crumbled off the dock roots and onto the path.

"Indeed," said Majordomo. The lines around his mouth (some of which were stitched on) deepened with disapproval. "Are you taking up gardening?"

"I might," said Molly. "But for now, Smiting and Blighting, you know. All in a Wicked Witch's work."

She slipped past him, dock leaf in her hand, and ran into the castle.

"Dock leaf, check . . ." she murmured, rereading the recipe in the Little Gray Book. "Candle . . . hair . . ." She yanked one out of her head, then slid the book into her sleeve. "Now, to go find one of their hairs . . ."

Molly had a goal in mind already, at the top of the highest tower, where the bats roosted. The ravens could already talk, but bats generally don't (or if they do, only to each other and sometimes to the moon).

"May I be of some assistance, Mistress?" asked Majordomo, stepping out of a doorway into the hall.

"I'm fine," said Molly. "Are you following me around?"

"It is the duty of the guardian to assist the Master in any way possible," Majordomo intoned.

"Maybe you could go oil Lord Edward's knees," said Molly.

Majordomo narrowed his eyes. Molly widened hers. (Her mother would have recognized that look and sent her to her room preemptively, since, as she said, "You've obviously done *something!*" but Majordomo did not have a great deal of experience with twelve-year-old girls.)

"We're all very eager to see some magic," said Majordomo. "All of us minions. It's been so long since there was a Master, you understand. And in order to complete the first of the Board's Tasks . . ." He trailed off.

Molly waved her hand airily. "Tonight, then. I prefer to work magic under the moon, you know."

Majordomo bowed. "We shall look forward to it."

That's done it, thought Molly, sprinting up the steps of the tower. *I've got to pull something off tonight. Majordomo's getting suspicious, and going invisible isn't going to be enough.* She gulped.

If she couldn't prove that she was a real Witch, she was going to be sent back home in disgrace. She'd have to share a room with her twin again. With pink stuffed animals and glittery unicorn posters.

Molly shuddered.

If only she'd been able to arrive in a carriage pulled by cockatrices or turn into a wolf or something impressive like that! Something that would have made Majordomo accept her as the proper Mistress of the castle, no questions asked.

Tonight, she thought. *If worse comes to worse, I'll do the spell where I spin off my shadow and dance with it. If we can get enough candles in the room, that'll look impressive, even if it is just a silly little trick . . .*

She pushed open the door to the belfry and entered the roost of the bats.

The top of the tower was lost into darkness. On every surface—the rafters, the walls, the rusting iron gratings—were dozens and dozens of bats.

Bats are actually very delicate little creatures. Molly was fond of them. These were brown bats. They looked, as they clung to the ceiling, like nothing so much as dozens of dried prunes.

Molly pulled the door shut and stepped carefully across the floor. A bat roost, no matter how diligent people are about cleaning it, smells like bat guano. It's an unavoidable problem. Angus came up once a week with a shovel and scraped the floor, then carted the scrapings down six flights of stairs to the gardens. (Bat guano makes the very best fertilizer in the world.) Then Serenissima would come up and steam the floors clean. But in a week, it would have to be done all over again.

The roost had been cleaned two days ago, which meant that it didn't smell too bad at the moment. Molly lit her candle, set it on the floor, and scoured the ground for a stray bat hair.

It wasn't difficult. Bats also shed. Molly, like most Witches, had no compunctions about handling icky things, but she made a mental note to wash her hands afterward.

She wrapped the bat hair in the flat green dock leaf, tied it off with one of her own hairs, then held the whole works over the candle.

With the Little Gray Book in one hand, she read off the magic words as clearly as she could. "Avack . . . Auilriuan . . . Arwiggle . . ."

The dock leaf burned slowly, being green. Molly held it as long as she could, then dropped it. There was a brief, acrid scent of burnt hair.

Molly held her breath.

Slowly, like someone tuning in a station on an old radio, sounds began to fill the air. They were high-pitched at first, but they gradually descended, growing deeper and louder, until the air was full of voices.

At first Molly could only make out one or two words. Then the words strung together and made sentences, and the sentences made a conversation.

"Is it the Witch?"

"Quit shoving, I can't see!"

"It sounds like the Witch."

"Get your wing out of my ear."

"What's she doing here?"

"She's not going to enchant us, is she?"

"She's a Witch. The Witches are always kind to us bats. I wouldn't mind if she enchanted me."

"The Mad Scientist experimented on Great-Uncle Humphrey."

"Yeah, and Humphrey could breathe fire after that. He ate all his bugs cooked."

66

"I wonder why she's here."

Molly was thrilled. She could understand the bats!

She cleared her throat. "Can you hear me, bats?" she asked.

The whole roost began to twitter and flutter.

"Can we hear her?"

"We can hear a mosquito in a drain pipe."

"We can hear moths talking a mile away on a windy night."

"Can we *hear* her?"

"I'm sorry," said Molly hurriedly. "I wasn't trying to insult you. I just want to make sure the spell is working."

There was a great twittering and rustling, and then a very old bat swung her way from the back of the roost, pushing past the other, younger bats. Her wrinkled face was even more wrinkled than is usual for bats, and her fur was streaked with gray.

"We hear you . . . Witch . . ." said the old bat. She stretched both her wings down over her head, then swept them up and crossed her claws over her chest. This is the formal greeting of bats. "I am the Eldest . . . of this Roost."

Molly bowed to the Eldest, because she knew that many beasts are easily offended, and it is important to return courtesy with courtesy. "It is an honor to meet you, Eldest."

"It has been a long time since anyone came . . . and spoke to us," said the Eldest. "How may we serve you?"

"I was hoping that you might help me," said Molly. "I can do magic—well, a little—but it's not very impressive-looking magic." (It seemed safe to admit this to the bats, since Majordomo clearly didn't know how to speak to them. In fact, on the tour he had simply opened the door to the belfry, said "The bats live here," and then closed it again.)

The Eldest cocked her head. "Go on . . ."

"I need to do something so that Majordomo—the guardian—believes I'm really a Witch."

She bit her lip. She hoped that admitting this to the bats wouldn't get her in trouble.

The Eldest nodded her head slowly, upside down, and rubbed her claws over her ears thoughtfully. "Go into the garden tonight . . . at moonrise. The Roost will see to it . . . that no one doubts you."

"Thank you very much," said Molly. She bowed again. "Is there anything I can do for you? Now that I'm the Mistress of the castle?"

The Eldest laughed, a high-pitched chittering. The other bats laughed as well, and the sound spread out like ghostly wings around her. "It is very simple . . . to be a bat . . ." said the Eldest. "We do not desire . . . things . . ." She turned and began to swing back into the mass of bats.

She paused, though, and turned her head, meeting Molly's eyes with her own tiny black ones. "You might . . . come and speak to us . . . sometime. It has been . . . a long time . . ."

The Eldest swung away into darkness. Molly picked up her candle, feeling very honored and very grown-up, and let herself out of the belfry.

CHAPTER 9

Dinner was held in the Long Hall. Molly would have preferred to eat in the kitchen, honestly—the Long Hall was cold, and her feet didn't touch the floor when she sat in the great dragon-footed chair at the head of the table—but Majordomo insisted.

Well, he didn't exactly *insist*. He said, "Dinner is served in the Long Hall, Mistress."

"Not in the kitchen?"

His scar-lines deepened, and he said, "The Master of the castle *always* eats dinner in the Long Hall."

So Molly climbed into the great chair and had dinner. Her solitary place setting looked very small on that vast expanse of table. The sea of candles glowed and rippled behind her.

There was a bowl of skulls instead of fruit on the table for a centerpiece. Molly approved of that. They were all grinning rakishly, as if they quite liked being skulls.

Cook clomped in, set dinner down on the table, and clomped back toward the kitchen.

"You're supposed to put it on the sideboard!" hissed Majordomo. "Then I serve her."

"Is stupid," said Cook. "Is one person, one dinner. Is getting cold on sideboard."

"I'd rather have it here," said Molly hurriedly.

"The last Sorceress would never have approved," said Majordomo. "Or the Warlock."

"Maybe they liked cold food," said Molly.

Majordomo sniffed.

Dinner was meatloaf. There was nothing particularly Wicked about meatloaf, but Molly loved it anyway. She liked the crusty red sauce, which Cook made with brown sugar and Worcestershire sauce. (There is actually something quite agreeably Wicked about Worcestershire sauce.)

She even ate all the green beans, partly because Cook's green beans were very good and had bits of bacon on them, and partly because refusing to eat your vegetables is not Wicked, but merely tiresome.

It would probably not help Majordomo's opinion of her if he had to lecture her about eating her vegetables.

Hopefully the bats would be able to do . . . something.

Hopefully whatever they did would be impressive to people, and not just bats. What if they started reciting poetry in Bat? Nobody would be able to understand it but her.

She pushed the last green bean around her plate with her fork.

Surely the Eldest would know that. The Eldest had seemed smart. Maybe smarter than Molly herself, which is an unsettling quality in a creature the size of a dried prune.

"We are all looking forward to your display after dinner," said Majordomo. "Or would you prefer dessert first?"

"Dessert first," said Molly, with an airiness she didn't feel. "And I'll be doing my magic at moonrise."

Majordomo bowed. Moonrise was apparently acceptable. He went into the kitchen.

Molly pushed the green bean around some more.

If all else fails, I can do the shadow spell. It won't look like much in a dark garden, but maybe the moon will be bright.

She hoped the bats came through. Detaching her shadow made her heels itch terribly, and she always felt weirdly hollow for a few minutes afterward, as if she hadn't eaten in days.

Majordomo emerged from the kitchen bearing a plate with a single slice of pie on it. "With Cook's compliments," he said, setting it down in front of Molly.

Molly popped the last green bean in her mouth, wiped her lips with the napkin, and tackled the pie. It was berry, with whipped cream oozing over the crust. "What're the compliments?" she asked.

"Beg pardon?"

"You said there were compliments. Like, uh—'Your hair looks good' or 'I hear you did very well in geometry' or something?"

"They're just . . . generally complimentary," said Majordomo, nonplussed.

Molly grinned around a mouthful of pie.

A few minutes before moonrise, she walked into the herb garden. Cook's garden might have worked too, but the overgrown jungle of herbs seemed better somehow. More Witchy.

Molly stood at the center of the garden, where the paths converged, and made a show of gazing up at the moon.

Please show up, please show up, please show up . . .

She could feel the eyes of all the residents of Castle Hangnail on her. Serenissima steamed in the cool air. Lord Edward the knight had, with many creaks and groans, clanked as far as the kitchen. Pins had even brought his goldfish down. She was bundled up against

the cold and carefully cradled in the arms of Angus the Minotaur.

Molly glanced behind her. She could hear them talking, but not loudly enough to make out the words. Cook gave her a thumbs-up with one hoof-like hand. Majordomo was expressionless.

He's waiting for me to fail . . . I have to do something or he'll figure out I'm barely a Wicked Witch at all . . . maybe even that I'm not really Eudaimonia . . .

She looked up, her heart in her mouth—and a bat flew across the face of the moon.

Majordomo watched glumly as Molly stood in the center of the ruined herb garden.

He didn't dislike Molly, but she was a little girl and nothing he'd seen her do had convinced him that she could rule Castle Hangnail. Or at least be a Master that the Board of Magic would find acceptable.

She was the only person who answered the invitation. No one else wanted to rule a castle with a leaking roof in the middle of a pleasant little farming community.

He pushed the thought away. That didn't matter. If Molly couldn't prove that she was truly a Wicked Witch, she'd have to go. The Board had very strong opinions about non-magical folk trying to run a magical castle.

"Is the magic happening yet?" asked Edward. "I can't see!"

"She's not doing anything," said Pins worriedly. "Not yet."

"Magic takes time," said Serenissima.

"But—"

"Serenissima is right," said Majordomo, determined to be fair. "Magic doesn't have to be fast to be magic."

Molly threw both her arms in the air.

Suddenly the night sky was alive with bats! They spiraled out of the air like falling leaves, they circled and swooped and skittered, they flew low over the heads of the onlookers.

It was an impressive display—but bats alone weren't really magic. Majordomo knotted his hands together.

A point of light appeared over the wall of the courtyard, then another. It moved like a bat, but it glowed like a shooting star. Another joined it, and another, and soon a dozen brilliant lights danced over the garden, performing sarabands and arabesques, leaving long glowing trails behind them.

"Ooooh . . ." said Serenissima and the goldfish.

"*Ahhhh . . .*" said Pins and Lord Edward.

"Hmph," said Majordomo. Dancing lights were all very well, but was it magic *enough?*

The lights came together and formed pictures. Dragons danced over the courtyard, skulls chattered their teeth, and the name MOLLY was written in elaborate cursive letters.

Cook began to applaud. So did Angus (carefully, so as not to upset the goldfish) and Serenissima and Pins. Lord Edward clanked. The goldfish blew excited bubbles.

The lights went out. The garden was bathed in the glow of the moon. Molly stood in it, five feet tall, round face, impressive boots.

The bats swooped inward. She was suddenly hung with bats like a Christmas tree is hung with ornaments or a beehive is hung with bees. Hundreds of tiny furry bodies clung to her cloak and her hair and her shoes.

The Eldest landed directly on her nose and spread grizzled white wings across her face, like a carnival mask.

A second passed . . . then two . . . then three . . .

The bats exploded outward, shrieking and chattering. The cloud dispersed into the sky.

Moonlight streamed through the garden and into the space where Molly had stood.

The Witch had vanished.

The servants gasped.

Where had she gone? Had she actually turned into a flock of bats?

"Pretty good, huh?" said Molly, behind them.

All the residents of the castle spun around, except for Edward, who could only clank in a circle. The goldfish sloshed in her bowl.

Molly grinned at them, with a confidence she didn't quite feel.

Would it be enough?

Then—

"Bravo!" cried Pins.

"Huzzah!" cried Edward.

They all began applauding wildly. Cook and Angus stomped their hooves and Serenissima whistled. Edward whistled too, and clattered all his armor until it rang like bells.

Majordomo let out a long, long breath and said, "*Well*, then."

Molly felt weak and slightly damp with relief. (And also because of the bats. As we have said before, it is not possible to housebreak bats. At least two of them had been rather nervous, and she urgently needed to change her socks.)

She also didn't want to stick around, in case somebody asked for an encore.

"If I may see the list of Tasks?" said Majordomo.

Molly pulled the list from her pocket and handed it to Majordomo.

He held it up for the other minions, and they let out a cheer.

A long red line ran through the first Task on the list. It was the same bright red as the seal from the Board of Magic itself, and it twinkled faintly in the starlight.

Majordomo gave the list back to Molly and she tucked it away again.

"I expect that tomorrow I'll want to get started with the Smiting," she said. "Or perhaps the Blighting. So I'd prefer to be well-rested." She feigned a yawn, waved, and turned away.

An Evil Sorceress would have swept out of the room, and a Cursed Beastlord would have prowled. Loathsome Hags slink and Vampire Lords prefer to turn into a mist and flow under doors.

The Wicked Witch of Castle Hangnail skipped.

She skipped out of the garden, reached the hallway, and took the stairs up three at a time.

When she got to her room, she made two separate discoveries.

The first was that Serenissima had already turned down the bed and slipped a hot pad near the foot, so that it was delightfully warm and snuggly.

The second was that there was a small, sleepy bat still hanging from her silver vulture necklace.

"Bugbane," he said. "That's my name. The Eldest said to stay with you. She said it'd be better. She said—oh—" He clutched his head between his wing-tips. "I'll remember in a minute—in just a minute—oh dear . . ."

"Take your time," said Molly, peeling off her socks. They were quite ruined. Nervous bats are hard on clothing. "May I hang you on the bedpost? There we go."

"Sorry . . ." He shook his head. "Nights make me so confused. I get so sleepy."

"You're a bat," said Molly. "I thought you got sleepy during the day."

Bugbane snapped his claws. "Daytime! That's it. I like being awake during the day. The Eldest said maybe you'd have some use for me." He yawned, showing a tiny pink tongue. "I don't like the night very much. I mean, I can *do* nights"—he yawned again—"but they're so tiring. I'd rather be awake during the day. But then there's no one to talk to." He drooped tragically on the bedpost.

Molly nudged the chamber pot under him with her toe. "Well, if the Eldest sent you . . ."

"She did—she did! She's my great-grandmother. Great-great-grandmother. Maybe more greats—oh, I don't remember. A lot of greatssss . . . sss . . . zzzz . . ."

Molly cocked her head to one side and waited, but it was clear that Bugbane had fallen asleep on the bedpost.

"In mid-sentence?" she asked.

"Zzzz . . ."

". . . well, all right, then."

She blew out the last candle and climbed into bed.

It was silent in the castle, except for the snoring of the bat. Nobody at the window. Nobody at the door. Nobody in hearing distance, except Bugbane.

Molly put her head under the blankets and shouted into her pillow: "*WOOOHOOO!*"

She and the Eldest had done it. Better than she had dared to hope.

Now, you have probably already figured out how Molly had vanished, but just in case, we must go back to the moment when the bats landed on her.

Molly had not had any idea what to expect from the

Eldest's performance. She had been surprised and dazzled by the lights, and it wasn't until a bat swept past her nose, holding a firefly carefully in its mouth, that she had realized how they were doing it.

When all the bats had landed on her, she had been startled. She wasn't frightened—she was enough of a Witch that bats didn't bother her, and she trusted the Eldest—but being covered in bats is a rather shocking experience at the best of times, particularly when one of them pees on your sock.

The Eldest had landed directly on her nose. Molly's eyes had crossed trying to meet the gaze of the ancient bat. She held her breath.

"That should give them something to think about," said the Eldest, chuckling. "Call on us again if you have need. We go to the hunt—now, children!"

And all the bats had flown away.

Molly had almost—almost—exhaled.

Then she turned around—and saw, instead of her shadow, moonlight on the ground.

I'm invisible. I'm holding my breath and I must have just faded out when the bats flew away—

Her boots would have clattered on most paths, but the herb garden was overgrown with mints and mosses. She hurried out of the center of the garden, snuck around the edge of the courtyard, and squeezed past

Edward. She was just starting to feel light-headed from holding her breath when Majordomo spoke and she saw her opening.

We did it. The Eldest put on an amazing show, and I helped out at the end.

She snuggled down under the covers. Bugbane made tiny squeaking noises on the bedpost.

If the ancient bat wanted Molly to take care of Bugbane—a bat who preferred daylight! How silly and wonderful!—then it was certainly the least Molly could do. She made a note to ask Cook to save some caterpillars for him, if there were any in the garden.

A bat flitted by her window, but no one was awake to see it.

CHAPTER 10

"Today," Molly announced at breakfast, "we really must see about some Smiting and Blighting." She put both hands flat on the table. "Does anybody know anyone who needs to be Smited?" (She wanted to put off the Blighting as long as possible. It's mostly good for killing vegetation, and Molly never felt quite right about Blighting an innocent wheat field or patch of daisies.)

"Smited?" asked Majordomo.

"Smitten?"

"I thought it was Smote," said Angus. His voice was so deep, it sounded like a church organ.

"Someone who deserves Smiting," said Molly firmly. "Whatever the past tense of that may be."

The kitchen fell silent. Cook flipped a pancake onto a plate and slid it toward Majordomo.

All of them stared at the table. Pins played with one of the needles on his head. Bugbane chewed on a caterpillar that Angus had located in the garden.

The problem was that, while they all approved of Smiting & Blighting in the abstract, when it came down to Smiting real people in the village . . . well, that was another matter. They were neighbors. Nobody wanted to see Miss Handlebram Smited or Smitten or Smote, and she would have been terribly upset to find her geraniums Blighted. And certainly it would be a bad idea to Smite the mercantile . . . or any of the ladies who brought Pins their washing . . . or the post office . . .

"Nobody?" asked Molly.

"What sort of person?" Majordomo asked.

"Somebody bad," said Molly. "Rude or mean or unkind to animals. I don't want to Smite someone who doesn't really deserve it."

Angus tapped a finger on the table. "There's Old Man Harrow. He beats his donkey."

"That's terrible!" said Molly. "That poor donkey!"

The Minotaur nodded. "Aye. I would stop him, but . . ." He spread his hands.

Molly looked blank.

"Is being monsters," said Cook, dropping a second plate of pancakes in the middle of the table. "Is always being very careful, if monsters. Is being good neighbors, very quiet, not making trouble. Otherwise is being blamed always, all things."

Molly froze with a pancake suspended on her fork.

"But you won't get blamed, will you? If *I* Smite someone?"

"It's different for the Master of the castle," said Major-domo. "People expect it. They might not want it to happen to them, but they like knowing there's a Master in the castle, in case something needs Smiting. Makes them feel good knowing the old traditions are being kept up."

"It's safer for monsters to be minions," Angus added. "Then everyone says 'That Wicked Witch, somebody should stop her!' instead of putting monster-hunting parties together."

"That doesn't seem very fair," said Molly in a small voice.

Cook shrugged. "Is *not* being fair," she said. She dropped another pancake on Molly's plate. "But is way things are being. Not like old days." She grinned sourly. "Not being like days of mazes and swords! But monsters is adapting."

"Well," said Molly after a minute, "it sounds like Old Man Harrow needs Smiting. I'll teach him not to beat a poor defenseless donkey! Angus, can you take me there after lunch?"

"Certainly," rumbled Angus, and it was agreed.

Molly had a plan. Mostly.

One of the spells in the Little Gray Book was for turning a cow into a dragon for one minute. It was an oddly specific spell, but it made sense when she thought about it, because a minute is enough time to get the point across (the point being "Look at my dragon!") without being enough time for the cow-dragon to go stomping across the countryside setting things on fire.

If she could turn Old Man Harrow's donkey into a dragon for one minute, that should throw a good scare into him. Then Molly could pretend to be passing by and turn the donkey back, but warn Harrow that it could happen again at any time, unless he treated the donkey better.

She examined this plan from all angles and could only find one flaw with it—namely that donkeys are not cows and cows are not donkeys. They both have hooves and large ears and live on farms, but there the similarities end.

"That, however, we can fix," said Molly, under her breath.

The invocation in the book required a hair of the cow's tail, a sprig of moonwort dipped in spring water, and six magic words. The hair would have to be a donkey hair, and she would get that at the farm itself. She had a bunch of moonwort sprigs that she'd brought from home, since moonwort is very common in potions, and Cook would give her some spring water from the kitchen.

That left only the magic words themselves . . .

"Accreus Illusus Bovine Accomplicia Margle Fandango," she read aloud.

87

"Eh?" said Bugbane, who was hanging behind her left ear.

"Magic," said Molly. "I'm tweaking the spell a little."

"Oh." The bat stretched. "Can I help?"

"Not with this," said Molly, pulling a dictionary down from the library shelf, "but I'll need your help when I actually cast it."

She opened the dictionary. The Q section had been carefully cut out with a razor blade. Molly sighed and flipped past it.

She had always been very good at vocabulary, so she already knew that *bovine* means "related to cows." She double-checked, however, because magic is tricky stuff.

There it was . . . *bovine*. She ran her finger down the page to a small drawing of a Holstein cow.

"Of, related to, or affecting cattle," she read aloud. *"Excellent."*

She flipped through the pages to the *E* section.

"Equine," she read. "Of, related to, or affecting horses or members of the horse family."

If she substituted a donkey hair for a cow hair, and then used the word *equine* instead of *bovine* . . .

"It's bound to work," said Molly, slamming the dictionary closed, and went to go find some spring water.

CHAPTER 11

The Smiting of Old Man Harrow went well . . . at first.

Angus led Molly through a low, scruffy wood off to one side of Castle Hangnail. He whistled as he walked and Molly hurried along beside him. The Minotaur took one step for every three of hers. Bugbane flitted overhead, nabbing at startled mosquitoes.

Molly felt like singing or skipping or laughing out loud. She was on a grand adventure with a bat and Minotaur. And to think only a week ago, she'd been at home, with her twin sister keeping her from Smiting so much as a fly!

The more sentimental sort of grown-up would have been surprised how little Molly missed her twin. Other than being identical, though, they had very little in common.

Comes of being the good twin and the Wicked twin, I guess.

The truth of the matter was that Sarah used to run and tattle whenever Molly did anything even remotely Wicked—even just Blighting the Brussels sprouts in the garden, which, after all, Sarah would have had to eat *too*. Now, without Sarah around, Molly felt . . . free.

"Here," rumbled Angus, turning off the path. He held back the branches so that she could scramble through. "This is the fence around Old Man Harrow's property."

Molly ducked out of the wood and blinked in the sunlight. The wooden fence (and the wood) stood at the bottom of a hillside, although "stood" was probably being overly generous with regards to the fence. Posts leaned at crazy angles and a few of the boards had gone missing completely. It was obvious that Old Man Harrow was not concerned about upkeep.

There was a dilapidated barn at the top of the hill.

"Bugbane!" said Molly.

The bat zipped in and landed on her head. He weighed almost nothing. "Yes, boss?"

Molly grinned. *Boss*. She liked that. "I have a very important job for you. I need you to go up and tell me what's going on in the barn. And I need a spot I can look inside without being seen."

Bugbane hummed happily. "Will do!" He launched himself from the top of her head and flittered up the hill.

A few moments later he flew back. This time he landed on one of Angus's horns and hung upside down so that he could gesture with his wings. "The donkey's in the barn. So's Old Man Harrow, and he looks angry. If you go up to the back wall, there's a lot of broken boards. I bet you could look right through one."

"Thanks, Bugbane!'

The bat grinned. He had tiny pointed teeth. "Also . . . uh . . . I thought you might want this . . ."

He stretched out a claw. Wrapped around it was a single coarse black hair.

"It's from the donkey's tail," he said. "You said you needed one for the spell."

"You're the *best*," said Molly. She stood on tiptoe and kissed him on his little wrinkled nose. Bugbane blushed and put his wings over his face. (You can tell a bat is blushing when his ears turn pink.)

"All right," said Molly. She took the donkey hair and tied three knots in it, then wrapped it around the sprig of moonwort. She had a bottle full of spring water from Cook's stash and dipped the sprig into that. All that remained were the magic words.

"I'll wait here," said Angus. "I, uh, don't hide all that well. But if you need me, yell, and I'll come get you."

Molly nodded. "I doubt it'll be a problem. I can turn invisible, after all."

Still, she was glad to know that the muscular Minotaur was waiting for her. Old Man Harrow was a grown-up, after all, and one who beat innocent donkeys, so it was good to have backup.

She hiked up the hillside. It was a steep slope, and she was glad that she didn't have to turn invisible, since holding her breath would have been difficult. When she reached the back of the barn, she peered through a crack in the slats.

The barn was filthy. Nobody had cleaned it for a long, long time. It smelled of old dung and moldy hay.

There was a wooden cart in the middle of the barn, piled high with firewood. It was stacked halfway to the ceiling.

An old man with knotted forearms was pulling a donkey toward the cart by the halter.

He can't really *expect that little donkey to haul all that wood, can he? There's more wood there than donkey!*

Apparently he did expect it. The donkey, on the other hand, took one look at the cart, set its hooves, and hauled backward.

This ridiculous tug-of-war continued for nearly a minute—Harrow was a big man, if elderly, and the donkey was very small—then Harrow balled up a fist, yelled something not at all nice—and punched the donkey between the eyes.

The donkey let out a tragic bray. Harrow lifted his fist again.

Molly had seen enough. She yanked the Little Gray Book out of her sleeve and read, quickly and clearly:

"Accreus Illusus Equine Accomplicia Margle Fandango!"

The sprig of moonwort in her hand leaped up in a tongue of flame and vanished before the heat even touched her skin.

"Eh?" said Old Man Harrow, turning his head. "Is someone there?"

He dropped the donkey's halter and started toward the back of the barn.

Molly sucked in a breath and prepared to vanish.

The donkey brayed again. It sounded . . . different.

Hotter, somehow. *Scalier.*

Old Man Harrow froze.

The next bray wasn't a bray at all.

Harrow was one of those people who is born mean and continues to lose ground. He took up farming because people hated him. Animals didn't like him very much either, but they weren't capable of telling him to go away. His wife *had* told him to go away, many years ago, and when he refused, she had gone away instead.

Harrow had gotten older and meaner and even though he had an adult daughter who kept urging him to move to the city and stay with her (she was as kind as Harrow was mean), he had planned to stay on the farm until he died.

The noise the donkey was making made him think that perhaps that might not take very long.

He turned around.

A dragon filled the space where the donkey had been. It was a small gray dragon with enormous ears, but it was definitely a dragon.

It shook the remains of the halter off its long reptilian snout and grinned at Old Man Harrow.

Its teeth were as long and thick as pencils. They gleamed in the dim light of the barn.

The former donkey charged.

Harrow dove behind the cart of firewood. The dragon smacked at the cart with its claws, but it was now too big to squeeze past the cart. It roared in frustration.

Molly wanted to cheer. The spell had worked better than she'd dared to dream!

"Go away!" screamed Harrow from behind the cart. "Go away! Bad donkey!"

The dragon knocked some of the firewood off the top of the cart. Logs flew like matchsticks. It roared triumphantly.

"Bad donkey!"

That should be enough, thought Molly. *The spell only lasts a minute. It'll turn back any second and then I'll go out and tell him that he's got to be nice to the donkey or it'll happen again . . .*

The minute certainly seemed to be taking a while.

More firewood flew. Old Man Harrow dove into one of the empty stalls, which was only empty in the sense that there were no animals in it. (There was a great deal of animal dung, however. Harrow did not keep his barn very clean.) The dragon tore at the stack of firewood with its claws.

A very long minute indeed.

More like two minutes.

Possibly even three minutes.

Molly had brought a watch just in case, and she pushed her sleeve back to look at it.

It had been four and a half minutes.

The dragon knocked the last of the firewood loose, tore the cart in half, and stomped toward the stalls.

"It's not supposed to last that long!" said Molly, panicking. "It's only supposed to be a minute—the spell *said* it was only supposed to be a minute—"

"I don't think it read that bit," said Bugbane.

The dragon roared and sent its tail smashing through an old water trough. Mucky water poured across the floor.

Five minutes.

Remember when we said that spellbooks are like cookbooks, and individual spells are like recipes?

Just like with recipes, sometimes you can substitute the ingredients in a spell . . . and sometimes you can't.

If you want to use less salt in a recipe, oftentimes you can get away with it—but if you try to substitute sugar instead, your eggs may taste very odd indeed.

Cows and donkeys are very different animals—as different as sugar and salt. Cows are large, placid, and not very bright.

Donkeys, on the other hand, are cunning. And very, very stubborn.

And this one *liked* being a dragon.

It took seven minutes and forty-three seconds for the

dragon to turn back into a donkey. They were the longest minutes of Old Man Harrow's life. He cowered behind the dung heap and put his hands over his head.

At the six-minute mark, the dragon figured out that it could breathe fire. If it hadn't already knocked over the water trough, the whole barn might have gone up in flames. It settled for scorching the rafters and setting fire to the remains of the donkey cart.

Molly was torn between running to get Angus—maybe he could tear some of the boards off the back of the barn and they could pull Old Man Harrow out before he got toasted!—and running in to help herself. What if the dragon got there before Angus did? There was no time! She was supposed to Smite, not commit *murder!*

She took a deep breath and charged around the side of the barn.

"Hey!" she yelled. "Hey! Dragon! Over here!"

The dragon, who was snuffling at the dung heap, turned around.

It was not a particularly vicious donkey. It had hated the cart and the barn and Old Man Harrow, but Molly had never done anything to it. And she looked a little bit like Harrow's daughter, who had always been kind.

It ambled toward Molly, although in its current state, it wasn't sure if it wanted a lump of sugar or a lump of coal.

"Uh—good dragon!" said Molly. "Nice dragon. You . . . uh . . . leave that man alone . . ."

"Growwrrrrhaaaawww?" said the dragon.

Molly, for lack of anything else to do, reached out and scratched it behind the ears.

"Growrhhaaaww . . . haaa . . . heeee-haww . . ." said the dragon, and in a very few seconds it was a small donkey again.

Molly let out a breath that came from the bottom of her very impressive boots.

"I think it's safe to come out now," she called.

Old Man Harrow popped up from behind the dung heap. "Safe? Is that brute gone? What in the name of tarnation just happened?!"

"Were-donkey," said Molly firmly. "Looks like it caught a stray bit of magic. It happens, you know." (This was a lie.)

"Magic?" Harrow looked around a bit wildly. "From where?"

"Could be anywhere," said Molly, still petting the donkey. It had a very soft nose. "Sunspots. Passing fairies. You know." (This was an even bigger lie.)

"Is it going to happen again?"

"It might," said Molly. "Once things turn into other things, they're liable to do it again without warning." (This

98

was actually true.) "I've turned him back for now . . ." (This was a gigantic lie.) ". . . but I wouldn't upset him."

"Upset him?" Harrow gave a horrible cracked laugh. "I'll *upset* him! Where's my axe?"

"Axe?" asked Molly blankly.

"I'm going to chop that monster's head off! I'm not keeping a dragon in my barn!" He began rooting through his tools.

"No!" said Molly, throwing herself in front of the donkey. "You don't want to do that! If it sees you coming with the axe, it might turn into a dragon again!"

Harrow paused, his eyes narrowing. "I'll get it in the dark," he said.

"Dragons can see in the dark," said Molly. "Like cats. Or bats." She took a step backward. "Besides, it—uh—"

Oh, what would be horrible enough to save the poor donkey's life?

Inspiration struck. She dropped her voice as low as she could, took a step forward on her very impressive boots, and leaned forward.

"*It might not stay dead*," she hissed.

"Eh?" said Harrow.

"You know how snakes thrash around for hours if their heads are cut off?" she said. "Dragons are worse. You can chop it into little pieces and bury them, and they still

99

might claw their way out of the ground and when you least expect it—when you're on the way to—to—to the outhouse, say—"

Old Man Harrow turned the color of cottage cheese. "Stop!" he said, taking a step back. "What do I do?"

"I'm a Witch," said Molly. "From Castle Hangnail. I'll take it off your hands. For—oh—five dollars?"

"Five dollars?" said Harrow.

"Disposal fee," lied Molly glibly. "I'm giving you a discount because it's a very small donkey."

Harrow looked from the donkey to Molly, then to the ruins of his barn. "Well . . ."

"I'd say take time to think about it," said Molly, examining her nails, "but I can't swear that the donkey won't turn back once it's rested up a bit."

There was a long minute while the old farmer teetered back and forth.

And then—

"Four dollars," said Harrow.

"Four fifty," said Molly. "I can't go any lower or I'll lose money."

Harrow might not have understood magic, but he understood money very well. "Fine," he grumbled. "But I don't want to see that donkey ever again, you hear? It slips away and comes back to the barn and I'll have you before a magistrate, you understand?"

Molly folded her arms. "I assure you," she said, in her frostiest and Witchiest voice, "that will not be necessary."

Harrow counted out four fifty into her palm. "Now get it out of here!"

"Come along," said Molly to the donkey, putting an arm around its neck. "Let's be a good donkey and not think about being a dragon . . ."

She led it away from the barnyard. When she was down the road, around the bend, and out of sight, she sat down in the road and laughed hysterically until she thought that she might cry.

She pulled out the letter from the Board of Magic. As she watched, a red line drew itself through "one (1) act of Smiting." For some reason, this made her laugh even harder.

Angus galloped up. "You've got a donkey," he said. "Is everything okay?"

"Fine, fine . . ." gasped Molly, wiping her streaming face. "Fine. Well, it's fine now."

The Minotaur looked at the donkey. The donkey looked at the Minotaur.

"Well," said Angus. "I guess Castle Hangnail has a donkey now."

Two days later, Majordomo went into town with a mixture of dread and anticipation.

He went into town once a week, to visit the mercantile and pick up the mail. Under normal circumstances, he looked forward to this—he would have a cup of tea at the little café and a nice chat with the woman who ran the post office and then he would take Cook's shopping list into the mercantile and pick up all the little odds and ends required to keep Castle Hangnail running smoothly, like sugar and dish soap.

Today, however, he was worried. Nothing travels as fast in a small town as news. Surely everyone must have heard about Old Man Harrow and the dragon-donkey by now.

The question was how they would feel about it.

If a donkey suddenly turns into a dragon and a Wicked Witch shows up a moment later, you'd have to be a pretty dim bulb not to guess that the two were connected. (Harrow had something of an excuse, since being trapped behind a dung heap by a fire-breathing monster tends to addle the mind a bit. He had figured it out by the next day, but was too frightened to go and ask for his four fifty back.)

When the old Evil Sorceress had been in power . . . well, she'd been old when most of the people in town had been born, and she hadn't done a lot of magic toward the end, even before she'd convinced herself she was a rosebush. Having an actual practicing magician in the castle was going to be new to many of the residents.

Majordomo had to admit that having a Master who wasn't senile was an improvement. There had been a bad few weeks when the old Sorceress had begun ordering things off the shopping channel on TV. He'd been returning them as fast as they arrived. Postmistress Jane had helped him stamp "Return to Sender" on everything, but there was a difference between packages and dragons.

Would the townspeople be impressed with Molly's magic, or would they side with Old Man Harrow?

In his pocket, he had an envelope addressed to the Board of Magic. He had carefully filled out all the boxes, printing the name Eudaimonia in purple ink.

Surely this would be enough. They wouldn't feel the need to send somebody out and check, would they? As long as their list of Tasks checked itself off and he'd sent in the form saying that there was a Master in the castle, the castle should be safe.

It had to be.

Majordomo ran a hand along the top of Miss Handlebram's white picket fence. Roses and dahlias and spires of delphinium twined through the fence slats.

Miss Handlebram herself came around the side of the house and waved. She was a stout, gray-haired black woman with a pleasant face. If she had ever been seen without gardening gloves and galoshes, he'd never heard of it. "Guardian!" she said. "How are you doing?"

"It's, um, Majordomo now," said Majordomo awkwardly. How did you go about telling everyone that you had a name instead of just a title? "The new Master—Mistress—the Wicked Witch named me—"

"That's a wonderful name," said Miss Handlebram firmly. "I like it. *Majordomo*. It sounds like something you might name a rose—a sturdy white one, I think, with good resistance to beetles."

This sort of compliment might confuse many people, but Majordomo had lived down the road from Miss Handlebram for eleven years and took it in stride.

"It's good that there's a new Mistress in the castle," she continued. "One likes to see the old traditions being kept up. I shall have to invite her to tea."

The old Evil Sorceress would have blasted Miss Handlebram on the spot for such presumption—at least, when she'd been in full possession of her wits. Majordomo could very easily picture Molly sitting in Miss Handlebram's garden, swinging her feet and eating scones.

He didn't know how to feel about that.

He waved to Miss Handlebram and continued down the road to the village.

The post office was his first stop. He nodded to Farmer Berkeley, who was coming out of the building.

"Guardian!" said Berkeley cheerfully. "Just the fellow I'd like to see. I've got an old donkey cart out in one of the sheds, you're welcome to it. Ha!" He grinned broadly as he walked away.

Majordomo sighed. Word had spread. Clearly.

"Won't be a minute," said Postmistress Jane. She took his letter to the Board of Magic, applied a stamp, and dropped it into the slot. Then she opened the post office box for Castle Hangnail. "A good bit of junk mail, I'm afraid—it's that time of year—another notice from the Board . . ."

Majordomo unsealed it. It had an official seal and stated that they had been given the absolute last extension possible under the Minions-in-Residence Act of 1481, and either they got a new Master in immediately or Castle Hangnail would be slated for decommission.

He shoved it in a pocket, where it joined six other

identical letters. Once Molly finished the Tasks, they wouldn't be a problem anymore.

"Oh, and a letter for someone named Molly?"

Majordomo took the envelope. It was addressed to Molly Utterback, care of Camp Hangnail. Someone had sealed the envelope with a sticker in the shape of a pink glittery heart.

"Camp Hangnail?" asked Jane. "Are you running a summer camp up there now? Not that that's not a good idea . . . all those rooms, and that lovely moat to go swimming in . . ."

"No . . ." said Majordomo. "I think there's been a mistake. Miss—Miss Utterback, is it?—is the new Mistress of the castle," he explained to Postmistress Jane. "She's an Evil twin. This must be from the good twin."

Camp Hangnail?

It's the good twin, he told himself. *Good twins are never very bright.*

"Oooh, an Evil twin!" Jane nodded. Her brown pony-tail bobbed up and down. "Just the sort of thing you like to see in somebody up in the castle." She grinned. "Is it true about Old Man Harrow?"

"I couldn't say," said Majordomo warily. "Is *what* true about Old Man Harrow?"

"Well, Mabel had it from Darcy that Harrow's donkey up and turned into a monster! And a little girl showed up and turned it back and led it away, gentle as a lamb."

"Oh," said Majordomo. "I . . . uh . . . guess that's true enough. The Mistress is quite young for her age."

"Child prodigy, I expect," said Jane cheerfully. "You'd expect that from an Evil twin, you would."

"She's a Wicked Witch," said Majordomo, feeling an unexpected glow of pride. "A child prodigy. Yes."

"And . . ." Jane looked from side to side. "We're not supposed to give out information about customers, but he came in today and filled out a change of address form! Says he's had enough and he's moving to the city to live with his daughter."

"Oh my . . ." said Majordomo.

"It's his daughter I feel sorry for," said the waitress at the café, a few minutes later, bustling up with his tea. "Your usual, Mr. Guardian."

"Thank you."

"On the house, Mr. Guardian," she said. "Anyone

who can get that nasty old Harrow out of town is tops in my book."

"I didn't do it myself . . ." said Majordomo.

"No, indeed, it was that nice Wicked Witch of yours. Still! Harrow used to come in here and it was shameful the things he'd say to the staff and he'd leave a penny as a tip."

Majordomo very wisely did not argue with this.

He enjoyed the tea and the steady flow of gossip from the waitress, who knew everything in town and not just the fate of Old Man Harrow. "And how is that Wicked Witch doing in her new castle?" she asked after a bit.

"Very well, I think," said Majordomo, standing up. "Also—" He cleared his throat. "It's Majordomo now. The new Mistress named me."

"Ooh, that's a posh name!" said the waitress. "Don't know if I'll remember that right off, but you just keep reminding me, Mr. Majordomo, and I'll get it straight."

He left her an especially generous tip and went off to visit the mercantile.

He was on his way home when Miss Handlebram ran out to meet him. "There you are!" she said happily. "Was afraid I'd miss you on the way back."

She was carrying a bunch of roses—deep, dark ones,

with vivid red hearts. "These are for you to take up to the castle. The rose is called Witchcraft and I thought, now what could be more fitting than that? You give those to your Mistress and see that she comes down for tea."

"Yes, Miss Handlebram," said Majordomo, accepting the roses.

CHAPTER 13

Molly took the letter and rolled her eyes. *"Sisters,"* she said, in deep disgust. But she was thrilled by the roses, and by the invitation.

"I'll go to tea tomorrow," she said. "Although—"

She glanced down at herself. The boots were still impressive, but wrangling the donkey had taken a bit of a toll on her outfit. Donkeys and lace simply do not go together, which is part of the reason you very rarely see a doily on a mule.

"As to that," said Pins, with a discreet cough, "I have just finished something up . . . if madam will step this way . . . ?"

It was a coat.

It was the greatest coat that Molly had ever seen in her life.

It was black (of course), but it was different *shades* of black. The fabric was charcoal black and the trim was metallic black and the lining was obsidian black and the buttons were tiny silver raven skulls with even tinier twinkling black eyes. The sleeves were swooping and edged with black lace, but because Pins knew how Witches were, the lace could be tied back out of the way and there were very practical tight black sleeves underneath.

Molly was almost speechless. "Pins," she said, and had to stop and wipe at her face. "This is—it's the Witchiest—it's the best thing I've ever had!"

She swooped him up and hugged him. Pins looked smug as only a stuffed creature can.

It was true that there was nothing any tailor could do about her height, but the coat somehow made five feet tall (with the boots) the exact height that a girl should be. Molly swept around the room. The top hugged in close while the outer reaches of the coat flared like a peacock's tail. There was even a little button under the fold of the collar where Bugbane could cling with his feet.

"*This* is magic," said Molly, turning in front of the mirror.

"Possibly a little," said Pins. "Mostly it's double stitching, though, and the black frogging on the collar. Now, let me just snip this loose thread—there! Wear it to tea tomorrow."

She wore it to tea the next day, and the day after that she wore it when Miss Handlebram came stumping up the road to the castle, armed with shears and a copy of *Gardener's Guide to Flowers.*

"Miss . . . Handlebram?" asked Majordomo, blinking.

"That's right, Guar—Major! Your dear little Witch asked me up to help her with the herb garden, and I'm here to set things right." The gardener adjusted her sun hat like a knight adjusting his helmet before battle. "You let me at those weeds!"

She stepped into the hallway before Majordomo could

protest. He wasn't used to middle-aged women carrying shears forcing their way into the castle.

"My!" said Lord Edward appreciatively. "At your service, madam!" The old suit of armor managed a creaky bow.

"Miss Handlebram!" Molly ran down the staircase, clomping on every step. Her coat flared out like wings. "You brought the book! And I found *Weeds of the World* and *Field Guide to Obscure Wildflowers*."

"Perfect!" said Miss Handlebram, raising her shears. "We'll figure out what's worth saving and send the rest to the compost pile. To battle!"

"To battle!" cried Molly, and giggled. "Taming the herb garden counts as 'securing and defending the castle,' doesn't it?"

Majordomo said, "Um?"

"We're defending it from weeds!" Molly charged out the door, with Miss Handlebram behind her.

Majordomo sighed. Well, it wasn't quite as impressive as an invading army, but perhaps the Board would consider that a Task done. And he would just as soon not have to deal with an invading army.

"Fine figure of a woman," Lord Edward whispered to Majordomo. "Why, if I were three hundred years younger—and had a body—"

Majordomo put a hand over his eyes.

It took Molly and Miss Handlebram three days to set the garden to rights. Majordomo would peek in occasionally and see the two of them bent over a page in a book, discussing a tricky ID.

"Now, the stem is square and the leaves are toothed—"

"But the leaves are set opposite each other, not alternating—"

"And that's a yellow *composite* flower—"

"Are there hairs on the underside of the leaf? That's how you tell the two apart—"

This sort of thing is really only of interest to Witches and gardeners, which is why the two groups get along so well, and why, if you want to find a real honest-to-goodness Witch, the best place to start is at your local botanical garden. Majordomo left quickly.

"Is good neighbor," said Cook firmly, sending a plate of sandwiches out to them. "Is knowing all little plants. Me, is knowing cooking. Is can spot cabbage at twenty paces. Any cabbage. Good with cabbage. Other plants, not so much." She shrugged.

Majordomo took the sandwiches and did not argue the point.

It was all going so *well*, he thought. The villagers seemed predisposed to like her, and she had undoubtedly worked quite an impressive bit of magic with the donkey—a dragon! Really!—and she was working hard to tame the herb garden, which had been sadly neglected for years.

And when you looked at the letter from the Board of Magic, there was a faint red line through the word *secure*.

"It's not all the way there yet," Molly said when she showed it to him. She wiped her forehead with her gardening gloves. "But we haven't gotten the east flower bed under control yet, either. I think it's working!"

Perhaps it was simply because he had a dour disposition, or because he was used to serving dark and dreary Masters, but when things went this well, a minion like Majordomo could not help but expect something to go terribly, terribly wrong.

CHAPTER 14

Molly woke up three days later to find her room icy cold.

She had been having a nightmare where the real Eudaimonia swept into the castle and everyone found out that she was just plain old Molly. In her dream, Majordomo had been staring at her, and his expression was so cold that when she woke up chilled, it just seemed like part of the dream.

Then she exhaled, and her breath fogged over the blankets.

"What . . . ?"

It was normally a bit chilly in the evenings, but the ancient boiler kicked on at night and by morning the castle was warm. This morning, however, there was frost on both sides of the windowpanes. Molly felt a small, hot lump on her neck.

"Bugbane?"

"It's cold," he said, shivering. "I had to come off the bedpost. My wing-tips were going numb."

"Don't bats hibernate when it's cold?"

"Not in summer."

Molly swathed herself in blankets and put her feet on the floor. The thick carpeting muted the cold somewhat. Her breath made a steamy plume in front of her.

"Something's wrong," she said. "I better go find out what."

She eyed the bathroom door. The tiles gleamed like ice.

"First, though," she said, "I'm putting on ALL my socks."

"It's the boiler," said Majordomo, when Molly finally came down to breakfast. Everyone in the castle was wearing everything they owned. Cook had on a parka that had to have taken at least an acre of material. Pins had brought his goldfish down before her bowl froze and set her near the stove.

They huddled around the table.

"The boiler's broken?" asked Molly. She wrapped her hands around her hot chocolate to warm them.

Majordomo shook his head. "Not exactly. The plumbing's broken, so there's no water. The boiler can't make steam to send through the radiators to heat things up. And all this stone keeps the castle so cold . . ." He leaned back and thumped one of the gray stones affectionately.

"I suppose we'll have to have someone in to fix it, then," said Molly. "Is there a plumber in town?"

117

There was a brief, embarrassed silence.

"There is," said Majordomo slowly, "and I'll go fetch him after breakfast. But plumbing can be expensive, and I don't know . . ."

"Oh," said Molly, who understood grown-up talk well enough to know that meant that there was a chance they couldn't afford to have it repaired.

She stared into her hot chocolate. It felt as if a hole had opened in her stomach and her heart had sunk down into it.

She was the Master of Castle Hangnail. It was her plumbing. She ought to pay for it.

The sum total of Molly's possessions, including the money from Old Man Harrow, was eleven dollars and seventeen cents. Plus a very small donkey.

"Do you know any spells to fix plumbing?" asked Pins, without much hope. Plumbing wasn't very Witchy.

Molly shook her head, and felt her heart sink even lower.

There was one person in the castle even more upset than Molly, and that was Serenissima.

Serenissima didn't need heat the way everyone else did. She carried her own heat with her. She could have stood in the middle of a blizzard, steaming gently.

But she was a creature of water and she felt an affinity with pipes and plumbing and most especially with the great steaming boiler. With the pipes not working and the castle rapidly emptying of water, she felt abandoned in a way that none of the other minions could really understand.

"You don't understand!" she cried. "All your water is on the inside!"

She retreated into her teakettle on the stove and sobbed bitterly. The kettle whistled sharply with every sob, which Cook was patient with for the first hour, and then finally Serenissima found herself lifted up and plopped down in the pantry. This made her sob even harder, until (as always happens) she eventually cried herself out and could only curl up in the kettle and sniffle.

Everyone tried to cheer her up, but to little avail.

"Come out, Serenissima," said Pins. "They'll fix it, you'll see."

"Is no good crying," said Cook. "Is better working!"

"C'mon, Serenissima, it'll be okay," said Molly.

"Really, this is most unseemly," said Majordomo. "As minions, it is our duty to accept whatever life has thrown at us!"

"Stiff upper lip, my girl!" advised Lord Edward. "Always darkest before the dawn, what?"

To all of these entreaties and more, Serenissima only

wailed "You don't understand!" The puddle under the teakettle (mostly condensation, but some tears too) grew wider and wider.

Steam spirits are generally very lively, but when they get depressed, they are very soggy indeed.

Eventually they gave up and left her in the pantry.

The repairman came out the next day. His name was Harry Rumplethorn, and he was very tall and very wide and his pants tended to ride down in the back, so that when he knelt to work on the boiler, you saw rather more of Harry than you wanted.

But for all that, he was a decent man and everybody in the village knew that he was fair. He had come out several times to fix the pipes over the years, and Majordomo trusted him. When Harry stood up this time and hitched his pants back into place, there was a regretful look in his eyes.

"It's bad," he said. "If it was just a blocked pipe or something leaking or backed up, I could rig something to make it work, but it's rusted through and the pump's burned out trying to compensate and . . ." (And here he said a great many more things that he understood and no one else really did.)

Majordomo gritted his teeth. Molly, who had been hovering near the boiler room, leaned around the edge of the doorframe.

"Is that bad?" she asked.

Harry sighed. He wasn't quite sure how to talk to Molly—she was young enough to be one of nieces, but she was also most definitely a Wicked Witch, and everyone in town knew about the incident with the donkey by now. So he decided to be blunt.

"It's pretty bad," he said.

He tried to explain how the plumbing worked, but rapidly veered into technical terms that made Molly's head ache. It was a different kind of magic from hers. The bit she took away was that there was a broken piece in there somewhere, and it had broken a couple of other things along with it. He could fix it, but it was going to cost a lot.

"How much is *a lot* in this context?" asked Majordomo.

"Eighteen hundred dollars," said Harry. (Molly sucked in her breath.) "Nine hundred for the parts, and nine hundred for labor."

"We'll have to think about it," said Majordomo. "Thank you for coming out. What do we owe you?"

"Nothing," said Harry, who knew that "we'll have to think about it" is grown-up code for "we don't have the money, but we don't want to admit it." He wiped his hands on a towel. "I'm sorry I don't have better news. You call me when you're ready to set something up."

"We will," said Majordomo, even though both of them knew that it wasn't going to happen.

The door closed behind Harry. Molly and Majordomo looked at each other, then at the walls.

"Time was," said Majordomo grimly, "time was that we had such a treasury that we gave charity, we didn't ask for it. Ungo the Mad had a whole vault of gold and diamonds and antique china he got from selling his inventions. When the library in town burned down, he paid to have it replaced."

"That was nice of him," said Molly.

"Well . . ." Majordomo shifted his feet. "It burned down because he'd been experimenting with fire-breathing bats."

"Oh! Like Great-Uncle Humphrey!" said Molly.

"What?"

"Err—nothing."

He gave her a funny look, but Molly felt a sudden tug of hope. He'd given her an idea. The bats had helped her before—could they help her again?

CHAPTER 15

"Treasure?" asked the Eldest. It was only an hour or two after noon, and the old bat was yawning. "We have no treasure. What would a bat do with treasure?"

"We couldn't lift it."

"Treasure is heavy."

"It doesn't taste good."

"Not like bugs."

"Don't you have any ideas?" asked Molly. "We need to make some money, fast! Otherwise Serenissima's going to flood the whole castle crying. And it's all salt water, so we can't even use it. Cook says that there's an inch of water in the pantry and she had to move the cheeses, and Angus is hauling in buckets from the well so we can all have baths."

"We have nothing." The Eldest yawned again and folded a wing over her face. "Treasure is a thing of earth. Plumbing is a thing of water. Bats are of the air. Ask someone else . . ."

Molly opened her mouth to protest that surely they

must have *some* ideas, but Bugbane tugged on her hair with one claw. She looked at him and he shook his head warningly. Apparently it did not do to keep the Eldest from her sleep.

Molly sighed and tried to squelch her disappointment. She bowed to the bats and said, "Thank you for your time, Eldest," as politely as she could.

The bats were already snoring when she left the tower.

She found Majordomo, Pins, and Cook pooling their money in the kitchen. Between the three of them, they had three hundred and twelve dollars and eighty-eight cents. Molly pushed her own eleven dollars and seventeen cents into the pile.

A few days ago, this would have seemed like a vast sum of money to her. Now it was dwarfed by a much bigger number—eighteen hundred dollars.

"Will be getting egg money next week," said Cook. "Probably . . . thirty dollars. And Angus is being helping Berkeley with the calves, is bringing home maybe a hundred dollars, if many calves."

"I have a shiny rock," said Pins's goldfish. She stroked a fin over a small pebble. "Perhaps we could sell it."

Nobody said anything. The goldfish sighed. "Air-breathers don't appreciate shiny rocks nearly enough."

"Mrs. Emmett wants her grandmother's wedding dress let out to fit her daughter," offered Pins. "That might be worth something."

"Unless it's worth fifteen hundred dollars, I don't think it's going to help," said Majordomo. "And if we can't fix it, we'll have to leave—you can't stay in a castle like this in winter without heat—and then the Board will get involved. It won't even matter if Molly has completed all the Tasks."

"Why would the Board get involved over a boiler?" asked Molly.

"They don't let magic places stand empty. The magic gets all . . . funny," Pins explained. He poked a pin into a crack in the table and began trying to pry a splinter loose with it.

"If a magic castle can't be inhabited, it's decommissioned," said Majordomo.

"Oh," said Molly. After a minute she said, "How do they decommission a castle, anyway?"

"Druids," said Majordomo gloomily. "A whole team of them, wearing goggles and rubber gloves. They pull the magic right out. Anyway, by the time they're done, it's just an ordinary old castle, and they usually wind up selling it to a developer to turn into apartment buildings."

This thought was so depressing that Molly wanted to hide under the table.

"Check the letter," said Majordomo quietly.

Molly reached into her coat pocket and pulled out the letter from the Board of Magic. She spread it flat on the table.

The thin red line that had appeared across "Secure and defend the castle" had vanished. Now there was a black underline under the phrase. It pulsed when Molly looked at it.

"Oh, come on!" said Molly. "I pulled every weed in the herb garden! I got slivers and thorns and Miss Handlebram got a rash! That doesn't *count*?"

Majordomo shook his head. "Not now. Not if the castle will be uninhabitable."

Molly put her hands over her head.

Pins worked the splinter loose from the table and stuck it into his head next to the other pins and needles.

"We've got some time, don't we?" asked Molly. "I mean, the plumbing's not going to get any *more* broken."

"That's true," said Pins. "We're not using it." (Flushing the toilets was becoming increasingly difficult, since you had to carry water from the well and dump it into the toilet tank, where it promptly froze because the castle was so cold. Using the bathroom was starting to require a lot of strategic planning.)

"As long as it's fixed by fall . . ." said the goldfish.

Unspoken between them was the thought that they

probably couldn't raise fifteen hundred dollars by fall. Even some of the money they had needed to be spent on groceries and chicken feed.

"Six weeks," said Majordomo.

They looked up at him, startled.

"It's a Task now," he said, tapping the letter. "Molly's only got six weeks to do the Tasks. If it hadn't broken until afterward, it wouldn't matter, but . . ." He sighed. "Maybe I can file another extension."

"We'll figure something out," said Molly, feeling horrible. She was the Master of the castle. She was supposed to be able to fix things!

A terrible little voice in the back of her head said: *The real Eudaimonia would be able to fix it.*

Majordomo rose and went out without saying anything. That only made her feel worse.

Cook took down a big jar and swept the money on the table into it. She wrote "PLUMBING IS BEING RE-PAIRED FUND" on the label and set it on the counter.

Pins and Molly nodded. They had work to do.

CHAPTER 16

When Majordomo went to town the next day, Molly went with him. She had a letter of her own to mail.

It wasn't a bad walk. They didn't say very much. The shadow of eighteen hundred dollars hung over them, and both Molly and Majordomo felt, on some level, that whatever their differences, they were in this together.

(Molly was feeling especially quiet because when she had tried to use the bathroom that morning, the toilet was completely dry. She'd gone to three different bathrooms in the castle before she found one that had enough water to flush. This lent a certain urgency to the plumbing issue.)

Majordomo held the door of the post office open. Before Molly could walk through, a man shouldered his way through the door and nearly ran into her.

"*Excuse* me!" said Molly, in the tone that really means "You're being very rude!"

"Oh!" said the man. He looked down at Molly. "Didn't

see you there." He was wearing a red checked jacket and a disagreeable expression.

There is really nothing you can say to this, so Molly didn't say anything.

"You're fine," said the man. He patted her on the head, which caused Molly to hate him immediately, at once, and for eternity. "Good little girl."

And then he simply walked away.

"What was that?" demanded Molly, shocked.

Majordomo shook his head. He had no idea.

"Good little girl?!" she said. "Am *not!* I've half a mind to turn him into an earwig!"

"Oh, *would* you?" asked the postmistress. "He's an awful man. Some time as an earwing might improve him immensely."

Molly peered over the edge of the counter. "I'm Molly." She slid a letter over the counter. (It was addressed to her parents, and it was asking for an advance on her allowance. She would have gladly given up her allowance for the rest of her life to save Castle Hangnail, but somehow, she didn't think they'd send her eighteen hundred dollars. Still, it didn't hurt to ask.)

"You'll be the new Wicked Witch, then," said Postmistress Jane. "The one with the good twin. It's a pleasure to meet you." She handed Majordomo a stack of mail. "That nasty fellow was Freddy Wisteria."

"Wisteria?" asked Majordomo. "Didn't his grandfather own that lake in the middle of town?"

"Indeed, and his father after him, and now Freddy owns it. But he's taken a notion in his head to put a hundred houses on it."

Majordomo frowned. The stitches on his forehead pulled together in an impressive topography of concern. "But . . . there's not enough land there. You could fit—I don't know, three or four houses. Maybe five or six. You couldn't put anything like a hundred houses on it."

"You can if they don't have yards," said Postmistress Jane. "Or proper gardens. And if you drain most of the lake and put in parking lots." She slammed a drawer shut. "People won't know it's not supposed to look like that. They'll just move in because we're a quaint little village with charming atmosphere, and then want to know where the *real* grocery store is and why isn't there a nail salon and pretty soon they're putting up more stores and we're just a faceless little town where the village used to be." She scowled. "I've seen it happen. I used to live over in North Hickory, and . . . well. It was the nicest little town. *Was*."

Majordomo shuddered. Molly thought of the town where her parents lived. It had nail salons and three grocery stores and parts of it were nice, but parts of it were hard and grungy and dirty and there was broken glass on the sidewalk. There weren't any places like that in the village. She ran a finger over the brass rail on the counter.

"I hear he's got an eye on your place too," Jane added. "When the old Sorceress went to the home, he got the notion you'd be selling it."

"No!" said Molly, shocked. "Nobody's selling Castle Hangnail!"

Majordomo said nothing. If the Board of Magic had to decommission Castle Hangnail, they'd put it up for sale, and Freddy Wisteria would be waiting. He'd put *three* hundred houses on it, and the village would change all out of recognition.

"That's what's going to happen, isn't it?" asked Molly as they left the post office. "If we can't fix things. If I can't do the Tasks."

Majordomo nodded. "Six weeks from now," he said. "Maybe two months, because it takes a little while to send out the druids. But not longer."

"We'll fix it," she said fiercely. "We *have* to."

The old servant glanced down at her and smiled, almost involuntarily. He knew that it was probably hopeless, and yet, the new Master loved Castle Hangnail. And that was a start, however small.

CHAPTER 17

Two days later, Majordomo went back to town to check the mail. He usually waited a few days, but he had sent the letter to the Board of Magic off over a week ago, and he was desperate to get the reply. Even just an acknowledgment that Castle Hangnail had a Witch and was now no longer slated to be decommissioned would be *something*. That way, when the boiler issue came to light, they'd be the castle with the Wicked Witch who was filing an extension and not the abandoned castle without a Master and he could stall the paperwork for weeks if he had to.

There was no letter. There was, however, plenty of junk mail, a flyer for a rummage sale, and a cheerful post-card of people water-skiing, with WISH YOU WERE HERE!! printed across it.

The second exclamation point disturbed him. Major-domo did not believe in squandering punctuation. He flipped the card over.

It was addressed to Molly Utterback, care of Camp Hangnail.

At that point, he should have stopped reading. He *meant* to stop reading. He really did.

But the writing on the postcard was a large, clear print, like a schoolteacher's, and the word *camp* leaped out at him from it, and as he started to turn it back over, he saw the last line. He couldn't *help* but see it.

And then Majordomo did a terrible thing.

He read a letter that wasn't addressed to him.

It was a betrayal of common decency, and furthermore, it was a betrayal of a minion's loyalty to his Master. He knew that even as he was doing it.

As he read, his free hand clenched into a fist, and the flyer for the rummage sale crunched as it was smashed into a ball.

"Something wrong?" asked Postmistress Jane. "Bad news?"

"No," said Majordomo. "No. Nothing." He crammed the postcard under the other junk mail. "Thank you."

He did not stop at the café. He did not stop at the mercantile. He walked home, up the long road to the castle, while the words on the postcard ran through his mind.

Dear Molly,
Hope you're having a good time at summer camp! We've

gone to Lake Whattamatta for two weeks, although we'll
probably be back by the time you get this. We went swim-
ming and your dad went water-skiing. Sarah picked out this
postcard. We miss you, and can't wait for you to come home.
Love,
Mom & Dad & Sarah

It was as if every cheerful letter was a weasel and it was chewing on his brain. (Majordomo was, in fact, one of the few creatures on earth who had had a weasel chew on his brain and lived to tell the tale, but that had been back in the old days, and Ungo had bought a new lock for the ferret cage the next day.)

Molly's parents thought she was at summer camp.

Her parents were expecting her to come home again.

He'd mailed a letter to the Board saying that they had a new Master, and the new Master, it turned out, was a twelve-year-old girl who was the next best thing to a runaway and was expected to leave at the end of the summer.

A twelve-year-old girl who had been lying to him this whole time.

He'd thought—just a few days ago, walking up this very same road with her—he'd thought there was a chance. He'd seen somebody who loved Castle Hangnail and thought that maybe here was a Master, however young, who could help him save the castle from de-

134

struction. Majordomo had stalled the Board of Magic for years, but with a Master to help him, maybe they could have saved the castle once and for all.

He'd almost started to believe. That was the worst part of all.

At first, he was angry. Being angry got him past Miss Handlebram's house, with a face that wilted several roses as he passed.

But then, as he looked up the road to Castle Hangnail, with its crumbling tower and tottering turrets, he thought, *She lied to all the others too.*

What was he going to tell the other minions? What was he going to tell Lord Edward, who had sworn fealty to Molly? What was he going to tell Pins, who had labored so lovingly over a proper outfit for a Wicked Witch?

What was he going to tell *Cook?*

His heart sank.

They were going to be devastated.

He trudged up the road to Castle Hangnail, moving like an ant under the unforgiving sun.

CHAPTER 18

M olly was in the library, looking for a spell.

The Little Gray Book was no use. She'd gone cover to cover, trying to find a spell that would turn something into gold, and all she could find was a spell that would turn real gold into fool's gold, which was no good to anybody.

The other spellbooks were just as opaque and complicated as they had been a week ago. As far as she could tell, nobody else had been able to turn things into gold either. One of the books had a recipe, but you had to start with diamonds and live lobsters, and the scrawled notes underneath said it didn't work and just made the lobsters very uncomfortable.

Occasionally she'd pull out the letter from the Board of Magic. It was probably her imagination that the black underline under "Secure and defend the castle" was spreading.

She was sitting in a chair, trying to puzzle out the

crabbed handwriting of *A Witche's Grimoire of Practicale Magicke* (written in an era when *E*'s were plentiful) when the door opened and Majordomo came in.

At first, she didn't look up. Reading books in the library was perfectly acceptable now. If he asked, she'd tell him the truth—that she was looking for a way to turn things to gold.

He set a small silver tray down on the end table beside her and said, in a chilly voice, "Your mail, madam."

"Mail?" said Molly.

She leaned over and picked up the postcard. It took her only a moment to read it, but she stayed, staring blankly at it, for several seconds.

Then she raised her eyes, very slowly, to Majordomo.

She knew at once.

"You read it," she said. It was not a question.

"Yes," said Majordomo.

"You shouldn't have read my mail."

"No."

"But you did."

"Yes."

People talk about tension so thick that you can cut it with a knife. You couldn't have cut this with a knife. A knife would have bounced off. You'd need a sledgehammer for tension like this.

Molly tried. She made a choking sound that was meant

to be a laugh and said, "Postcards. I never thought of postcards. Ha."

"When did you plan on telling us that your parents expected you back?" Majordomo asked. His voice was very calm and very even.

"I thought I'd find a spell to change their minds," said Molly in a small voice. "I've got weeks and weeks to look for it. I've *been* looking . . ."

She trailed off. From the way that Majordomo's eyes had gone wide, she realized that she'd managed to shock him.

"You can't change people's minds with magic," said Majordomo. "For an hour or two, maybe, you can muddle them—but to actually make them think something else? You have to break their minds open, turn them into thralls . . ." He trailed off, horrified.

Making someone a thrall is well past Wicked. It's deepest, darkest Evil. An Evil Sorceress who thought nothing of freezing someone in ice for a thousand years might balk at turning them into a thrall.

"Didn't they teach you that in Witch school?" asked Majordomo.

Molly gave him a small, guilty glance and looked away.

He collapsed into one of the reading chairs and put a hand over his eyes.

"You didn't go to Witch school," he said.

"I *wanted* to!" She leaned forward. "My mom wouldn't let me! There's not that many Witch schools left, and they're mostly expensive or far away, and she didn't think it was nice. But I tried!"

"So you lied about it."

"I thought you'd like me better," she said uncomfortably. "It's not like I'm not really a Witch! You've seen me cast spells! Ask Angus about the donkey! It's just . . . I'm self-taught, is all. And I learned a lot from Eu—from a friend of mine. I'm really a Witch!"

"Yes," said Majordomo wearily. "I suppose you're really a Witch. There's still that."

He got up. He looked older and more tired than Molly had ever seen him look.

"Are you going to tell everybody?" she asked.

He shook his head slowly. "Why? What does it matter now? We can't fix the plumbing. The Task will fail, you'll have to leave, and the Board will have us decommissioned. Whether or not you went to Witch school . . . when or why you're going to leave . . . it just doesn't matter."

He went out, shutting the library door behind him. Molly waited until the door was closed and promptly burst into tears.

CHAPTER 19

Molly cried hard and ugly, the way people do when the world is utterly broken and can't be fixed. Her nose was red and runny and her face was blotchy and scrunched up and her eyes ached and still she cried.

Bugbane hunched up against her neck and extended one wing over her shoulder. "It's okay," he said. "I'm still your friend. Even if you have to go somewhere, I'll come with you."

This only made Molly cry harder.

She'd let everybody down.

She'd ruined *everything*.

The only thing that could make it worse would be if he found out I'm not really Eudaimonia.

She knew she had to stop crying. Someone might come into the library and find her, or hear her, and then they'd ask what was wrong and she'd have to tell them, or Majordomo might tell everybody and then they'd *all* hate her.

It wasn't easy. She bit down on her knuckle to slow the sobs.

She thought, *Eudaimonia wouldn't be crying.*

Yeah, but Eudaimonia wouldn't have screwed everything up in the first place.

Molly took a deep, shuddering breath.

Eudaimonia would have swept in and probably kicked Majordomo aside as she did, and he would have loved it because that's how he expected a Master to behave. And no one would have questioned, because Eudaimonia was tall and pale and had exciting cheekbones and was an Evil Sorceress to her fingertips.

And the servants would have loved her and hated her in equal measures for it. Pretty much the way that Molly did.

If she could see the mess I've made . . . she'd say, "But it was so simple, *Molly dear! Can't you even get that right?"*

And then she'd laugh.

The memory put steel in Molly's spine. She straightened up and took another breath and refused to let it catch in a sob.

Eudaimonia—the real Eudaimonia, the one Molly had known in her hometown—had been perfect and Wicked and seventeen years old. She'd had almost a dozen invitations to come and be an Evil Sorceress.

Molly was not seventeen and not perfect, but she was

the one at Castle Hangnail, so she was the one who was going to have to muddle through.

"There's got to be a way through this," she muttered, standing up. "There's got to be a way to keep the Board of Magic away. I don't care *how* cold it gets in winter or how far I have to walk to flush the toilet, and I won't let *anybody* make me leave!"

Bugbane clutched at her hair. Molly swiped at her face with the back of her hand and turned up the collar of her jacket.

She wanted to go outside. If she was out in the air, maybe things would be different.

She went through the castle without saying anything. No one stopped her.

At another time, the garden might have been a comfort. Molly trailed her fingers over the mint and the sage as she passed, so that she walked in clouds of sweetness and spice. But the thought that she might have to leave the garden—just when they'd gotten the weeds out and the stinking horehound was happy and it looked like the manticore artichokes were going to flower this year—made her want to cry again.

Molly went out through the garden gate, into the pasture where Dragon the donkey was grazing. (They had named him Dragon, because there was really no other choice.)

She picked a spot largely free of donkey droppings and sat down. Bugbane stretched his wings and took a few cautious turns over the flowers, snapping at passing flies.

Molly flopped over on her back and stared up at the castle.

Clouds drifted by. The main tower rose like a tree above her. One of the ravens had found a bit of shiny ribbon and was showing it off. A bit of rock fell off the side of one of the turrets and thumped down into the grass. The shallow moat glittered in the sun, casting wet shadows on the squat little detached tower.

She loved it.

She loved the towers and the sense of elegant decay, the not-very-bright ravens, the grassy hills that tried so hard to be a blasted heath but were really just grass, spangled with clover blossoms and dandelions.

"I won't leave you," she told it fiercely. "If they try to make me go home, I'll run back to you. If the Board of Magic tries to decommission you, I'll tie myself to the front door and make them go through me!"

The ground trembled.

For a split second, Molly thought that the castle had heard her, and was responding—or that the Board of Magic had heard her, and a druid in rubber gloves and a breathing mask was going to erupt from the ground under her feet!

Then her more practical side exerted itself and she thought that they were having a very minor earthquake.

Then the ground trembled again and a little bit of earth heaved itself up onto the grass, and a long pink nose poked out of the ground.

It was a mole.

Molly rolled on her side to look at it better and the mole dove back underground, startled. The disturbed dirt lay in ruffles around the entrance to the hole.

Molly sighed. She hadn't meant to startle it. She knew people didn't like moles because they dug tunnels in the lawn, but she'd always thought the tunnels were more interesting than the lawn anyway. Lawns were *boring*.

The mole had left in such a hurry that there was a tiny tuft of velvety fur left on the edge of the tunnel. She picked it up between her fingers.

And then she had an idea.

Treasures are a thing of earth, the Eldest had said. And: *Ask someone else.*

By now Molly knew the talking to animals spell backward and forward. There were dock leaves growing wild in the grass already. She had the ingredients together in no time at all.

"Avack! Auilriuan! Arwiggle!"

She leaned over, put her mouth close to the hole, and said, "Oh please, mole, *please* come back and talk to me."

She waited.

The mole must not have gone very far down the hole, but he emerged very slowly, nose twitching. "Eh? This isn't a trick, is it? Eh?"

"No trick," said Molly. "I'm Molly. I'm the Wicked Witch."

"Witch, eh?" said the mole. "Got it. Explains why you talk Mole." He ran a heavy clawed foot over his snout. "Whatcha want?"

"While you're down there, in the dirt," said Molly, "have you ever seen any treasure?"

"Treasure . . ." said the mole slowly. "Eh? Worms. Rocks. Lotta rocks."

Molly sat back, disappointed.

Well, what did you expect him to say? "Oh, yes, we're sitting on a giant trove of gold and jewels and small unmarked bills"?

"Okay," she said. "I'm sorry to have bothered you then."

"No bother," said the mole. "Always time for a Witch, eh?"

He dove back into the earth.

She put her chin on her hand and her elbow on her knee and stared at the castle.

"Maybe we can have a bake sale," she said out loud, without much enthusiasm. Whenever her school wanted to raise money, it seemed like they always had bake sales. Cook could probably whip something up . . .

Bugbane danced over the flowers. Butterflies veered out of the way, wondering why a bat was chasing them in daylight.

She'd have to take him home if she failed to save the castle. It would be hard to explain, though. Usually if you saw a bat wandering around in daylight, it was sick. Her mom was going to have a lot to say, and the word *rabies* would come up at least three times.

And Sarah . . . Molly didn't even want to think about it. Bugbane was very handsome for a bat, with his squished-up face and his wrinkled nose and his big ears . . . and Sarah was going to scream until she lost her voice when she saw him.

Molly wiggled her toes inside her boots. That might not be all bad . . . No, if Sarah lost her voice, she would just write notes demanding that the bat be removed from the bedroom.

"And she'd dot the *I*'s with hearts too," muttered Molly. "*And* use pink paper."

The ground stirred again. The mole came up practically between her feet.

"Gotta question," he said.

"Sure," said Molly.

"Treasure," said the mole. "Not sure. Don't know you'd call it treasure. But bits of things, eh? Not like rocks."

He dumped something at her feet.

It was a coin. It was so crusted in dirt and mud that she couldn't read the face on it. Molly picked it up with growing excitement and scrubbed it on her tights until she could make out the design.

She'd never seen anything like it before. It looked like an octopus wearing a crown.

"This too," said the mole. "Have to dig around them. Annoying, eh?"

Another molehill erupted a few feet away. A second mole backed out of it, dragging an ancient bottle. It glittered red in the sunlight.

"Maybe," said Molly, who was more excited by the coin. Still, sometimes antiques stores had displays of fancy glass bottles in the window, and charged lots of money for them. "Yes! Can you bring me more?"

The moles went back underground and consulted. Molly could hear them talking, although she couldn't make out the worlds, a snuffly, muttery kind of talk.

Finally one of them put his head back up and said, "Witch, eh?"

"Yes!"

"Need magic," said the mole. "For Wormrise. We make you a deal, eh? Give you things. Give us magic. Eh?"

"You'll bring me things like this . . . but you want me to give you magic? For . . . um . . . Wormrise?"

The mole nodded.

"I'd love to," said Molly cautiously, "but I don't know any spells about worms."

The other mole came up. "Not a spell," he assured her. "Not like that. You Witch, you know—give other Witch some magic, eh?"

Molly thought about it. Witches often did spells together, and when that happened, one Witch would do the spells and the others would give them power. She'd done it with Eudaimonia lots of times—"Fine, Molly dear, if you can't do it *yourself*, let me do it *right*"—but she wasn't sure how much of that was her and how much had been the older Sorceress.

Honesty seemed to be the best policy. She'd seen where lying got her. "I'll try," she said. "I'm not sure if I know how, but I'll do my best, and I'll keep trying until we get it right."

The mole crossed his claws over his chest. "Good! Not

asking more than that!" he said. "Tomorrow night. Mole bargain!"

Molly hesitantly crossed her arms over her own chest and said, "Mole bargain?"

"Right!"

The mole dove back into the earth, and Molly wondered what had just happened.

CHAPTER 20 ◆

"There appears to be a small army of moles digging up the south lawn," said Majordomo at breakfast the next morning.

"It hasn't been the south lawn for years," said Pins. "You couldn't play croquet on that if your life depended on it. It's the donkey pasture right now."

Majordomo shrugged. When the plumbing's broken and your Master is leaving and the Board of Magic is in imminent danger of repossessing your castle, the state of the south lawn is not high on anyone's list of concerns.

Cook absentmindedly turned on one of the faucets. There was a clunk and a rattle and several chunks of ice fell out into the sink, followed by sputtering noises. She said something in a language Molly didn't understand.

"Mother!" said Angus, quite shocked.

"Is getting tired of broken plumbing! Is being no way to run a household!"

Molly, who had been avoiding meeting Majordomo's

eyes, took a deep breath and straightened her shoulders. "The moles are with me," she said.

The old servant raised one eyebrow. "Really," he said.

He didn't sound angry, just curious, so Molly plowed on. "They found some coins and some old bottles. I thought those might be worth money. They agreed to help."

The silence around the table was thoughtful. Finally Pins said, "You know, people have lived here a long time. Sometimes you find odd things buried. Mostly it's garbage, but not always."

"At my school, when they were putting in a new parking lot, they turned up all kinds of things," Molly said. "Old pill bottles and arrowheads and rusted cans and even a cat skeleton." (She'd wanted to keep the cat skeleton, but Sarah had thrown a fit and told her it was stinky and disgusting, even though the bones were so old, they didn't smell like anything but dirt.)

"Ah, yes," said Majordomo, "your . . . school."

Molly slid down a little in her chair.

"Is good plan," said Cook, setting down the omelets. "Is being good thinking." She waved a spatula at Molly. "But is keeping moles out of my garden! Is not sharing food with them!"

"I'll be sure to tell them," said Molly. "I'm supposed to go out tonight and help them with some kind of magic called Wormrise."

She looked around the table, but none of the others had heard of it either. Everyone shook their heads.

"Whatever it is," said Pins, "it'll be interesting."

"Interesting perhaps," said Majordomo, "but whether there is anything worthwhile in the ground hereabouts . . ." He shrugged.

"Is being a little far inland for pirate treasure," admitted Cook, "but one is never knowing."

"They brought me this," Molly said, setting the octopus coin on the table.

She'd rubbed as much dirt off as she could. It needed silver polish, but she had a vague notion that you weren't supposed to polish really old things, that they had a valuable "patina" (which she *thought* meant the sort of blackish silver film over it, but "pa" was too close to Q in the dictionary, and Cook's removal of the Q section had also claimed most of P and some of R on the other side.)

Majordomo picked it up and turned it over in his fingers. "I've never seen this design before."

Edward, who didn't eat but who liked to take part in the conversations, said, "Bring it over here, old chap, will you?"

Majordomo held it up for him. The enchanted armor squinted his eyeslits at the coin. "That's an Imperial Squid!" He let out a low whistle. "I haven't seen one of those in . . . well, centuries, come to think of it!"

"Is it valuable?" asked Molly hopefully.

"Haven't the foggiest." Edward shrugged his shoulders with a clatter. "Used to be worth quite a lot, but I don't know about now. Not a numismatist, you understand." (Molly forgave him for using the word *numismatist*, which simply means "coin-collector," on the grounds that it was a very good word and opportunities to slip it into conversation are rare.)

"There's an antiques shop in the village," volunteered Pins. "Two doors down from the sewing shop. Mr. Davenport runs it. He might be able to tell you how much it's worth."

"I'll see what else the moles come up with, and take them all in at once," said Molly firmly. She wanted very much to run to the village right now and see if the coin was valuable, but she'd promised the moles she'd lend them magic, and she wanted to get into the library and see if she could figure out how it worked.

"An Imperial Squid . . ." said Edward nostalgically. "Ah, that takes me back. Mad King Harold it was who printed those."

"Why was he mad?" asked Molly.

"Well, he thought he was a cuttlefish. Declared himself the Emperor of All Oceans and tried to declare war on the clouds for failure to pay tribute."

Despite several history classes in school, Molly had

never heard of Mad King Harold. This struck her as a dreadful oversight.

"You don't get that sort of thing today," said Edward sadly. "All these Presidents and Prime Ministers and Parliamentarians . . . If any of them think they're a cuttlefish, they have to keep it quiet. Politics used to be so much better."

"Messier too," said Majordomo. "Didn't Mad King Harold cut your head off?"

"Well, yes, but he didn't *mean* anything by it."

Molly reluctantly slipped away from the conversation and went to go read about moles.

By that evening, she was no closer to learning about Wormrise. If any of the magicians had known about it, they hadn't left notes in the library. Apparently none of the earlier Masters had much contact with the moles.

On the subject of giving magic to someone else, however, there were lots and lots of notes.

Most of them said NEVER EVER EVER EVER EVER EVER DO THIS, in big capital letters with underlines and exclamation points. (Except for the book that said it backward and in Latin, which read *!!!coh tnui-caf non.*)

A few had extra notes underneath that said: "But if you absolutely have to, this is what you do . . . But don't do it. Ever."

This was because most Wicked magicians are much too paranoid to work together. That is why the world is ruled instead by Presidents and Prime Ministers and Parliamentarians, who may or may not believe that they are cuttlefish.

The Little Gray Book had a page about it, near the back. It said: "This can be dangerous, but sometimes it's necessary. You have to trust the other person won't take all your magic and leave you empty. If you absolutely must lend your power to another, look to the place under your breastbone where magic lives, and picture a silver cord running from it to the other person. And think, as firmly as you can, *Yes.*"

The book went on to explain that once you were done giving your power away, you pictured the cord again and thought *No.* And if at any time you thought that the person on the other end was taking too much power, you should think *No!* immediately, because taking too much magic away could burn a Witch out until she was nothing but an ordinary person who used to be a magician.

Molly frowned over the book. It seemed easy . . . but she couldn't remember ever doing that with Eudaimonia. The older girl would just grab her wrist and then the magic would flow out of Molly and the spell would work. And she usually felt tired afterward.

Maybe she was doing it wrong.

This thought was so shocking that Molly hardly knew what to do with it. Eudaimonia knew dozens of spells. She'd been *born* an Evil Sorceress, and Molly had thought she knew everything. She'd even been born with a caul. (A caul is a piece of membrane over the top of your head when you're born. It's rather nasty, but it usually means that magic—or at least second sight—will follow.)

All Molly had at birth was a twin, who grew up to be the kind of girl who sings while she cleans and says "Hello, Mr. Bluebird!" or "Hello, Missus Rabbit! You're looking very fluffy today!" (It could be argued that this sort of behavior was bound to turn Molly to Wickedness in sheer self-defense.)

I won't know if she was doing it wrong until I try it myself. The moles must know something about it, since they suggested it. She nodded to herself and closed the Little Gray Book.

"Come on, Bugbane," she said to the bat, who was already yawning. "It's time for Wormrise."

CHAPTER 21

Molly went out onto the south lawn (aka the donkey pasture) with Angus following her. "In case something goes wrong," he rumbled, taking up a position by the fence.

Molly, her mind still humming with the warnings in the books about giving your magic away, nodded. She couldn't think of any reason why the moles would want to hurt her, but it was nice to have Angus around just in case.

Dragon the donkey had been put in the old stable, where he seemed quite happy and showed no signs of wanting to breathe fire. The sun had almost gone down behind the hills, and the sky was darkening into the shivery blue of twilight. Bugbane snored gently in Molly's ear.

Dozens of little piles of dirt gave testimony to the activity of the moles. There was a small pile of muck-encrusted objects off to one side. Molly had to restrain herself from running to look at it.

There's probably nothing, she told herself, trying to stave off a future disappointment. *Or it won't be worth much. Or we'll find out that an Imperial Squid is only worth about a dollar now.*

A mole popped his dark head out of a mound. "Witch!" he said.

"Witch?"

"Witch!"

"Eh?"

"Witch?"

The pasture was suddenly full of moles, their twitchy pink noses sticking out of the molehills. One—she thought it was the one from yesterday morning—waved his claws at her.

Molly picked her way toward that one, trying to avoid stepping on any molehills.

"Eh!" he said. "Witch! Come for Wormrise!"

A thin, snorfly cheer went up from the other moles. Her mole waved his claws over his head like a prizefighter.

"Do we do this now?" Molly asked. "Only I'm not sure how . . ."

"Waiting," the mole assured her. "Waiting for Stonebreaker."

"Stonebreaker!"

"The Stonebreaker!"

"Eh! Eh! Eh!"

The moles were clearly in a good mood.

They didn't have to wait long. Molly's mole tapped her boot with one claw and pointed.

A few yards away, dirt was being thrown into the air like a fountain. Two burly moles climbed out and stepped away, and then even more dirt flew into the air and the biggest mole Molly had ever seen erupted out of the ground.

His fur was jet-black, but there were pale patterns on it—loops and swoops and spirals and swirls so that he looked almost white. His claws were long and sharp and gleamed in the last light. He was easily twice the size of any mole in the field . . . which made him slightly larger than Molly's foot.

"Stonebreaker!" cried the excited moles. "*Stonebreaker! Eh!*"

Molly fought back the urge to giggle and composed her face into an expression of solemn dignity. This was clearly the moles' magician, and it wouldn't do to laugh at another magician, even if he was fuzzy and serious and adorable.

Stonebreaker crossed his claws over his chest and bowed to the moles. "My moles," he said, which set off another round of cheering.

Molly's mole tugged at her boots and urged her forward.

Molly took a deep breath and walked forward. When she was a few feet away from Stonebreaker's hill, she thought for a moment, then crossed her arms over her chest and bowed.

"Witch! Witch!"

"Stonebreaker and Witch!"

"Eh! Eh! Eh!"

Apparently this was the right thing to do.

Stonebreaker's muzzle wrinkled in a smile. "Witch," he said, bowing back to her. "Come for Wormrise?"

"As we agreed," said Molly. Honesty compelled her to add, "Although I'm not sure what it is you want me to do."

"Painless," said Stonebreaker. He climbed out of his burrow and waddled toward her. Molly crouched down to be on his level, and noticed that the spiral patterns appeared to have been shaved into his fur, revealing the pale skin underneath. "You give magic. Done before?"

"Sort of . . ." said Molly. "But she—the other person did all the work."

"Will do my work," Stonebreaker assured her. He reared up and patted her knee with his claws. "Painless," he said again, kindly.

"What is Wormrise?" she asked.

He smiled. "Luck for moles. Thankful moles. Witch sees, eh?"

"I guess I will . . ."

"Moles!" cried Stonebreaker. "Moles, in position!"

"Eh!" cried the moles as one, and they all dove into the earth.

Molly waited, her hands folded together in her sleeves. She was a little afraid that Wormrise was going to involve millions of earthworms. Molly, like any gardener, was quite fond of earthworms, but she preferred them one or two at a time. A million writhing earthworms would be a bit much, even for a Wicked Witch with a *very* large garden.

As it turned out, the reality was . . . somewhat different.

Sprays of dirt showed where the moles were digging. The last light was fading, but she saw the lines forming a spiral, with Stonebreaker and Molly at the center.

Moonrise was early. The moles finished the spiral as the first moonlight washed over the field.

Molly looked up and saw the moon was a fat, grinning crescent. She shivered inside her jacket.

Dark gray heads popped out of the dirt, lining the spiral. Molly's mole came up beside her and sat, his tiny eyes bright in the starlight.

Stonebreaker nodded. "Good," he said. "Good work, moles." He turned to Molly. "Now, Witch work?"

Molly steeled herself.

I'm supposed to picture a silver cord . . . a silver cord . . . like that . . .

Picturing the cord was easy. It was thinking *Yes* after all those dire warnings that scared her.

Stonebreaker set his claw on her knee again. "Witch," he said, his voice formal, "you consent? Stonebreaker borrows magic for moles?"

And suddenly it was easy. He'd *asked*. He'd asked, and she could say *No*, and that meant that she could also say—

Yes.

She was never sure afterward if she spoke out loud. The silver cord in her mind's eye pulsed, and then she felt power flowing out of her.

The pale patterns in Stonebreaker's fur began to glow like foxfire. As Molly watched, the light grew out of him, running along the line of mole hills, until the spiral burned as if it had caught fire.

"Wormrise!" cried the mole magician.

"WORMRISE!" thundered the assembled moles.

The ground began to shake.

Molly was already crouching, but she sat down, hard. Her mole laughed happily and patted her boot. "Good!" he told her, in a small, exultant voice. "Witch work! Wormrise!"

The shaking intensified. Something huge and pale breached the surface of the earth, far down the pasture, just for a moment, like the back of a whale coming out of the sea.

"Enough," said Stonebreaker. "All power moles need." He brought up his claws and snipped the silver cord that Molly had thought was only in her mind. The sense of magic flowing out of her stopped at once.

Molly exhaled. She was tired, as if she'd run up a flight of stairs two at a time, but not exhausted. And what on earth was going on?

The pale leviathan surfaced again, at the entry to the moles' spiral.

"What *is* that?" whispered Molly.

"Mother of Earthworms," said Molly's mole. He paused, then shrugged. "Also Father of Earthworms. Worms complicated that way."

The giant worm—and that's what it was, a worm thicker than a python and longer than a bus—reared out of the ground. Molly saw a great blunt head lashing back and forth under the moon—and then it plunged forward, into the spiral.

The spiral with Molly at the center.

However grateful Molly was for the work earthworms did in the garden, a forty-foot specimen was . . . well, it was a little much.

I'm a Wicked Witch. I'm Wicked. A Wicked Witch isn't afraid of worms.

The thought rose unbidden that even Eudaimonia might be afraid of this worm.

Stonebreaker did not seem afraid. He stood on top of the molehill in the center while the Mother (or Father) of Earthworms plowed through the earth toward him. It moved sometimes deep underground and sometimes right under the surface, leaving a vast wake of broken earth behind it.

The massive worm threaded through the spiral, coil on coil, until it was so close that Molly could have stood up, walked over, and touched it. Its side was huge and slick.

*I could go invisible. I could go invisible and . . . What?
It's got no eyes, it can't see me anyway.*

It reached the center of the spiral.

The blunt head moved back and forth, between Molly and the mole. For a moment, despite the creature's lack of eyes, Molly had a feeling that the worm was *looking* at her.

What's it seeing? What's it doing?

The Mother of Earthworms reared up, far over Molly's head (she caught her breath), and Stonebreaker moved forward.

The mole magician took several waddling steps, crossed his claws . . . and bowed to the Mother of Earthworms.

The worm lowered its massive head. Stonebreaker reached out very lightly and laid his paw on the worm's head.

Patterns erupted down the length of the worm, silver spirals and swoops and swirls, like those on the magician's body. The worm suddenly glowed as if it had been inlaid with pearl.

The pasture went mad with whoops and cheers.

"WORMRISE!"

"Stonebreaker!"

"Mother of Earthworms!"

"EH EH EH!"

(Even Molly was suddenly delighted to hear "Witch!")

The moles scurried forward, all of them fighting for a chance to touch the great worm. Dozens of furry bodies glowed briefly as the magic passed on to them—and then faded. The moles, still laughing and cheering, dove into the earth.

When the last had burrowed away, and only Stonebreaker and Molly's mole remained in the pasture, Stonebreaker touched the great worm again and said something in the language of moles. Molly didn't need to speak the language to know that it was "Thank you."

The Mother of Earthworms bowed its (her? his?) head. For a moment its eyeless gaze swung back to Molly, and it dipped once—almost a salute—and then dove once more into the earth.

The rumbling of the worm's passage faded. Molly saw that Stonebreaker was no longer glowing.

The mole magician looked exhausted, but happy. He turned to her. "Thank you," he said.

"I'm glad I could help. But"—Molly hugged herself tightly inside her jacket—"but what did it *do?*"

"Ah." Stonebreaker smiled. "Many questions, eh? Good. Witches ask questions."

"Well—why? Don't moles eat worms?"

"Yes. *Exactly.*" Stonebreaker tapped her boot with his claw. "Moles eat worms. Moles are *thankful* for worms."

Molly was getting more confused. "But if you eat

worms, why would you summon the Mother of Earth-worms? Doesn't she *mind?*"

Molly's mole laughed. Stonebreaker smiled. "She does not mind worms being eaten," he said. "Someone must eat worms, or worms eat the world, eh?"

Molly, already a little on edge about the whole giant-earthworm thing, twitched a little at the thought.

"What worm wants is *respect,*" said Stonebreaker, leaning forward. "Not just eat a worm, eat a worm, never think about it, eh? Mother of Earthworms wants to know that moles are *grateful.*" He clapped his claws together. "Moles make offering of magic. Open the way. Then . . . hope, eh?" He wrinkled his muzzle. "Thought she'd come, though. *Good* magic."

Molly took that as a compliment. "And because she showed up . . . ?"

"Luck," said Molly's mole, speaking up. "All moles here. Luck. Grace. Mother of Earthworms a great spirit, knows that these moles honor her. All moles . . ." He sought for a word. ". . . *blessed.*"

"Oh," said Molly. She could understand that, at least a little. "Then . . . I'm glad I could help."

"Ever need mole work," said Stonebreaker, "ask a mole. Eh?"

"I will," said Molly.

Stonebreaker gave her a thoughtful look. "Good," he

said. "Good magic. Could make mole shaman of you, eh? Too tall, though."

"I'm afraid I don't like to eat worms," said Molly. "And I'm not very good at digging."

Stonebreaker gave her a sympathetic look and patted her boot kindly. It occurred to Molly that he considered this a terrible handicap.

"Still," he said. "Good magic. *Fierce* magic."

And then he and Molly's mole dove into the earth, and left her alone in the middle of the field.

Angus helped her gather the moles' treasure up and take it back to the castle. There would be time tomorrow to sort it out and find what, if anything, was worth selling.

For Molly's part, she thought that even if there was hardly anything in the treasure, it had been worth it. She'd never seen anything like that before. And the moles had been very grateful.

Majordomo was waiting when they reached the castle. He held up a candle to light their way in as Angus (who had thoughtfully brought two buckets) carried their prizes into the kitchen.

"We felt a rumbling," he said to Molly.

"Yes," said Molly. She met his eyes. "I just helped them summon the Mother of Earthworms."

Majordomo could have laughed, but there was an odd

168

silver light dancing in Molly's eyes, although she herself seemed unaware of it. "Did you indeed?"

"Yes," said Molly. And then, still meeting Majordomo's eyes, she said, "They wouldn't have taught that. Even in Witch school."

Majordomo inhaled sharply.

Then—"No," he said. "They would not have taught that. Not even in Witch school."

Molly nodded and went inside, with the silvery molelight still playing around her shoulders.

CHAPTER 22

M r. Davenport's Antiques Emporium looked as if it were an antique itself. There were dusty, dark-stained shelves covered in old photographs and small porcelain statues. There were doilies and antimacassars (which are like doilies with ambitions) and quilts made by the Daughters of the Hangfish Revolution and paintings of cherubs and framed prints of uncomfortable birds. Behind the counter, in a locked case, Mr. Davenport kept antique firearms and old swords with dark, stained blades.

The entire store had *patina*.

Everyone at the castle had stayed up very late, cleaning dirt off coins and shaking it out of the bottles. Serenissima had been persuaded to come out of her teakettle and help steam dirt loose—"Oh, very well," she said, "if you think it'll—gulp—help!"—and had been very effective, even if she left a trail of scalding tears on the pantry floor.

Cook hadn't even complained about the mess all over her nice kitchen table.

Their final tally was thirty-six coins, including the Imperial Squid, nine glass bottles, an empty tin of something called "Doctor Mawkin's Shoe Polish & Revivifying Tonic," a porcelain statue of a fisherman missing its nose, and a Complicated Metal Thing that no one could figure out.

Looking around the antiques emporium, Molly thought that the mole treasure might fit right in.

Angus carried the entire load in a cardboard box, and Pins rode on his shoulder to make the introductions.

Mr. Davenport was the only thing in the store that didn't look like an antique. He was a black man in his late twenties and looked entirely too young to be surrounded by so much age and dust.

"Mr. Pins!" he said as they came through the door. "So good to see you again! And Mr. Angus, how is your mother doing?"

"She's very well," rumbled the Minotaur.

"Still—err—not happy about the letter Q? I had a marvelous old cookbook come in the other day, but it's by a Miss Daphne Quaylinghurst . . ."

Angus shook his head.

"Ah, well . . . Now you, miss, I don't think I've met." He leaned over the counter and extended a hand to Molly.

Molly shook it. "I'm Molly. I'm the Wicked Witch up at the castle."

To Mr. Davenport's credit, he did not get that look in his eye that so many adults (even the very nice ones) did at this news. The look that said "Oh, aren't you precious?" and "My, what a big imagination you have!" Molly, like most intelligent children, could pick out a look like that a hundred yards away.

But to an antiques dealer like Mr. Davenport, who was used to objects that might be a century old or more, the difference between twelve and twenty was insignificant. Compared to the stock in his store, *everyone* was young.

"We were hoping you could help us," Molly said. "We've got a bunch of old coins and things that were dug up behind the castle, and we were wondering if they were worth anything."

She crossed her fingers for luck.

Mr. Davenport knew all about the boiler, of course—Harry Rumplethorn had told his wife, and his wife had told Postmistress Jane, and once you told Jane, you told the world. So he didn't ask any questions about why they might want money or why they were bringing him things to sell.

"Let's take a look," he said.

The porcelain statue he dismissed immediately. The bottles he held up to the light and turned, checking their bottoms for stamps.

The Complicated Metal Thing had him baffled as

well. "It's . . . um . . . maybe a . . . could be . . . you know, I have no idea what this is."

"Cook thought it was an egg-beater," said Molly. "I thought maybe it was some kind of farm equipment."

"Can't imagine any animal letting you get near it with that," said Angus. He prodded the Thing with one hoof-like finger. It went *clunk!* and a little gizmo on the side turned and a little metal lever popped out and did nothing whatsoever.

"Are you sure it's not one of old Ungo's?" asked Mr. Davenport. "We can't sell magical artifacts, you know, it's against the law after all those people wound up with cursed monkey's paws."

"How were they cursed?" asked Molly, professionally interested.

"They'd give you whatever you asked for, but they'd just take it from somewhere else. So if you asked for a million dollars, it would disappear out of a bank vault, and the police would turn up and start asking a lot of questions."

"Ooh . . ."

"It's not one of Ungo's," Pins put in. "Majordomo'd never part with those. And anyway, those tend to explode if you move them."

Mr. Davenport spent the longest with the coins. He had a large book and he kept looking back and forth from the pictures to the coins in front of him, moving them into separate piles.

"I'm not a coin collector," he explained. "There are people who spend their whole lives doing it, and could tell you how much these are worth just by glancing at them. But here's what I know.

"These"—and he indicated the largest pile—"aren't worth more than a dollar or two apiece. There's a lot of them around."

Molly sighed. There were more than twenty coins in that pile, including the Imperial Squid.

"These"—and he indicated the next-largest pile—"might be worth a bit more. Five or ten apiece, say."

This was a little better. There were eleven coins in that pile. That might be a hundred dollars for the boiler fund.

"Now, these last three . . ." He indicated the remaining coins. "These might be valuable. Twenty or thirty dollars apiece, at the very least, but possibly more. There's an antiques show this weekend up in Rumbling Falls, and with your permission, I'd like to take them up there and see if I can't find a buyer."

Molly perked up. Maybe one of them would be really valuable! If they could get the money to fix the plumbing, she'd be able to cross the item back off the list—and she wouldn't have to go down three flights of stairs and a hallway to find a toilet that wasn't solid ice.

"Some of the bottles are actually worth more than the coins," Mr. Davenport said. "This one here is a fine example of New Bedford milk glass. I'll give you thirty dollars for this one alone."

Molly glanced at Pins. Pins nodded—he didn't know glass, but he knew that Mr. Davenport would give them a fair deal.

"Sold!" said Molly. "What about the others?"

They settled on a final price of one hundred and seventy-three dollars for the bottles and the less valuable coins. (Molly kept the Imperial Squid.) Mr. Davenport also agreed to take the rare coins and the Complicated Metal Thing to the antiques show, and to sell them there if he could get a good price.

He dropped the coins and the Thing into the tin of Revivifying Tonic. "That'll remind me they're yours," he said. "Pleasure doing business with you! Come back Monday and I'll have news!"

Molly was practically skipping as she left the store. A hundred and seventy-three dollars! That was a lot of money toward the plumbing—and maybe those rare coins would get them the rest of the way!

Her mood diminished somewhat when she tried to do the math . . . even with the new money, it was a long way to eighteen hundred dollars . . . but it was more than they'd had before.

CHAPTER 23

They were walking down the street when Angus let out a startled grunt.

"Stop him!" cried Pins.

Molly turned, and saw Freddy Wisteria standing just outside a cottage fence. He had a rock in one hand, pulled back to throw at a window.

"Hey!" yelled Molly. "What are you *doing?*"

She stomped toward him. Angus followed closely behind her, which gave her a confidence that she wouldn't have felt otherwise. There is nothing like three hundred pounds of bovine muscle to really level the playing field.

Freddy looked up, startled, and dropped the rock on his own foot. He let out a yelp and jumped up and down.

"You attacked me!"

"Did not," said Molly. "You dropped your rock on your own foot, and served you right!"

"I wasn't doing anything," said Freddy, shoving his hands in his pockets and hastily kicking the rock into the bushes.

"You were about to throw a rock through that house's window!" said Pins indignantly.

"Oh yeah? What are you supposed to be, some kind of puppet?" He sneered at Pins. "And a little girl, and . . . um . . ."

His eyes traveled slowly over the Minotaur. His sneer didn't vanish, but it did get rather weak around the edges.

"A valued member of the agricultural community?" Angus suggested mildly.

"Uh . . . yeah. That."

"Look, we saw you with the rock," said Molly. "It's not like people just wave rocks in the air at people's windows for no reason."

"Maybe I do! Is there some law that says a man can't wave a rock around?"

Molly stared at him. For a grown-up, he was acting . . . well, *childish* didn't seem like the right word. Most children she knew would have had more sense.

"Seriously?" she said.

"I'm sure the police would know whether there's a law about rocks being waved around," said Pins. "Why don't we ask them?"

Freddy went a little green around the gills. "Look, don't get all uppity . . ."

"*Uppity?*" said Molly.

The real-estate developer rubbed the back of his neck.

"Sorry. Look, there's no need to bring the police into it, is there?"

"I don't know," said Molly. "Is there?" She gave him a hard look. "Is that window going to get broken? Because if it is, I think there's a very good reason."

"Look, the window's business. The old woman who lives here needs to sell me her house. I'm just trying to make sure she understands that."

"By breaking her windows?" said Pins.

"Some people don't take hints well. It's all part of the business." Freddy waved a hand. "Look, never mind that. You're the Witch, aren't you? The one up at the castle."

She was hardly going to deny it, since she was walking around with a talking burlap doll and a Minotaur, in addition to wearing several pounds of Witchy silver jewelry. "I'm the Witch, yeah."

"Great!" said Freddy. He leaned down to try and look honest. It was not an expression that came easily to him. "You own Castle Hangnail, right?"

"I'm the Master . . ." said Molly. She was quite aware that ownership was complicated, and one could just as easily say that Castle Hangnail owned *her*. She didn't think Freddy Wisteria was the sort of person who would understand that.

"How would you like to sell me your castle?"

Molly stared at him. Angus snorted.

"I'll give you . . ." He paused and made a flourishing gesture with both hands. ". . . a *thousand* dollars!"

It was bad enough, thought Molly, that he thought she would sell Castle Hangnail. But for such an insultingly low price?

"How about I give you a thousand legs?" she asked. "It'll require turning you into a millipede, but I think I can manage it."

"That's a lot of money," said Freddy.

"It's a lot of legs."

"Fine. *Two* thousand dollars."

"Houses cost hundreds of thousands of dollars," said Molly. "I might be twelve, but I'm not stupid."

"You want a hundred thousand dollars for that decrepit old castle?" Freddy scowled. "No way. It'll cost that much just to pull it down. It's a fire hazard."

"Pull it *down?*"

"Well, obviously. Who would want to live in an old wreck like that?" Freddy stuffed his hands in his pockets. "Fine. Suppose I offered you fifty thousand dollars for the castle and the surrounding lands—"

Molly shook her head. "It's not for sale!"

Freddy Wisteria shook his head. "Don't be ridiculous," he said. "I know for a fact that it nearly went on the market before you showed up. It'll be for sale again. This is your chance to actually make money off the deal."

Molly took a deep breath and let it out in a long sigh. It was a lot of money. Her parents would insist on putting it in a college fund. "No," she said.

"Oh, come on!" Freddy took a threatening step forward.

Molly folded her arms. Angus put a hand on her shoulder.

"The lady said no," the Minotaur rumbled.

"Seventy-five, and that's my final offer."

"Get lost," said Pins. "Find someplace else to ruin."

"You'll be sorry," said Freddy. "We could have done this the easy way." He turned and stalked away.

Molly sighed again.

She'd done the right thing. Castle Hangnail wasn't hers to sell. It didn't belong to anyone, except itself.

"That was a lot of money," said Pins, a bit sadly.

"Yeah," said Molly. "But some things aren't for sale. Or at least they shouldn't be."

If the Board of Magic decommissioned it and it wound up in the hands of Freddy Wisteria . . .

"C'mon," said Molly. "Let's figure out how to keep that creep from getting his hands on the castle."

CHAPTER 24

As it happened, Molly made one more trip to town that afternoon. She needed to get a couple of things, in order to do one more spell.

Her first errand was simple. She went to the hardware store.

Hardware stores are marvelous places for Witches, almost as good as botanical gardens. Most Witches, even the Wicked ones, enjoy feeding the birds, and all of them usually need bits of copper pipe and useful bits of wire. All of these things—birdseed and pipes and nails and wire of all varieties—can be found at a good hardware store.

Molly did not actually need any of these things. She needed to buy a box of nails and get a hole drilled. Mr. Jensen, who ran the store, was happy to drill a very small hole for her. He had cordially despised Old Man Harrow and was so tickled about the dragon-donkey incident that he didn't even charge her.

She took the box of nails back up the hill to the castle. In the garden, she sawed off a branch of rosemary nearly as long as her arm.

Then she trudged out to the far side of the donkey's barn and drove a nail into the ground.

"Zizzible zazzible," she murmured, waving a sprig of rosemary at the nail. "Watch-and-report!"

It was a simple spell. Molly had learned it when she was just seven years old, when her sister Sarah kept going over to her side of the room and trying to "tidy up," which mostly involved throwing away anything that

Sarah didn't approve of. (Sarah did not approve of bones, comic books, or chewing gum, although Molly had always suspected that she was keeping the gum for herself.)

It was an alarm spell. If anybody came onto the castle grounds without permission, Molly would know who it was.

The fields around Castle Hangnail were too large to surround with just one box of nails, but she made a rough oval around the barn and castle. (It wasn't like anyone could do much harm out in the fields anyway—what would they do, kick down the weeds?)

The only hard part was driving the nails. On the high side of the castle, the dirt was rock-hard and she had to use her boots like a hammer to sink them into the ground.

When she'd gotten all the way around the castle, she dusted off her hands and wedged the rosemary sprig under a convenient rock. The spell would last as long as the rosemary stayed in place.

She took a roundabout path back to the castle. A mole popped out of the ground and waved to her. Dragon grazed contentedly in the meadow.

A dragonfly droned overhead. Molly banished the last thoughts of the seventy-five thousand dollars from her mind.

Something, she thought grimly, was going to have to be *done* about Freddy Wisteria.

CHAPTER 25

Two nights later—Sunday night—Molly was lying in bed, thinking. Bugbane snored on the bedpost, and Molly wound a lock of hair around her fingers. (It was a bit oily. She kept forgetting there was no running water. She'd tried to take a shower earlier and the shower-head had gone "Cluh-GUNK!" and then fallen off on her head, frozen solid. She'd had to take a bath down in the kitchen instead, with water Cook heated on the stove, and it was hard to get all the way clean.)

She had counted down the days to the six-week deadline three times, and wound up with twenty-eight days, no matter which way she counted. She sighed. Doing the math over wasn't going to help at all.

Mostly, though, she was thinking about magic. The Wormrise spell had gone beautifully, and even though she had given magic to Stonebreaker for it, she hadn't been exhausted afterward. She'd been a little bit tired, but she felt great.

That was the thing that was puzzling her.

She'd given magic to Eudaimonia before. She'd done it a lot. And every time, afterward, she felt *exhausted*. Drained. Feeling like she'd spent all day weeding the garden and then doing laps around the neighborhood.

But the spells she'd done for Eudaimonia were such little things. The older girl had borrowed Molly's magic for spells that Molly couldn't do herself—and they were such minor spells! Mending tears in fabric or changing the color of the paint on the walls. Changing a C on Eudaimonia's report card to an A. (Molly knew this was bad, but Eudaimonia was, after all, an *Evil* Sorceress. And Sorceresses are expected to summon ice and fire and ride dragons, not do algebra.)

Spells like that couldn't possibly be as big a magic as summoning the Mother of Earthworms. So why hadn't she felt tired?

Maybe Stonebreaker only needed a little magic. Maybe he almost had enough himself.

Molly twisted the lock of hair around her finger in the other direction.

Maybe Eudaimonia wasn't very good at borrowing magic.

She frowned into the darkness.

Maybe—

And then something went *BONG!* in her head and she smelled a sudden overpowering scent of rosemary.

Someone was trespassing on the castle grounds!

She concentrated. If it was just somebody out for a late-night walk . . .

Come on . . . come on . . . where are you and what do you want?

The spell wasn't very specific, but what Molly got back involved the barn.

And fire.

Molly sat bolt upright in bed, threw the blankets off, and dove into her clothes. She had to get down there— and fast!

She snatched Bugbane off the bedpost—he went "Hnrrhg?! Whazzit!?"—and ran down the stairs. "Angus!" she yelled. "Angus, come quick!"

Lord Edward woke up with a clatter of armor. "Eh? What? Who goes there? Are we under attack, my lady? I'll rout the devils! Where's my sword?"

"Somebody's breaking into the barn! Where's Angus?"

"I know I put it somewhere in here . . . big sword, blue gem on the handle, can't miss it . . . forget my own helmet next . . ."

Molly ran past him and into the kitchen. *"Angus!"*

Fortunately the Minotaur had only just gone to bed. He clomped out into the kitchen, wearing his pajama bottoms. "What? What's wrong?"

"What is being ruckus?" cried Cook from her room. "Is needing sleep!"

"Somebody's breaking into the barn! I think they want to burn it down! We have to stop them!"

Angus gave an angry snort. "We will! No time to lose!" He opened the door to the garden. "Come on—"

The smell of rosemary was getting awfully thick now, and even though it was all in her head, she wanted to sneeze. The barn was at the bottom of the pasture, well away from the castle, and even as she watched, Molly thought she saw a light.

"Have you ever ridden a horse?" asked Angus.

"Well—yes, once, but it was at a pony ride—"

He snorted again, this time with amusement. "This will be different." He reached down, grabbed Molly around the waist, and slung her up on his shoulders.

"Whoa!" Molly grabbed his horns to keep from falling off. "What are you—"

"Hold on," said Angus. "Hold on very, very tight."

He dropped to all fours.

Humans can't run on all fours, at least not very well. They're not built for it. But Minotaurs have strange, twisty joints and long arms and extraordinary muscles. A Minotaur can run on all fours as easily as he can walk upright . . . and much, much faster.

Molly found herself riding a bull down the pasture.

There were a few awkward moments when she tried to find the right way to sit, and it was a good thing that Angus's horns faced forward, because otherwise her career as a Witch might have come to a sharp, pointy end. But there was an intruder and Angus and Molly were the only ones who knew it, so she sat up straight and gripped the horns tight and yelled, "Run!"

He ran.

The barn stood dark and apparently quiet at the end of the field, but Molly never doubted that someone had broken in. She might only know a few spells, but she could have set the alarm spell in her sleep. She just hoped they'd arrived in time.

Angus slid to a great splay-hooved halt in front of the door, and Molly leaped off his back and ran for the barn door. "Go around back!" she hissed over her shoulder.

The door was ajar. Molly knocked it open with her elbow and stepped inside.

CHAPTER 26

Witches are brave. Witches walk in dark places. And there was a Minotaur with her. Molly lifted her chin and walked forward.

Her boots wanted to stomp, but she lifted her feet and set them carefully instead.

The barn was quiet—almost. Dragon the donkey was restless in his stall, shifting from hoof to hoof. At the end of the line of stalls, in the little room where all the straw was kept, Molly saw a flicker of light.

They're still here. Whether it's Freddy or someone he hired—they're still here.

Great! I can catch them red-handed!

Err . . . if they don't catch me first . . .

She took a deep breath and held it until she was sure that she was invisible, then poked her head around the doorframe.

A dark figure stood in a beam of light. There was something in his hands that Molly couldn't make out.

It was Freddy. He was wearing black clothes, and had set a flashlight on the counter to see by.

Molly reached out, groped along the wall—the light switch should be there, shouldn't it?—and heard a chilling sound.

Scritch. Scritch. Scritch.

It was the sound of someone trying to light a match.

"Strike anywhere matches," Freddy muttered. "Huh! Strike nowhere is more like it."

Was Angus in position? If Freddy lit the straw on fire, would they have time to stomp it out? Molly didn't know and couldn't take the time to find out.

If he sets the barn on fire—if he scares Dragon, I'll— I'll—I'll do something!

Her fingers found the light switch.

"Stop right there!" yelled Molly, and flipped the light on.

Freddy let out a yelp and dropped the match he was holding.

It's not lit, it's not lit—whew!

It has to be said that Molly wasn't a particularly imposing figure. She wasn't wearing her coat or her Witchy hat and she hadn't had time to put on any silver jewelry. Her hair was tangled from the wild ride down the hill, and the pounding smell of rosemary was making her nose run.

"Oh," said Freddy, "it's *you.*" He folded his arms. "What are you doing here?"

"Stopping you!" said Molly. "What are you doing breaking into the barn in the middle of the night!"

"I could ask you the same question," said Freddy. "You're here too!"

Molly stamped her foot, which might have been childish, except that the boots made it a fierce stomp. "I'm the Master of Castle Hangnail! You're breaking and entering!"

"You can't prove that," said Freddy. "I might just have been passing by."

"You're wearing all black! You've got a flashlight!"

"You're wearing black too."

"I saw you trying to light a match! You're trying to burn the barn down!"

Freddy folded his arms. "So you *say*. I say it's dark and I wanted a light. It's your word against mine, isn't it?"

Molly gritted her teeth.

I'm a Wicked Witch. Witches don't lose their tempers over stupid people. Witches fix things. Wickedly.

"You're right," she said, wonderfully calm. "You're absolutely right. We'll just call the constable to sort this out, shall we? There's a phone up at the castle."

Freddy took a step back. "I don't think we need to do that."

"I'm pretty sure we do," said Molly. "Since one of us is lying and I know it's not me."

"But if the constable comes, I'll say *you* were going to burn down the barn. They'll think you're a juvenile delinquent."

Molly grinned. Freddy thought he could scare her with *that?* You didn't grow up with a good twin without learning a thing or two about blackmail.

"I'm willing to take that chance," she said. "After all, I'm twelve. What are they going to do to me? But you . . ." She half turned toward the barn door, keeping an eye on Freddy.

She made three steps toward the stalls—and Freddy yelled "STOP!" and tried to tackle her.

Molly saw him move. She'd been half expecting it. Somehow, though, expecting someone to attack you doesn't prepare you quite as well as you think it should. Molly dove sideways, into an empty stall, and hissed the first spell that came to mind.

"Shanks and shadows—

up and down—

inner and outer *and*

magic unbound!"

Her chest felt fizzy, as if someone had poured a bottle of soda over her heart. Molly never liked that feeling, so she didn't do the spell often, and she wasn't quite sure why she'd done it now.

Freddy yanked the stall door open.

"Now I've got you—"

Molly's shadow stretched, yawned, and peeled itself away from Molly.

Freddy blinked.

The shadow grew. Molly had never tried the spell except in daylight, when the shadow was sharp and clear and firm, and not much taller than she was. But surrounded by darkness, cast by the light from the flashlight, the shadow was large and blurry and indistinct.

It rose . . . and rose . . . and rose . . .

Its head brushed the ceiling, then slid along it in the manner of shadows.

Molly was lying on her back against the wall, straw poking through her clothes, and couldn't see over the wall, so she wasn't sure why Freddy suddenly whimpered and cowered back.

When she summoned the shadow, she danced with it. That was all the spell did—peeled your shadow off and made it a dance partner.

So why was Freddy bone white?

"Get back!" he yelled. "Get back! You can't take me there! That's not a real place—*go away*—"

What's he talking about? It's just a shadow . . .

Well. You can't leave a spell half finished.

"Dance with him," Molly croaked.

The shadow stood up straight and lifted one arm in the opening positions of a waltz. The moonlight through the window and the light from the end of the hall combined to give the shadow long grasping fingers.

It reached for Freddy.

The real-estate developer let out a shriek and whirled, running for the back door—

—straight into Angus's arms.

CHAPTER 27

The town constable was not fat and jolly, despite many stereotypes about policemen. Constable Singh was tall and thin and he took his job very seriously. But he was also a very intelligent man, and when Molly explained about the rosemary spell and why she'd done it, he nodded and took careful notes and called her "Miss Utterback."

"Seems pretty cut-and-dried," he said. "We found matches and a can of gasoline. We'll press charges and have him up for breaking and entering and attempted arson before the end of the week."

"Will that work?" asked Molly anxiously. They were all sitting at the police station, and the constable had fetched her a mug of hot chocolate and a blanket to put around her shoulders. (She didn't really need the blanket, but apparently it said somewhere in the police handbook that if you found someone in a traumatic situation, you put a blanket around their shoulders. Molly didn't feel like arguing with police procedure.)

"Yes," said the constable. "You won't even need to come and testify. He's made a full confession." He smiled. "You've done us a great favor, Miss Utterback. He's a nasty piece of work and we've been trying to catch him for something for quite a long time, but he's as slippery as an eel."

Molly nodded. Since there seemed to be nothing else to say, she finished her hot chocolate and carefully folded the police blanket. "Err . . . Constable Singh?"

"Yes, Miss Utterback?"

"When I threatened to call the police, Freddy said he'd tell them I was the one breaking in. He said it would be my word against his . . ."

A rare smile split the constable's long, sallow features. "First of all, Miss Utterback, Freddy had what we'd call a *definite motive.* He's got a history of trying to harass people into selling their property to him, and his interest in Castle Hangnail was well documented. Secondly, you've the word of a respected member of the community"—he nodded to Angus, who looked startled and gratified—"and so that's two against one. And third . . ."

His smile faded, and he scratched his forehead. "Well, you're a Witch, so you probably know more than I do about what went on in there. But he didn't even try to claim that you were up to any mischief. He confessed to everything and begged us to lock him up—'where the monster can't get him,' he said."

"Oh," said Molly. "I—I guess I scared him. It wouldn't have hurt him, but he was trying to grab me . . ."

Constable Singh nodded. "Completely understandable," he said. "And as long as you're not scaring off good *law*-abiding citizens—well, I shan't complain about a little wickedness in a good cause."

He smiled and patted her on the knee. Molly and Angus left the station and began the long climb up the hill to the castle.

"*Would* it have hurt him?" asked Angus.

Molly shook her head slowly. "I don't think so," she said. "Well . . . it never hurt *me* . . ."

But she made a note to look the spell up in the library just as soon as she got a chance.

CHAPTER 28

Majordomo was just emerging from the kitchen when he heard someone bang the knocker on the door.

He hurried into the Great Hall and reached the door just as Molly came skidding down the banister. (She'd been up in the belfry, chatting with the bats. The Eldest had been telling her a fascinating story, but had fallen asleep right at the good bit. Molly didn't mind because the belfry was currently one of the warmest places in the castle.) "Is it Mr. Davenport?" she asked breathlessly. "He said he'd come today—he'll have just been back from the antiques show—"

"I don't know," said Majordomo. Despite his desire to keep Molly at arm's length, he couldn't fault her recent efforts. "Only one way to find out . . ."

He turned and opened the door with a proper slow *creeeeeaaaaaaak* of hinges.

"Wonderful old hinges," said Mr. Davenport appreciatively. "You don't get a creak like that anymore."

"We try to keep up the old traditions," said Major-domo, pleased.

Mr. Davenport stepped inside—and right behind him, a bit pink from the walk up the steps, was Harry Rumplethorn.

"Mr. Rumplethorn?" said Majordomo. "I wasn't expecting—"

Molly clasped her hands together. "Mr. Davenport! Did you go to the antiques show? Did anybody buy the coins? What about the Complicated Metal Thing?"

Mr. Davenport shook his head. "I am afraid that I was unable to find a buyer for the Complicated Metal Thing. The coins did reasonably well, but not spectacular."

Molly's face fell.

"However," said Mr. Davenport, giving her a slow smile, "I did find a buyer for the tonic tin."

"The tonic tin?" asked Molly blankly.

"The tonic tin?" asked Majordomo.

"Dr. Mawkin's Shoe Polish and Revivfying Tonic," said Mr. Davenport. "I'd never heard of it, but apparently Dr. Mawkin was the most famous swindler and snake-oil salesman for a hundred miles around. But there are precious few tins left, since they exploded if you left them out in the sun too long."

Molly did not approve of snake oil—it tended to make the snakes very cross when you tried to extract oil from them—but she grasped the point immediately. "It was rare?"

"Rare and very valuable." Mr. Davenport took off his glasses. "Twelve hundred and forty-five dollars, to be precise. I took the liberty of bringing Mr. Rumplethorn with me, as I expect you've some business with him."

Harry Rumplethorn touched an imaginary cap and nodded to Molly. He spoke to Majordomo, however. "With your permission, sir, I'll be ordering replacement pipes. My apprentices and I can get started tomorrow."

Majordomo was struggling to keep up with this unexpected fortune. His math skills, however, were very much intact. "I'm afraid we still don't have eighteen hundred dollars," he said. "I'm very sorry you've come up here for nothing—"

Harry shook his head. "Fifteen hundred," he said. "For the parts, for the company that makes them won't take any less than nine hundred. But my apprentices have agreed to work for half-wages on this job. We'll have the parts installed in a trice."

"But—but you have to pay your apprentices—" Majordomo knotted his hands together.

Harry smiled down at Molly and ruffled her hair. (Molly permitted this, although she generally detested adults ruffling her hair, because she knew that it would be very foolish to offend the plumber when he was offering to fix the plumbing cheaply.)

"We talked it over. For the Wicked Witch who drove off Freddy Wisteria!—we're willing to put in a few days of work on half-wages. We'd no way to do that ourselves, you see." He nodded to Molly. "A nasty piece of work he is, and been hanging around town hassling people far too long. But pipes we can fix. And we take care of our own."

Majordomo opened his mouth, and Molly cringed internally—was he going to say something foolish and grown-up about not taking charity? Grown-ups were very stupid about accepting help sometimes. But however proud Majordomo was, his love of Castle Hangnail was stronger.

"Thank you," he said simply. "We're very grateful."

Mr. Davenport smiled and handed him the Complicated Metal Thing. Both of them took themselves off.

"Well!" said Lord Edward, who had been watching from the hall and approaching at a slow clank. "Well! Bless my soul, did you ever hear the like?"

Majordomo shook his head. He thought he might cry, and that would never do. For one thing, when Ungo the Mad had been sewing him together, he'd put the tear ducts in completely the wrong place.

"I knew it would work!" said Molly jubilantly. "I knew we'd figure something out! And here—look—"

She pulled the list of Tasks out of her pocket. The red seal from the Board of Magic flapped as she unfolded it.

The black line under "Secure and defend the castle" was fading away.

"It won't go away until they actually fix the plumbing, I guess," said Molly, "but it knows that we're trying."

Majordomo nodded. The Tasks were much more intelligent than any of the normal paperwork he filled out for the Board.

"But look," said Edward, pointing to the next line.

The line that read "Win the hearts and minds of the townsfolk" had been crossed out.

Molly looked up and met Majordomo's eyes, astonished.

"Well," said Majordomo. "It's not keeping their hearts in jars, or grinding them underfoot, but I suppose driving off a nuisance is pretty good. At least, it counts as a Task done."

"That's the way to do it!" said Edward. "Fine tactics, doing one thing to do another."

Molly folded up the list again, looking at Edward. "I didn't really mean to—oh! I almost forgot—wait right here—"

She ran up the steps two at a time, the boots clattering

and clonking on each step. Edward creaked his head toward Majordomo.

"Bless her heart," said the enchanted armor. "I know you were worried at first, her being so young, but she's a proper Witch, isn't she?"

Majordomo exhaled. "Yes . . ." he said slowly, and continued, only in his mind, . . . *yes, but she's leaving us at the end of the summer, and however will I explain it to you?* Edward had always been the most sentimental of the minions.

Molly came pounding back down the stairs. "This is for you, Lord Edward," she said. "Pins gave me a ribbon to hang it on. It was your idea to take the coins to a numismatist."

She held up the Imperial Squid. The man at the hardware store had drilled the hole right at the top of the squid, and the black ribbon threaded through it made it look like a medal of honor.

For a moment, Edward could hardly speak. Then he said, very slowly, "I'll wear it with pride, my lady. It's been a long time since I won a lady's favor in a joust, and I never won one that I'd treasure half so much as this."

Molly grinned. It's hard to hug a suit of armor—they aren't made for it—but she gave one of his gauntlets a squeeze and reached up to place the Imperial Squid around his neck.

"Let's go tell Cook," she suggested.

Majordomo watched them walk away—Molly stomping, Edward clanking—and thought again, *How am I going to explain it to you when she leaves?*

CHAPTER 29

The workmen took three days to fix the pipes. It was three days of banging and clanging and a little too much of Harry Rumplethorn on display. The ravens retreated to the roof of the tower in the moat, and the bats complained about not being able to sleep and Cook flatly refused to cook anything, so they dined on sandwiches in the evenings.

Even when you are in a very good mood, having pipes worked on is hard on the nerves. And the apprentices were nice boys, but they could never remember that frozen toilets don't flush very well, so Angus had to get out a plunger and a blowtorch at least three times a day.

Molly set herself to finishing some of the other Tasks. She turned three pigeons in the park into glossy gray rats with marvelously twitchy whiskers. She Blighted a stand of daylilies and turned them into thistles. (Thistles are actually much more useful than daylilies, particularly if you are a butterfly.) And, with the aid of the Little Gray Book,

205

she worked a complicated spell and gave one of the statues in town the gift of speech. It was a statue of a Roman soldier, just outside the post office, marking the place where some old ruins had been found.

The statue mostly just muttered insults—it was a Wicked spell, after all—but he muttered them in Latin, so they sounded very grand and impressive.

"*Malum! Spurcifer! Malus nequamque!*"

"He's better than the radio," said Postmistress Jane. "Lets you know whenever anyone's coming. Postmistress Emma over in Foggy Heights wants one for her office."

"*Pessime et nequissima!*" grumbled the statue.

Molly was rather proud of the statue. She'd always been able to Blight plants, and pigeons-into-rats was a very easy spell from the front of the Little Gray Book, but the statue had been complicated and she'd had to come back at dawn and dusk and do the spell twice over to make it work.

Best of all, the thistles and the statue counted as two acts of Blighting for the Tasks. (Turning pigeons into rats didn't count—apparently rats were a step up from pigeons, as far as the Board of Magic's paperwork was concerned.)

"Very good," said Majordomo, watching a red line grow through the word *Blighting* on the list of Tasks.

Blighting the daylilies was a fairly standard bit of witchery, but the statue was quite impressive. "One more ought to do it."

"Does anyone need anything Blighted?" asked Molly, pushing up her sleeves.

"Pediculose!" the statue yelled after them.

As it happened, the waitress down at the café did need some Blighting done. "I'm not sure if you can Blight this," she said, wringing her hands. "Only, we've got mushrooms in the carpet in the office."

Majordomo blinked.

Molly, however, laughed. "Carpet mushrooms! Oh, I've heard of those! Can I see one?"

"We keep a very clean café," said the waitress, looking quite upset. "I don't want you to think we don't. I vacuum every day. These are *extremely* clean mushrooms. But they do keep growing out of the office carpet. It's the most embarrassing thing. I'd hate for the customers to find out, but—well—you're a *Witch.* You know all about mushrooms, don't you?"

She cast Molly a pleading look.

Molly grinned. "I've read about them in garden books," she said. "It's okay. It's not that you're not cleaning enough, honest. There may be a leak somewhere."

"It's under the coffeepot," said the waitress, sighing.

"Sometimes the owner splashes water when he's making coffee. He's a dear, but he's absentminded. Do you know, I shampooed that rug *four times?*"

"Sometimes they just settle into a place," said Molly kindly. "I'll see if I can't get rid of them."

(She herself would have been perfectly happy with mushrooms growing out of the carpet in Castle Hangnail, but she could understand not wanting them in an office.)

Funguses don't respond easily to Blighting. It took Molly three hours before the mushrooms agreed to go away and bother someone else.

"Perfect!" said Majordomo, watching the red line grow until it struck through the word *Blighting* completely. "And that's a Task done!"

The waitress loaded them up with armfuls of cookies, and begged them not to tell the other customers.

"Certainly not," said Molly. "A Wicked Witch is always discreet." She adjusted her hat.

And then, on the afternoon of the third day, the banging and clanging stopped and Harry hitched up his pants and said, "It's all done."

All the minions gathered round the toilet in the bathroom off the Great Hall.

"Would you like to flush it, miss?" asked Harry, nodding down at Molly.

Molly felt a trifle awkward flushing a toilet—even a

toilet with nothing in it—in front of everyone. But she realized that it was a grand occasion nevertheless.

"Serenissima?" she asked. "I think you should do it."

"Oh—well—oh—if you're sure—" The steam spirit let out a long teakettle whistle of a sigh, then glided forward. (Cook hastily threw a tea towel over the puddle she'd left on the stones.)

Serenissima took a deep breath—and depressed the handle.

There was a distant rattle and bang. "Air in the pipes," said Harry. "It'll sort itself out in a bit—you always get some on a start-up."

They waited.

Water gurgled into the tank. It hissed . . . it clanged . . . and then it flushed.

Molly let out a long sigh. You never knew how much you relied on indoor plumbing until it stopped working.

Harry hitched up his pants again. "You give me a call if it isn't working up to spec, but those pipes should last a hundred years." (He pronounced "hundred" as "hun'rd.")

"Thank you," breathed Serenissima, leaving a fine fog of condensation on the mirror.

Harry blushed—Serenissima was lovely, in a grown-up, misty kind of way—and mumbled something. He nodded to Majordomo, ruffled Molly's hair again—she bore this stoically—and let himself out.

"Well!" said Cook. "Is being a fine thing. Is having hot water again." (Molly nodded vigorously to this. Bathing in a bucket in front of the stove is all very well in theory, but it gets old quickly.)

And indeed, the boiler worked better than ever before and the hot water was delivered so piping hot that Molly nearly scalded herself the first time she went to take a shower.

In the days while the plumbing was being fixed, Molly herself had not been idle. She had gone through all the spellbooks and encyclopedias of magic, looking for references to the shadow dancing spell.

It hadn't gone well.

There were references to shadows, of course—lots of them, in book after book. There were spells for wrapping shadows around yourself so that you became hard to see (which is easier than invisibility, if you can't just hold your breath as Molly could). There were spells that called for shadow milk as an ingredient, and a whole article in the *Encyclopedia Thaumaturgica* about how you milk a shadow. (Carefully.)

There was even, in a square book with a greasy leather binding, a deep dark spell for stepping into the Kingdom of Shadows, where the shadows that have escaped from their Masters go to slide and slither and whisper together. Molly shuddered when she read that spell, and put the book on a high shelf. The greasy binding made her fingers itch. That was an Evil spell, not merely a Wicked one.

My shadow wouldn't do that, she told herself. *So I'll never have to go to the Kingdom of Shadows to get it back. Mine just likes to dance.*

And indeed, her shadow lay docilely across the rug, shifting slightly in the glow of the hill-giant candle.

"It *must* be here somewhere," she said to Bugbane. "It's such an easy spell!"

Eudaimonia had taught it to her, Molly remembered. *It was just after I'd gotten a spell right for once—I turned that sheet of paper into an origami tiger without touching it. And she laughed, and she said "So good, dear Molly! Getting to be quite the little spellcaster, aren't you? You'll be teaching me magic next. Here, why don't you try this one, since you're doing so well . . ."*

It was in that big spellbook she had, the one bound in griffin leather. Near the back. She wouldn't let me look at the spellbook, of course, but she told me the words . . .

Molly stifled a sigh. She could have been twice the Witch she was, if she'd just had a good spellbook. *If I'd had the Little Gray Book then, I bet I could have done all those spells . . .*

Well, some of them . . . she probably wouldn't have wanted a cow or a dragon in her bedroom . . .

She frowned. "It *can't* be a hard spell! It doesn't have

211

any components, just the words and your shadow, and if you say the words, it happens!"

She sighed and ran a hand through her hair. "So why can't I find it in the books?"

"What was it called?" asked Bugbane, hanging from a shelf near the ceiling. He ran a claw over a dusty binding. "Maybe I can help look."

Molly shrugged helplessly. "Eud—um. I mean, the girl who taught me didn't show me the book. She just recited the words for me."

"And then her shadow came off?" said Bugbane over his shoulder.

Molly felt as if she'd been standing in cold water and it had only just soaked through her boots. She could feel a realization climbing very slowly up her body, starting at her feet, until it finally reached her brain.

"No . . ." she said slowly. "No, it didn't. Her shadow didn't. Mine did, when I said the words, though."

"Maybe she couldn't do the spell," said Bugbane.

"But—"

Of course she could do the spell! She was—why couldn't she? It's a simple spell!

Molly tried to summon up the memory of that afternoon—of Eudaimonia's bedroom, with the dark blue wallpaper and the dark blue bedspread and the light coming through the glazed window and shimmering like ice.

Eudaimonia had been sitting on the bed, with the great black spellbook open on her lap, and Molly had been sitting cross-legged on the floor, with the origami tiger still wandering around in front of her.

I said the words back to her. I didn't do anything special. My shadow came off and bowed to me. My heels tingled like they were falling asleep and I got that weird fizzy feeling in my chest. And Eudaimonia—

Just for a minute, Eudaimonia had looked surprised. Frightened, even. She'd rocked back on the bed and put up a hand as if to ward the shadow off.

And I said, "Is that right?" And then she tried to look like nothing had happened and said, "Well? Order it!" and I stood there with my mouth open like an idiot and said, "To do what?" and her voice got all high-pitched and she said, "Tell it to do something!" and so I said "dance" and then my shadow did a saraband and a fox trot and then she said, "Now tell it to come back!" and I did.

And she said, "So good, dear Molly! Two spells in a row! You're a perfect little child prodigy, aren't you?"

Molly hadn't liked it when Eudaimonia used that tone. It had a lot of Sorceress in it, and icicles dripped off the edges. She'd said, "No, Eudaimonia," and then the older girl had laughed and said, "Well, they *were* very simple spells. Try this one!" and it had been a hard spell, something where you knit up the wind into knots, and Molly had gotten her tongue tangled up and the wind turned into a sock and then into a sweater with five arms and then unraveled into air in her hands.

Eudaimonia had laughed merrily and closed the spell-book. "It was a good try, Molly dear," she said. "But I suppose you're not quite ready for that yet." And then she had knit the wind into a scarf the color of nothing and wrapped it around her shoulders, and her hair moved in an endless invisible breeze.

Molly had forgotten the origami tiger spell and never tried knitting the wind again, but she remembered the dancing shadow spell. She'd done it four or five times, until the fizzing in her chest started to bother her, and then she didn't do it very often anymore.

"Everybody thinks that if they can do something, it has to be easy," said Bugbane, yawning. "I can fly and you can't. You can do magic and eat with a fork and I can't. Maybe the spell's not easy for everybody."

"But why did she want *me* to do it, then?" asked Molly.

Bugbane shrugged. "Maybe she didn't think you'd be able to."

Was that it? Did she set me a spell she thought I couldn't do, because she wanted me to fail?

It wouldn't be a nice thing to do, but Eudaimonia hadn't always been nice.

She really did seem surprised when it worked . . .

But if it's a hard spell, why did it work for me and not her? I'm bad at magic compared to her! I can't knit the wind or do anything.

Molly slowly flipped through the Little Gray Book. There was a spell in there about shadows, but she didn't much like the name of it.

To feed the hunger of shadows, it said. And it called for a drop of your own blood.

Even Molly knew that blood magic is one of the oldest and strongest kinds. Only bone magic is older and stronger and deeper and darker.

Use only in emergency, said the Little Gray Book, *when life and limb is at stake. She who feeds the shadows risks waking a greater hunger.*

Why would I even want to feed a shadow? thought Molly, putting the book down. *My shadow's not hungry. It just likes to dance.*

But she remembered Freddy Wisteria shrieking and backing away from the shadow, and suddenly she wasn't so sure . . .

"Don't take me there! It's not a real place!" What was he talking about? *Did he mean the Kingdom of Shadows? Could my shadow even do that?*

Her shadow lay dozing on the floor, giving no sign that it felt hunger or anything else at all.

CHAPTER 30

"There's someone at the door," said Edward.

"Yes," said Majordomo. "It was the hammering that gave it away. I'm surprised the door knocker hasn't fallen off—" And before he had quite finished, there was another series of knocks.

CRACK! CRACK! CRACK!

"I'd have let them in," said Edward slowly, "only I don't like the look of them."

Majordomo raised an eyebrow.

"It's a Sorceress," said Edward. "Um. Not a very nice-looking one, though."

Majordomo raised the other eyebrow. "A Sorceress? Here?"

"Perhaps she's one of Molly's friends from Witch school," said Edward hopefully.

"Er," said Majordomo, ". . . Witch school. Yes." Molly was out in the garden with Miss Handlebram. "Yes. I suppose—"

CRACK! CRACK! CRACK!

"Well, it wouldn't do to keep her waiting," said Majordomo. He opened the door.

He'd gotten about halfway through the long, drawn-out squeal of hinges, when the door simply slammed the rest of the way open. The hinges let out an offended "*Sqrrrk!*" and Majordomo rocked back on his heels.

The Sorceress was young and had white-blond hair and skin the color of ice. Her eyes were glacial blue, and she had very long fingernails.

Her gown was floor-length and shone all the colors of coldness, from the deep blue-violet at the heart of a glacier to the snapping green of an iceberg.

There were two men with her, both of them rather large and rather vague around the eyes. They hardly registered at all next to the woman dressed in ice.

"Dog!" snarled the Sorceress. "How *dare* you keep your new Mistress waiting!?"

A large part of Majordomo, the part that had served a great many Masters, said, *Yes! This is how a Master behaves!* His knees wanted to bend. His shoulders wanted to hunch. Large parts of his back and spine tried immediately to grovel.

A somewhat smaller part of Majordomo—which included the vocal cords—said, "Err—what?"

"I'm afraid we've already got a Master, miss," said Edward.

"WHAT?" The Sorceress drew herself up to her full height. She was *very* tall.

(Generally, when you are much taller than everyone else, you do one of two things. Either you rather enjoy looming over people, or you spend a great deal of time hunched over, trying not to run into doorframes and doing your best to make yourself look smaller so that people don't panic and run away. It was clear that this Sorceress did not spend any time trying to make herself smaller.)

"Do you know who I am?" roared the Sorceress. Her two bodyguards took up positions on either side of her. Edward began, slowly and clankingly, to try to put himself between the men and Majordomo.

"I am the Lady Eudaimonia!"

Into the sudden terrible silence came a very ordinary

noise. It was the sound of Molly and Miss Handlebram laughing together as they came out of the garden.

They entered the Great Hall together. Molly had dirt on her knees and a pair of gardening shears still in one hand.

"And *you* thought it was mugwort!" she said, laughing.

"Well, it looked like mugwort," said Miss Handlebram stoutly. "And anyway, it'll grow back. Plants usually do . . . hello, what's this?"

Majordomo was watching Molly.

She looked up, puzzled, and caught sight of the visitors. And then her face went very white, almost as white as the Sorceress, and her lips formed a name.

Eudaimonia.

And Majordomo knew.

Molly was an imposter.

All that time, as angry as he'd been, he'd never once suspected that she wasn't who she said she was.

As if it was not enough that she was leaving, now it seemed that she was never supposed to have been there at all.

Eudaimonia caught sight of her and trilled a laugh, a high, swooping sound like a bird of prey about to fall on a pigeon. "*Dear* Molly! So this is where you got off to!"

"Yes, Eudaimonia," whispered Molly. Her whisper kicked up echoes that went rustling like blown bits of paper through the Great Hall.

"But—but there must be some mistake—" said Edward. One mailed hand crept toward the coin hung around his neck.

Molly shook her head.

Edward slumped. He turned toward Majordomo, the eye slits of his helmet wide and baffled.

"Apparently," said Majordomo coldly, "we have been laboring under a misapprehension."

"So you've been playing house here, have you?" said Eudaimonia, strolling into the Great Hall. "I don't *mind*, dear Molly—you know, we've always been such great friends!—though I did wonder where my invitation had gone—"

Molly went even whiter, then flushed a sudden, ugly red, as if she were about to cry.

"But you said—"

Eudaimonia waved a hand at her and said, "Bygones, dear, bygones." Her gaze traveled over the Great Hall and the ruined staircase. She clucked her tongue. "How shabby. I see it's been far too long since this place had a proper Master."

"*Far* too long," said Majordomo, looking daggers at Molly.

"Now see here!" said Miss Handlebram, stepping forward. She brandished her shears the way a knight might brandish a sword, and lowered her sun hat to do battle. "I don't know what's going on here, but I *do* know that

Castle Hangnail's got a Master! Molly's in charge here!"

"Molly?" said Eudaimonia. She stifled a patently fake yawn. "Dear Molly. Such a talented little girl . . . but run a whole castle? *Do* be serious."

Molly shrank.

"She does a fine job!" roared Miss Handlebram. "And as for you, young lady—does your mother know you're leaving the house dressed like that?"

Eudaimonia's lip curled. "I left my mother's house to get away from carping old women. I won't put up with another one in my own castle."

She clicked all of her fingernails together, dipped two into a pocket, and came out with a little black wand about four inches long.

"Guar and Grappa," she chanted. "Avocet! Rattle bone, still tongue and tone!" And she waved the wand at Miss Handlebram.

It is possible that if someone had moved quickly enough, they would have been able to stop her. Spells that need words can often be broken if you can keep the spell-caster from saying the final word. But everyone was too caught up in the awfulness—except for Molly.

"Eudaimonia, *no!*" she shouted, and at the word *Avocet* she was flinging herself toward the older girl.

One of the bodyguards picked her up by the scruff of the neck like a kitten.

The air went stiff and then there was a noise rather like *thwang*.

Frost crystals formed on Miss Handlebram's clothes and on her hat and on her face. Frost—and then more than that. The frost became a zigzag of ice, and then the ice thickened until it was as thick as ice on a treacherous road, then as thick as an ice cube, then finally as thick as a frozen lake in winter.

And then there was a block of ice four feet thick with Miss Handlebram frozen in the middle of it. Her pruning shears were held up in front of her defensively, and the look on her face was the same one she wore when battling weeds.

"Interfering old biddy," muttered Eudaimonia. She clicked two long fingernails together and her bodyguards each picked up a suitcase from just outside the door. "Now. Someone stable my basilisk."

It was nothing short of miraculous, Majordomo thought, that they got through that evening in one piece.

Eudaimonia—the real Eudaimonia—was not pleased with her quarters. Her four-poster bed was too small, her bathtub was an old claw-foot and not a deep bathing pool, the tapestries were moth-eaten and the wrong color and there was not enough deep blue velvet for anyone.

"Really," she said over her shoulder at Majordomo, "you should have rooms in every color. What if a Purple Djinn should wish to stay here? Or a Midnight Hag?"

"It's never come up, Mistress," said Majordomo. "Purple Djinn are extinct, for one thing—"

"Are you contradicting me?" said Eudaimonia, turning on him. Her face was calm, but there was something terrible in her eyes, something that Majordomo couldn't quite identify.

"Err—no, of course not, Mistress! I shall—um—have Pins see to redoing the rooms at once—"

"And one in plaid," said Eudaimonia, turning away. "In case we've a Scottish Haggischarmer come to stay. I plan to entertain a great deal, but not while the castle is in this deplorable run-down condition! Really, it might be easier to pull it all down and rebuild from scratch!"

Majordomo took this blow without wincing. Partly he was too stunned by the evening's events, and partly it was that he was picturing an entire room in plaid, from floor to ceiling. He'd only met a Haggischarmer once, a pleasant little man with a troop of well-behaved performing haggises. Certainly neither the Haggischarmer nor his troop had done anything to deserve being shoved into a solid plaid room.

He would have put her in Molly's room—it was the best in the castle, and clearly Molly had no rights to it—but it only had a shower and Eudaimonia was very clear about her need for a nightly bath.

"And I shall require donkey's milk once a week," she said. "For bathing."

". . . um," said Majordomo.

"Will that be a problem? I believe I saw a donkey in the field as we approached?"

"No—no, Mistress—well—only—it's a *male* donkey, Mistress."

"I see." Eudaimonia drew herself up and glared down

at Majordomo. Her eyes glittered like ice. "I see that this place has become *slack*."

"Yes, Mistress."

"I will *fix* it."

"Yes, Mistress."

"Because I deserve better than to live in this—this *hovel*. Is that clear?"

"Absolutely, Mistress."

She narrowed her eyes, tapping her wand on her thigh. Majordomo, who had lived through Sorceresses and Beast Lords and Vampires, kept an expression of absolute humility on his face.

"You may go," said Eudaimonia, turning away. "Have the kitchen send me up a quiche, and tell the maid to draw a bath. I am fatigued."

"Yes, Mistress," said Majordomo, his heart sinking.

"And send Molly up. I see we've got a lot to talk about."

He hurried away. Her bodyguards sneered at him as he scurried from the room.

"Quiche," he muttered, limping down the stairs. "Hot bath. Oh, blast, blast, why did it have to be a Sorceress? Another Witch—a real Witch—and we could have muddled through, a Hag even, but we're in no shape for a Sorceress!"

Witches liked nature. Witches liked gardens. Witches

were a little bit shabby around the edges and they *liked* cobwebs in the corners.

Sorceresses liked ice and palaces and luxury. There was never anything remotely shabby about a Sorceress.

"Oh blast . . ."

He didn't know what he was going to tell Cook. But worse than that, he'd finally identified that glitter in Eudaimonia's eyes.

It was *anticipation*.

The moment that any of them in the castle failed—and with such standards, how could they help but fail?—she was going to encase them in ice.

And she was *looking forward* to it.

"Quiche?" growled Cook, slamming a ladle down. "*Quiche*, she is wanting?"

"Egg pie?" said Majordomo. "With, um, vegetables in it?"

"Is not fooling me! Is being *quiche!*"

Majordomo looked at the Minotaur, her horns quivering with outrage, took a deep, deep breath—and begged.

"Cook, *please*. We—the minions—we're all having some problems settling in. This has not been a smooth transition."

"*Transition*," said Cook, mouthing the word as if it were poisonous. "Not wanting transition. Was liking Molly."

"But she wasn't the real Master," said Majordomo. "She was an imposter. This is the real Master. Real has to be better, doesn't it?"

Cook snorted and tossed her head. If Majordomo had been a Greek hero in the middle of a labyrinth and saw a Minotaur looking like that, he would have turned around and sailed back to Greece and taken up fishing.

"Please? For me?"

"*Egg pie*," grated Cook. "All right. Is only doing this because *you* are asking, not because Master is asking. Is not being *my* Master."

I have to keep them separated, thought Majordomo. *Otherwise Cook is going to wind up frozen into a block of ice. Oh, poor Miss Handlebram!*

He took the "egg pie" up to Eudaimonia, and found Serenissima leaving the room ahead of him. The two bodyguards were standing there, so he couldn't speak to her, but she looked near tears.

Then again, steam spirits are always a bit drippy, so maybe—

"Steam girl!" snapped Eudaimonia as he brought the tray into the room. "Warm my water another ten degrees. It's getting cold."

"Forgive me, Mistress," said Majordomo. "I will send her up immediately. I shall just set your tray on the bed, shall I?"

"Don't bother," said Eudaimonia, emerging from the bathroom. She was wearing a dark blue bathrobe and her hair was dripping wet. "Clearly she can't do that right. I see that we shall have to see about training a proper maid-servant, and then the steam girl can tend to the stables or something." She waved a hand. "Where is my quiche?"

"Here, Mistress."

Even the Sorceress could find no fault with Cook's handiwork. She nodded to him. "Acceptable. You may go."

"Yes, Mistress."

He dragged himself back down to the kitchens, and found all the minions assembled around the table. Serenissima was crying and Pins was sewing and Angus was nursing some Wicked claw marks where the basilisk had scratched him.

"*Steam girl,*" said Serenissima, sniffling. "She didn't have to say it like *that.*"

"It's not a nice basilisk," said Angus. "Hasn't been treated well at all. I don't blame the bird, you understand."

Pins was sewing pale blue bedhangings out of velvet. "I had to take apart some old dresses in trunks," he said. "There's not enough material. Do you think she'll notice if I edge them in lace?"

"Do your best," said Majordomo heavily.

"I'm going to need a tetanus shot," said Angus.

"Miss Handlebram's frozen up solid," said Edward. "I put a sheet over her so those bodyguards won't gawk. Such a fine woman, and to come to this! We'll have to find a way to thaw her out."

"I don't know if the new Mistress will like that," said Majordomo.

"She didn't trust me to steam the wrinkles out of her dress," said Serenissima. "She said I'd probably set it on fire. Me!"

"Quiche," said Cook grimly.

"And it's a male donkey," said Angus. "Nothing I can do about that. And who bathes in donkey's milk, anyway?"

"Cleopatra did," said Pins. "But then an asp bit her."

"Wish I had an asp right now . . ."

"Angus!"

They all looked at Majordomo. The old servant took a deep breath. "Look. I know this is hard. We've all had a bit of a shock, and this new Master will take some getting used to. But if we pull together, we can manage. We've had demanding Masters before, and the castle was better for it afterward, wasn't it?"

There was some dispirited muttering around the table. Majordomo decided to treat this as agreement, because it was the best he was going to get.

"We'll manage."

No one would meet his eyes. They all stared at the table instead.

"I can't believe Molly lied to us," said Edward sadly.

And then, for the first time that long, horrible evening, someone looked up and asked, "Where *is* Molly, anyway?"

CHAPTER 32

M olly was with Eudaimonia.

She was also feeling about two inches tall.

She sat on the edge of the bed while Eudaimonia paced back and forth, like a hungry tigress in a cage.

"Molly, my dear, what were you *thinking?*"

"You got *lots* of invites," mumbled Molly. "You said you didn't want this one."

Eudaimonia tapped the wand on her palm. "As it happens, those other castles have *also* been filled." Her eyes narrowed. "You remember my mother?"

Molly nodded. Eudaimonia's mother had been . . . weird. She always seemed angry.

"She'd barge into your room all the time," said Molly. "I remember that. Like she thought she'd catch you doing something."

"I had to set that alarm spell on the stairs just to get some privacy!" Eudaimonia scowled. "And she'd never let me go anywhere. If I so much as stepped a foot out the

door,

door, she thought I was going to run off and do something awful." She slapped the wand in her palm.

Evil, thought Molly, *not just awful.*

Well, I'm Wicked partly because Sarah's the good twin and that means I have to be the bad one. Maybe Eudaimonia's Evil because her mother assumed she would be too.

"So of course my dear mother wasn't happy with the notion of me going off by myself, and she kept me home until—well, until I persuaded her to change her mind. By then most of the posts had been filled . . ."

Something about the way she said "persuaded" made Molly shrink back a little. Thoughts of Majordomo talking about thralls and holding people's minds down filled her mind.

Maybe she didn't know what it does, Molly thought. *Maybe she didn't know it was Evil.*

Looking up at Eudaimonia, Molly wasn't entirely sure that it would have mattered.

It was hard to think that she might be Evil. They'd been friends—maybe not *great* friends, maybe more like "Do this for me, and I'll be your best friend!" than real friends—but *still.*

You don't think of your friends as Evil. Even if you know they're in training to be an Evil Sorceress.

I always sort of assumed she wouldn't be Evil at me.

She sighed. *Which was a stupid thing to assume. It's not like she was very nice to me anyway. I mean . . . well . . .*

She looked up at Eudaimonia. And up. And up. Eudaimonia had always been taller.

"The Wizard at the last castle was very kind," she added. "He was, I daresay, a little overwhelmed. He gave me this as a gift."

She held up the wand and smiled.

Molly had a glum feeling that she knew just how that poor Wizard had felt.

Overwhelmed. That sounds about right.

"I don't mind you hanging around the castle when I wasn't using it, of course," Eudaimonia said over her shoulder. "But now that I'm ready to take possession—now that the castle is *mine*—"

She strode dramatically to the window and tried to throw the shutters back so the moonlight streamed down across her face.

It would have worked if the damp hadn't made the wooden shutters swell. One shutter banged back in proper dramatic fashion, and the other scraped, groaned, bucked a few times, then fell off onto the floor.

"Um," said Molly. "They do that sometimes. You have to work them gently 'til they're over the sticky spot."

Eudaimonia let out a long, exasperated sigh. "And of course it didn't occur to you to fix it?"

Molly's face felt hot. "I don't know how to fix shutters."

"Not *you*, stupid," said Eudaimonia. "You tell the servants—oh, I see." She sat down on the bed next to Molly. "The servants. They're terribly slack and they took just awful advantage of you."

"Everybody seemed to be trying hard," mumbled Molly.

Eudaimonia sighed again. "Dear Molly . . . you never could give anybody orders, could you?" Then she put her arm around Molly's shoulders and it was *just* like being friends again, like when Molly did something stupid and Eudaimonia picked up the pieces and did it right for her.

Part of Molly cried out for that. To go back to having someone else in charge! To have Eudaimonia make all the

234

decisions so that Molly didn't have to! To go back to just playing at being a Witch, instead of having a whole castle that was *hers*—her problem, her responsibility, her fault if it all fell apart.

For a minute she leaned against Eudaimonia and felt the way she had when she was nine years old, and the older girl had showed her how to do her very first grown-up spell.

But deep down inside, the Witchy part said, *No.*

The Witchy part said, *Nobody can do this all alone, which is why the minions were helping me.*

The Witchy part said, *We were doing good. We fixed the boiler—all of us helping. We'd almost finished the Tasks. The Board of Magic was going to accept me.*

And she remembered the silvery glittery splendor of Wormrise and the patterns the bats made in the sky over the garden, and the burning smell of the dragon.

She'd done that. Not Eudaimonia.

The Witchy part said, *You could do it again, if you had to.*

She pulled away from her former friend and stood up.

Eudaimonia gave her a searching look, and her ice-blue eyes narrowed. "What I don't understand, dear Molly," she purred, "is why you pretended you were *me.*"

"I had to use the invitation," Molly said.

"Silly," said Eudaimonia. "You must have known they'd

find you out eventually. Anyone can see you're *nothing like me.*" She gave a high, tinkling laugh, like icicles shattering on stone. "And did you see the look on the old minion's face?"

"Yes," said Molly, putting her hand on the doorknob. "I did."

CHAPTER 33

"She's not in her room," said Serenissima, coming back down to the kitchen. "And her clothes are gone."

"She's not in the garden," said Angus. "Nor the belfry."

Cook said nothing, but hunched her shoulders up and wadded her fists into her apron.

"She's not in the Great Hall," said Edward. "Or anywhere else I could get to, with my knees."

"It doesn't matter," said Majordomo savagely. "Good riddance. She lied to all of us. She was never supposed to be the Master here!"

They all looked at him. The silence went on for almost half a minute, and then they all looked away again, as if they had all silently agreed to pretend that Majordomo had never spoken.

Majordomo's face felt hot.

"We'll have to check Miss Handlebram's house," said Edward. "She may have gone there. Serenissima—?"

The steam spirit nodded. "I'll make sure her cat gets fed too, and see that the place is all locked up and the roses get watered. She'll appreciate that when—when we unthaw her."

"I'll check the stables and the hayloft," said Angus. "And the moles may know something—not that any of us can talk to moles, but they're smart little fellows, and perhaps we can work something out—"

Pins walked slowly into the room and climbed up onto the table. He set a sheet of paper down in the middle of it, very carefully.

It was covered in Molly's slightly loopy handwriting.

"She left this in my workshop," he said.

Dear Pins,

I have to go. I'm taking the coat you made me, even though I probably shouldn't, because it's the best thing anyone's ever done for me. I will think of you all whenever I wear it, even though I know you probably won't want to think of me.

I'm sorry I made a mess of everything. I never meant to hurt anyone. I will miss you all forever.

Love,
Molly

Serenissima burst into tears.

Edward put a gauntlet to the coin around his neck.

Pins tapped the paper. "We have to find her," he said.

"No, we don't," said Majordomo. "She went *home*, don't you understand? She wasn't supposed to be here at all! She's a little girl, and she ran away from home to come here—her parents thought she was at summer camp, for the love of Hecate! She's gone back where she belongs and that's the best for everyone!"

Pins folded his burlap arms. "Is it? I liked Molly. I don't know this new Sorceress at all, and she froze Miss Handlebram in ice."

"But she's the rightful Master of the castle," said Majordomo. "The invitation went to her. And she's an Evil Sorceress—a real proper old-school Evil Sorceress! You just don't get Evil like that anymore."

"We're part of Castle Hangnail too," said Pins. "We're as much part of it as the mortar and the stones and what's left of the moat. Don't *we* get some say in who the Master is?"

Majordomo stared into his cheese, as if hoping to find the answers written there. They were not.

"But Molly lied to us," he said finally. "She wasn't who she said she was. Or what."

Pins shrugged. "I'm not saying that was right," he said. "I wish she hadn't, and I'm upset about that too.

But the old Vampire Lord used to drain the blood out of villagers."

"Ungo the Mad once replaced your brain with a live hamster," added Angus.

"The Vile Hag made slime come out of the taps so you couldn't get a bath," said Serenissima.

"Lord Edward's had his head chopped off."

"Beastlord's thugs is eating and throwing bones onto floor," grumbled Cook from the doorway. She tossed her empty basket down on the counter. "And also being stealing sheep. Is not liking bones on my floor!"

Majordomo shuddered. It had taken him weeks to get the smell of sawdust shavings out of his skull, following the hamster incident. Still—

"That's all true," he said, "and they did a lot of bad things, but they were Wicked. They're supposed to chop off our heads and things. We're minions. It's what we *do*. At least they didn't lie to us."

"Ungo the Mad lied *all the time*," said Serenissima. "Usually he said 'this won't hurt a bit' and 'no, it's perfectly safe.' And then you'd wake up wired to a lightning rod while he screamed 'It's ALIVE!'"

Majordomo shoved the last bit of cheese in his mouth. "Maybe you're all right," he said, "but Molly's gone. She lied to us and then she left us. And *I* still remember what's due to the proper Master of this place."

Once again, everyone looked at him. It was getting a little unnerving. But this time Cook stood up.

"Is not mattering where she came from," said Cook. "Is not mattering how long she is staying or who is being told what. Molly is belonging here. *Molly is being Master of this place.*"

She stared Majordomo in the eye.

"All that is mattering," said the Minotaur, "is finding her again. And bringing her home."

CHAPTER
34

B ut they did not find her.

They went from the top of the castle to the bottom, from the bats in the belfry to the Bees by the boiler, and found nothing. Serenissima opened every cupboard and every wardrobe (and found, incidentally, eighteen bedsheets and a full tea service for twelve). Pins checked every crawl space and secret passage, and his fish sat in a bowl in a high window, watching over the countryside for a small figure in black.

"It is drafty," the goldfish announced, wedged into her tiny sweater, with her waterproof scarf pulled up to her eyes. "The breezes are cold and smell of mold. I shall take a lung infection or an ague and be ill for months, assuming I don't die of it. But none of that matters! We must bring Molly home! She looked up the scientific names of sixteen different diseases for me once—and their most obscure symptoms—and that is how I found that I likely had Ich-Borne Fin Paralysis and was able to stop it before it became too far advanced. I shall not leave my post until Molly is found!"

Everyone agreed that this was remarkable heroism for a goldfish, and Cook sent up a thimble-full of hot chocolate, which Pins offered to the goldfish in an eyedropper.

Majordomo didn't pay too much attention to the search. He was kept busy making sure that the bodyguards had their own rooms on either side of Eudaimonia's suite, a task made more difficult by the fact that one of those rooms had a hole in the ceiling as big as a sofa.

He didn't much like the look of the bodyguards. It wasn't that they looked like thugs—they did, of course, but that was fine. One doesn't serve a magical castle for centuries without seeing any number of thugs, minions, henchmen, lackeys, servitors, and mercenaries. Majordomo had been thugged at by the best, and these gentlemen were not it.

"Bargain-basement thugs. Not like the old days," muttered Majordomo, dragging a tarp into the room with a hole in the floor that corresponded to the hole in the ceiling below. "Now, the Cursed Beastlord, *he* had a thug worthy of the name. Blast. Kicked me down the Grand Staircase once, for breathing too loudly on a Wednesday."

He dragged the tarp over the hole and weighted the edges with iron candlesticks. The end result looked depressingly shabby. Majordomo sighed and found a carpet from farther down the hall and rolled it out over the tarp, which hid things rather better.

Now I just need a sign so people know not to walk on it—

There was a crash from downstairs. Majordomo heard Edward yell something, and then there was an even louder crash, followed by a clatter, followed by that horrible teetering noise that a plate makes when it's spinning slowly to a halt.

"Blast!" Majordomo limped hurriedly down the stairs.

Angus was standing in the Great Hall, his arms folded, glaring down at one of the bodyguards. There was a pile of armor on the floor behind the Minotaur, and the sheet had been yanked off Miss Handlebram's ice cube.

Majordomo came in just as the bodyguard said, "Oh yeah? What are you gonna do about it?"

Angus leaned forward and snorted, a full bull's snort.

"You're just some jumped-up cow," said the bodyguard. "My Mistress'll have you ground into hamburger if you don't leave off."

"Oh no, no, no . . ." muttered Majordomo.

Angus scraped a hoof along the ground, just for a few inches.

"Excuse me!" called Majordomo, hurrying down the stairs. "Your room is ready now, sir!"

Angus rumbled something under his breath. The bodyguard sneered and slouched up the stairs.

244

"Now, what happened here?" asked Majordomo. He hurried to where Sir Edward lay in multiple pieces on the ground. "Oh dear! He hates it when this happens—last time we got his elbows mixed up and he kept hitting himself in the face when he tried to wave—oh dear—"

"I'm not sure," Angus admitted. "I came in just as he was knocking Edward over. I wanted to knock *him* over, but I suppose it's not for the best right now."

"Oh, dear . . ."

They got the suit of armor spread out over the floor. Majordomo rolled the helmet back onto the shoulders, taking care to get the bits of chain mail inside the neck all tucked back down into the body. "Edward? *Edward!*"

The suit's visor fluttered. "Major . . . ?" asked Edward. "What . . . oh . . . Oh!" The bits of armor began shivering and rocking with agitation. "You have to stop him!"

"Stop who? Quit wiggling, I nearly dropped your knee plate . . ."

"That awful man! He was defacing Miss Handlebram! We can't allow that sort of thing to go on!"

Majordomo and Angus turned and looked at the block of ice. Someone—presumably the bodyguard—had chipped a handlebar mustache into the ice over Miss Handlebram's face, and had been working on writing "Gordon Wuz Here" on the side.

"I tried to stop him," said Edward. "But I don't have my sword. Why can't I find my sword? It was just here a moment ago . . ."

"It's all right," said Majordomo, patting Edward's shoulder plate. "We'll find it. And I suppose we just—just have to accept that some of the Mistress's retainers are . . . um . . . uncouth. But we'll adapt."

"But it's Miss Handlebram," said Edward, sounding bewildered. "We can't let them do that. Not to *her*."

"Those men aren't *real* minions," said Angus. "You can't tell me they're part of the Minion's Guild. I won't believe it. It's a disgrace, having non-minions doing minion jobs."

"I'll speak to the Mistress tomorrow," said Majordomo. "I'm sure we can get this all sorted out then."

Angus leaned down, got both arms around Edward's breast plate, and set the armor on his feet. Edward rocked uncertainly, checked both knees and his elbows, and then nodded.

"I'm fine," he said. "All together. All in the right place— except—"

His gauntlet went to his neck. The slits in his visor went blank.

"The Imperial Squid," he said. "The one Molly gave me. It's gone."

CHAPTER 35

They searched the Great Hall high and low, but the Squid was truly lost. "First Molly, now the coin," Pins said glumly. "What's next?"

"She hasn't turned up, then?" asked Edward. They had found his sword stashed in the umbrella stand and he was clutching the hilt tightly. He looked less like the armor of a mighty warrior and more like a small child with a security blanket.

"Goldfish hasn't seen anything," said Pins. "She's been watching all night. And nobody's seen Bugbane either, so he must have gone off with her."

He sighed and drew himself to his full height, which was about halfway up Edward's shin. "We should all get some sleep. I imagine tomorrow will be quite a day."

And it was.

Eudaimonia slept late, that was about the best thing you could say. Everyone got an extra few hours of sleep.

248

They needed it, because the minute she woke up, she began making demands.

"One egg," she said. "Lightly poached. Three stalks of asparagus. White toast."

"Not having asparagus," said Cook. "Is being wrong season for asparagus."

"Can you find some?" asked Majordomo. "Perhaps frozen asparagus—?"

Cook gazed at him as if he had just asked her to do something indecent.

"Quite right," said Majordomo, "don't know what I was thinking. I shall inform the Sorceress."

The Sorceress took this news by throwing a poached egg at his head. Fortunately Majordomo had dealt with this sort of thing before—Ungo the Mad had been able to hurl a test tube with pinpoint accuracy—and ducked. The egg splattered against the wall and leaked yellow yolk down the wall.

"Very well," said Eudaimonia, as if she had not just thrown an egg at his head. "How does the renovation of the guest bedrooms proceed?"

"Pins is working on the curtains now, Mistress. He shall bring the colors to you for approval this afternoon."

"Good," she said. "I shall wish to throw a masked

ball soon, to celebrate my investiture. The castle must be ready by then."

Majordomo winced. "Err . . . how soon, Mistress?"

She tapped one blue nail on her knee. She was wearing a dressing gown of blue silk the color of frozen cornflowers. "I was thinking next Saturday."

Majordomo did some quick mental calculations about how much labor would be required to rebuild the castle and refurbish the guest rooms by next Saturday. The numbers began to rise alarmingly and he had to carry the one multiple times. "Saturday?" he asked.

"Is there a *problem* with Saturday?" asked Eudaimonia, taking a delicate bite of toast.

"Errrr. Perhaps, Mistress, you would consider a date with more . . . ah . . . occult significance?"

A thin line appeared between her eyebrows. "Such as?"

"All Hallows' Eve is an excellent date," said Majordomo. "Very—erm—Witchy. Not like Saturday. No one bars the church doors and lights the lanterns to drive off the Evil forces of Saturday."

And All Hallows' Eve is also three or four months off, he thought, *and we might have some chance of having things ready then.*

"There is something to what you say," said Eudaimonia, "but All Hallows' Eve is much too far off."

"Autumnal Equinox?" asked Majordomo hopefully. "Very occult, your equinoxes."

"Lugnasadh," said Eudaimonia (and to her credit, she pronounced this very alarming-looking word correctly, *Loo-nas-uh*). "August Eve. The first of the harvest festivals. Farther off than I would like, but it shall give us time to make a few embellishments."

Majordomo gritted his teeth. It wasn't much time, but it was better than next Saturday.

Eudaimonia smiled. That is to say, her lips curved up and her eyes sparkled, but it was the sparkle of sunlight on ice. "That is a fine idea," she said. "Thank you, minion."

Majordomo felt a flush of gratification, despite his panic.

"You understand, Mistress—we will do our best, but things have been in poor repair—we have not had a proper Master in a long time."

"I can certainly see that," said Eudaimonia. "Dear little Molly! So young. Such a silly prank to pull."

Silly, thought Majordomo grimly. *Yes.* Silly *would be one word for it.*

"I'm amazed she managed to do any magic here at all."

"Nothing of consequence," said Majordomo. "Things with bats and plants." Basic honesty forced him to add, "And she summoned her shadow to chase off a rather bad man."

Eudaimonia looked up, startled. Majordomo realized that he'd been praising the old Master to the new one and hurriedly said, "Nothing important."

"Yes . . . shadows. *Not* important." Her laugh sounded a bit forced. She tapped her wand against her knee. "Send her up, will you? I shall speak to her this morning. Make sure that there are no misunderstandings."

"I don't think there will be any more misunderstandings with Molly," said Majordomo. "I'm afraid she has left the premises."

Eudaimonia halted in mid-stretch. "What?"

"She left a note," said Majordomo. "She was returning home. I believe—ah—she was rather attached to Castle Hangnail, you understand . . ." He trailed off.

"Dear Molly always was sentimental," said the Sorceress. "The type to cry all night over an injured spider instead of swatting it with a shoe. Well." She frowned. "You're quite certain she's gone?"

"We have been unable to locate her," said Majordomo cautiously.

"How vexing." Eudaimonia drummed her blue nails on the bedpost. Almost under her breath, clearly to herself, she added, "I can't believe she remembered the shadow spell . . ." There was a fine line between her eyes. "Very well! See that I am not disturbed for at least an hour."

"Yes, Mistress," said Majordomo, bowing. He shut the door behind him. The two bodyguards sneered at him, and behind the closed door, he could hear the sounds of chanting.

CHAPTER 36

"I don't understand," said Serenissima. "A girl like that can't just disappear."

"Of course she can," said Angus. "If she holds her breath, that's exactly what she can do. I imagine she snuck out last night." He sighed heavily and flexed his hooves. "I hope she's okay."

Cook stomped across the kitchen.

"Cook," said Majordomo from the doorway.

"What?"

"I was going to ask if you could make a sandwich—"

The Minotaur snorted. "Cheese and crackers on table. *No* sandwiches."

She stormed out the door.

Majordomo sighed heavily and began slicing cheese to put on crackers. "Do you think she's mad at me?"

"Gee," said Pins, "what was your first clue?"

It was a hectic afternoon. Majordomo ran back and forth, bringing the Sorceress spell-components and assuring her that yes, the redecorating was going just swimmingly, it would doubtless be done in no time. (Pins was still sewing curtains and said only, "If she wants it done faster, she will have to do it herself." Majordomo decided not to pass this along.)

The first serious crisis came when Eudaimonia decided to check on the redecoration herself.

"Um," said Majordomo. "Well, nothing is hung yet, Mistress. We're still—err—taking measurements—"

"Indeed," said the Sorceress. "Did I not give this order yesterday?"

"We have a very small staff at present," said Majordomo. "A full redecoration of the guest suites is somewhat beyond our manpower—"

She swept past him. "Show me."

The guest rooms were worse by daylight than by night. The light through the windows was unforgiving. While Serenissima steamed each room faithfully, there was nothing that could be done about the cracked paint or the worn carpets.

He expected Eudaimonia to say something cutting, but she merely pressed her lips together tightly and her face grew more and more pinched with every room.

This was much more alarming than insults.

When he closed the door to the last room—and it wasn't Serenissima's fault, really, but all that steam hadn't been kind to the wallpaper, which was bubbling rather oddly and starting to peel off in broad strips—the Sorceress folded her arms. "I see that nothing has been accomplished. Bring me the servants responsible."

"Servant," said Majordomo. "Err. Singular."

Eudaimonia slapped her wand into her free hand. It made a small, dangerous sound. "Bring him to me, then. *Now.*"

Pins was not happy to be dragged from his sewing room. "You can't tell me that she really expected the whole thing to be done today!"

"I think she expected us to start it," said Majordomo. "Perhaps we should have hung some curtains—something to show we were making an effort." He sighed. "And she likely expects that we have a bigger staff than we do. I don't think she realizes yet that there's only the six of us. And your goldfish, of course."

"She had best leave my goldfish out of this!"

"She hasn't mentioned your goldfish."

He pushed the door to Eudaimonia's room open and let Pins walk inside.

"You wished to see me, ma'am?" said Pins. (Not *Mistress,* Majordomo noted.)

Eudaimonia opened her mouth, looked down, saw Pins, and whatever she was saying died on her lips.

"You?" she said. "What are *you?*"

"My name is Pins," said the doll, executing a small bow. "I do all the sewing and mending for Castle Hangnail."

"You! You made that marvelous coat for Molly!" Eudaimonia clasped her hands together.

Pins nodded warily.

Eudaimonia snaked out a hand and caught Pins by the fabric at the back of his neck, holding him aloft like a kitten. Her sharp blue nails dug into the burlap. Majordomo winced.

Pins folded his arms and gave the Sorceress a level look.

"What *are* you? How did you come to exist?"

"That's a bit personal, don't you think? Ma'am."

Majordomo expected Eudaimonia to say something rude, or worse, to throw Pins across the room the way she'd thrown the poached egg, but the Sorceress laughed and set the doll down again. "How fascinating! I must certainly discover what makes you tick."

"I do not tick," said Pins with dignity. "If you want something that ticks, the Clockwork Bees live in the basement."

"Do they? I see that I am overdue for a tour of the grounds." She tapped her wand against her hand again. "And you, Pins—you must certainly prepare a new ward-

257

robe for me at once!" She flicked the edge of her ice-blue robe. "I will require a coat, I think—like the one you made Molly, but in the proper colors. And of course, it will be much easier to work with a figure like mine, don't you think?"

Pins twisted one of the needles in his scalp and made a noncommittal noise.

Majordomo hurried forward. "Perhaps . . . err . . . you would like a tour of the grounds now, Mistress?"

"I think so," she said. "Yes. And then have the staff ready in the Great Hall when we have finished, so that they may meet their new Mistress."

"Certainly, Mistress," said Majordomo.

CHAPTER 37

The tour went badly.

Majordomo started with the library, in hopes of putting Eudaimonia in a good mood. And she did seem to be pleased with the shelves of books and the candles and the comfortable chairs.

"Shabby chic," she said. "It will do. One can hardly ever go wrong with walls of bookcases, can one?"

Unfortunately, it went downhill from there.

The short tower with its moat intrigued her, but she was less than pleased it was not accessible. "Have the causeway rebuilt," she said. "The moat will need water lilies, and perhaps a sea serpent."

"Um," said Majordomo. Sea serpents were very expensive, and building a causeway even more so. The moat was only about three feet deep, but the mud underneath went down a long way. "I shall add it to the list of required renovations, Mistress?"

And then she smiled at him and said, "I should cer-

259

tainly be lost without you, Majordomo!" and he promised himself that there would be a causeway if he had to lay every stone himself.

Eudaimonia had no interest in the kitchens or the stables (Majordomo breathed a sigh of relief), but the sight of the south lawn annoyed her. "Gardens," she said. "Formal ones. With a hedge maze, I think. Perhaps some man-eating plants."

"I am afraid this climate is not really suitable for man-eating plants, Mistress. Um. If the Mistress would like to step this way, the Clockwork Bees are next . . ."

They ran into Cook on the way to the Clockwork Bees. Majordomo wrung his hands. "Ah—Cook, this is—no, wait. Mistress Eudaimonia, may I present Cook?"

Cook towered over even Eudaimonia, although she had to hunch down in the low corridor. She looked down and gave one explosive snort.

"A Minotaur!" said the Sorceress. "I thought your kind were mostly dead."

"Not being dead yet," said Cook.

"The quiche last night was quite good," said Eudaimonia.

Cook's horns scraped gently against the ceiling. "Is cooking," she said. "If is boiling over, is making dinner late." She pushed past them, turning sideways to avoid touching Eudaimonia.

Majordomo opened his mouth to apologize, but Eudaimonia gave another little tinkling laugh. "Minotaurs!" she said. "How quaint. Well, you can hardly expect the courtesies from them, can you? I imagine it's so hard for them to remember all the proper words."

She strolled down the hallway. Majordomo dashed a glance over his shoulder, hoping that Cook had not heard.

The second crisis came a few minutes later.

Cook and Angus waited in the Great Hall. Pins sat on Edward's shoulder. The knight was guarding the block of ice with Miss Handlebram in it. Serenissima sat on an increasingly soggy sofa and wrung her hands.

Eudaimonia strode into the room and stopped. She turned back to Majordomo. "I thought I made it clear that the entire staff was to join us?"

"Um," said Majordomo. "Yes. Err. This is them."

Her gaze fell across the minions like a lash. "This? The entire staff of this castle is two people, two Minotaurs, and an enchanted doll?"

Angus and Cook stiffened.

Implying that Minotaurs and Pins aren't people. Oh dear. Majordomo wrung his hands.

"Well," said Eudaimonia. "I suppose that changes things." She smiled, and it was almost kind. "I see now that it isn't your fault that things are such a ruin. There are so few of you, and so . . . ill-suited. You must think you are doing the very best you can."

The minions said nothing.

"But the old way of doing things will have to change. You will have to actually work for a living. We will have no *parasites* in this castle, do you understand?"

The minions continued to say nothing.

"Very well, then." Eudaimonia gave a bright, brittle smile. "I'm sure we'll get along splendidly . . ."

She tapped her wand against Miss Handlebram's block of ice.

". . . or else measures will have to be taken. Now, then. Are there any questions?"

"Excuse me," said Angus. His voice was calm and he didn't paw the floor. Only someone who knew him well would know that he was angry. "I do have one question, Sorceress."

Sorceress, Majordomo noticed with despair, *not Mistress.*

"What would you like us to feed your cockatrice? We're running out of chicken feed."

"Minotaurs are so *stupid*," said Eudaimonia. She smiled as she said it, and her voice was caressing, as if she were saying something else entirely. "I suppose you can't help it. Must I make all the decisions?"

She tapped her wand on her palm. Her smile grew wider.

"Why don't you feed it the donkey?"

"She's got to go," said Pins.

Everyone nodded.

"What are you talking about?" asked Majordomo. "She's got to stay! If she leaves, we've got no Master! The Board will have us decommissioned! We're out of options! She's our last chance."

"Did you give her the Tasks?" asked Pins.

"Um." Majordomo paused. "Well, no. Molly must have taken her list with her. One ought to be mailed here automatically—there are spells at the Board of Magic that handle that—but I haven't had a chance to get to the post office, since she'd had me running around—"

He stopped, since that might sound like a criticism of the new Master, and that was the last thing he wanted to do.

Angus folded his arms. "I'm *only* a stupid Minotaur," he said heavily, "but I'd rather go live somewhere else than stay here with her."

"You'd leave?" Majordomo felt his mouth sag open. "But—but this is your home!"

"Not while *she* is being here," said Cook.

"You're minions! Minions don't betray their Master!"

Pins spoke for all of them when he said "I'm not *her* minion."

"We took the Minion's Oath, same as you," said Angus. "We all pay our dues to the Minion's Guild. And we have a Master, and just because she's gone missing doesn't mean we're not still loyal."

"If anything," said Pins softly, "we're more loyal than you are. You never liked Molly. As soon as a new Master showed up, you threw her over, without even bothering to ask her side of the story. You'd never have done that to Ungo."

Majordomo's breath hissed between his teeth. He could not think of a single thing to say.

"Anyway," said Angus, "I'm not feeding that poor donkey to that ill-tempered cockatrice. I'll take the donkey to Berkeley tonight and see if he can't spare me some of last season's mutton."

Cook left the kitchen. Majordomo could hear her hooves clomping down the stairs toward the basement.

He pushed his chair back. "I will go and attend the Mistress," he said. His voice sounded hollow in his own ears.

It was a long walk up the steps to Eudaimonia's suite,

and for once, Majordomo was glad of it. *There are two Masters of Castle Hangnail now. There cannot be two Masters. One is gone—but a Master is never gone when the minions loyal to her remain.*

What do I do?

He tapped on the Sorceress's door. One of the bodyguards—Gordon, was it?—opened the door.

Majordomo was vaguely aware that the man was sneering, but his gaze was caught by a thong around the man's throat, and dangling from it—

The Imperial Squid.

A flash of rage went through the old minion's heart, and his hand shot up. He grabbed the coin and yanked hard.

The bodyguard wasn't expecting any kind of assault. Majordomo might look like a tired old man, but Ungo the Mad had rebuilt him well. Gordon went to his knees, choking, as the thong was yanked tight around his neck.

"That wasn't yours!" hissed Majordomo. "That belongs to Sir Edward!"

"Ghhrgghkk!"

"What is going on here?!"

Cold so intense that it burned struck Majordomo's face and froze his right arm. He could not have let go if he wanted to. The leather throng, made brittle by cold, snapped as Gordon crawled backward.

"I will not have my servants fighting!" shouted Eudaimonia. A second blast of ice knocked Majordomo sideways onto the carpet.

With her wand in her hand, her eyes glowing with rage and magic, her blue robes whipping around her, Eudaimonia looked every inch an Evil Sorceress. The old minion's heart seized with pride.

A Master. A Master like the old days. This is what they are supposed to be like.

He dragged himself to his feet. Gordon rubbed his throat and eyed him vengefully.

"He took something that didn't belong to him," said Majordomo.

She shook her head in disgust and turned away. "When you are done rolling around on the carpet, I have compiled a list of repairs that will need to be made immediately."

"Yes?" said Majordomo. His right arm still wasn't working, but it would thaw out quickly enough. "I would be glad to, Mistress, but we are—err—temporarily embarrassed in the funding department . . ."

"Yes, I know," said the Sorceress. "We will fix that."

Did she have money? "We will?"

Eudaimonia leaned back. "We will begin by selling the foolish metal Bees in the basement."

"You . . . you want to sell the Clockwork Bees . . . ?

But those were inventions of Ungo the Mad . . . they've been here forever . . ."

"Indeed. They look it too. I shall prepare a list of potential buyers." She waved a hand. "Should they prove insufficient, we shall have to find a buyer for the male Minotaur."

Majordomo thought perhaps he'd misheard. Then he thought perhaps he'd gone mad.

"Mistress?"

"I would prefer not to. I know the creatures don't like to be separated." And she gave him what she probably thought was a kind smile. "But we cannot live in a castle that is falling down around our ears, can we?"

She's talking about Angus as if he was something you could sell. He's a minion, not a piece of furniture!

"Mistress," said Majordomo. It wasn't agreement or disagreement, but at least he was saying something.

"As I said, we'll leave that on the table. How many Bees are there to sell?"

There were one hundred and sixteen, each of which Majordomo knew individually, but he said only "I will go and count them at once, Mistress."

He bowed. His last view as he turned from the room was of Eudaimonia in front of the window, the sunlight turning her hair into a pale white flame.

She looks like a Master like the old days.

But . . . it isn't the old days anymore. And even then, a castle couldn't have two Masters.

And you weren't allowed to sell your minions. It was a sacred trust.

His right arm was still frozen, but that didn't bother him. Clenched between his frozen fingers, an icy weight against his palm, lay the Imperial Squid.

Majordomo paused on the landing above the staircase. The Great Hall lay before him, and drifting up from it, he could hear voices.

"Shhhh!"

"Can you do it?"

"Keep your voice down! She'll hear you!"

"Of course I can do it! It's only ice! But how are we going to move her?"

"Quiet!"

Majordomo cleared his throat loudly and began walking down the staircase, setting each foot down with a thump. There was a flurry of activity, followed by the sound of people being very quiet down below, which is not quite the same as silence.

When Majordomo plodded out into the Great Hall, Edward was standing at attention beside the block of ice, Pins was sewing quietly on the couch, and Serenissima was cleaning the floor.

It was a scene so innocent that Majordomo would have been wildly suspicious, even if he hadn't just overheard them talking.

He trudged past them, toward the staircase that led down to the boiler room and the Clockwork Bees.

They're plotting . . . and they didn't tell me about it.

It would have been obvious even to the donkey that the other minions were plotting to melt Miss Handlebram out of the block of ice. Majordomo stomped down the stairs to the boiler room.

Why hadn't they told him?

Did they really think I'd try to stop them? Miss Handlebram is my friend too! I don't want her to be encased in ice!

They don't trust me.

They're afraid I'll tell the Sorceress.

He almost missed the next step, and had to catch himself on the handrail.

And get everyone else in trouble? Let her punish Pins and Serenissima and sell Angus, like he was a cow?

Majordomo pushed open the door to the boiler room. Clockwork Bees droned happily around him. Dark, metallic honey dripped between the gears and made sticky rivers down the far wall.

He could not imagine the castle without them.

Eudaimonia is a terrible Master.

We have to get rid of her.

If we get rid of her, Castle Hangnail is doomed. We'll never get the Board of Magic to give us another extension. It's the end.

In the heat of the boiler room, his frozen arm began to thaw. He slowly pried his fingers open and stared at the coin in his palm.

We'll have to leave. It's over. It's finally over.

He put his back against the stone wall and slid down it. The Bees thrummed around him.

Majordomo put his face in his hands and began to sob.

He had always known his place in the world. Now he had never felt more alone.

The touch on his cheek was as light as the feet of a Clockwork Bee. Molly put her arm around his shoulders and said, "Don't cry."

"You're here," said Majordomo, sniffling. Molly fished out a tissue and handed it to him. "You came back."

"I didn't ever leave," Molly confessed. "I've been down here in the boiler room and going out into the garden at night. Bugbane tells me when someone's coming, but he's out in the garden trying to catch some lunch. Cook's been bringing me sandwiches."

Majordomo wiped his eyes. "I suppose everyone else knows you're here and didn't tell me. Not that I blame them."

She shook her head. "Just Cook. She said nobody else was mad at me—except you—but I didn't see how they couldn't be, so I asked her not to tell."

She sat down next to him. Majordomo pressed the tissue to his eyes and took a deep breath.

"Why did you stay?" he asked.

Molly leaned her head back against the stone wall. "I didn't want to leave you guys alone with her."

There was no need to ask who Molly was talking about. Majordomo nodded.

"She doesn't care about us," he said hopelessly. "I'm used to bad Masters—we've had all sorts of Evil and Wickedness, it's what we *do*—but at least they loved the castle. They'd have died to defend it. Some of them did. The old Vampire Lord died defending the castle eleven and a half times."

"What was the half?" asked Molly.

"Someone put a stake through his spleen. They weren't very clear on anatomy. He was grumpy for weeks."

Molly nodded. After a minute she said, "I used to look up to her a bunch. She was so pretty and she knew magic, and nobody else did. She was mean to me, but then sometimes she'd be sort of nice too."

Majordomo sighed. "And then you think that if you could just do what she wanted, she'd be nice again."

Molly nodded vigorously. "Yes! You understand!"

"Yes."

The Clockwork Bees droned overhead. Molly sighed. "But I don't think it matters what we do. I think she's just mean when she wants to be mean. I used to try really, really hard at the spells to get them just right, so she'd be impressed, but it didn't matter. It was like she just got more and more sarcastic. Sometimes she was nicer when I messed up . . ."

She trailed off, with an odd expression on her face, as if someone had just handed her a great truth.

"What?" said Majordomo.

"She *was* nicer when I messed up. I think she wanted me to fail. When I did the shadow spell right, that first time, she was really mean, but in that way that sounds like she's being nice, but really she isn't."

Majordomo raised an eyebrow. "Well, that's not surprising, is it? Magical folk, particularly the Evil ones, don't like other people to be as powerful as they are."

"*I* don't care if other people are more powerful than me, as long as they leave me and Castle Hangnail alone."

"Yes," said Majordomo, "but you're Wicked. Wicked is different from Evil." He waved a hand. "You know."

Molly nodded. *Wicked* was turning somebody into an earwig and letting them run around for a week to give them a good scare. *Evil* was turning someone into an earwig and then stepping on them.

When Eudaimonia talked to you, you felt like an earwig looking up at the underside of a shoe.

"There was another thing she used to do," said Molly. "When I'd get a spell wrong, she'd take my magic to do it right."

Majordomo sat up. "*What?*"

"She'd take it. You know, the way the mole shaman did for Wormrise, only not like that, because he asked first and he only borrowed it. And Eudaimonia didn't really ask. I mean, she kind of told me that I had to let her."

Molly scowled. It sounded weak when she said it like that. Her twin sister would have said "Well, stand up to her and say no!" but her sister also said things like "Ignore them and they'll go away," and Molly knew perfectly well that if you ignored people, they generally figured they were getting away with something and got ten times worse.

Whereas if you turned them into an earwig, their manners improved *amazingly*. She really had to figure out that earwig spell.

"Did you ever tell her not to?" asked Majordomo.

"I tried to once," said Molly. "She sort of talked me into

it. I mean . . . well, you know. She said she wouldn't like me anymore and I couldn't come over and learn magic. So then I had to apologize and beg her to take my magic before she'd forgive me." She scowled again. "That's just the sort of person she is."

"I know exactly what you mean," said Majordomo, thinking of the curtains. "She asked me to do something impossible, and I knew it was impossible and instead I wound up apologizing because it hadn't gotten done."

"It's like a weird kind of magic," Molly agreed. "Like a spell that makes you feel like it's all your fault."

They both sighed at the same time.

"Anyway, I thought she was just taking my magic to do the spells right, because I couldn't do them myself. But now . . . I don't know. Maybe she was keeping the magic for herself."

"Maybe," said Majordomo. "Maybe they were the wrong spells for you. Witches and Sorceresses aren't the same. Just because she could do a spell doesn't mean you could. Or vice versa."

"Wish I'd known that two years ago," said Molly glumly.

Majordomo remembered suddenly why he was mad at Molly. "Did you just steal an invitation at random?"

"Um," said Molly, staring at the floor.

He waited.

She wouldn't meet his eyes. "I . . . well . . ."

"Just tell me," said Majordomo tiredly. "I can't feel any worse."

"She told me to throw yours away," mumbled Molly. "Said Castle Hangnail was too . . . um . . . small."

(Actually the phrase she'd used was "pathetic run-down little backwater," but Molly wasn't about to say that to Majordomo.)

"So I fished it out of the wastebasket," Molly said, "and came here because I thought—well—I thought you needed somebody, and I'm small too, and maybe a small castle needed a small Witch." She hunched her shoulders. "I really didn't mean to lie. I thought I'd figure out a way to stay."

There was a long silence in the boiler room, broken only by the buzz of clockwork. Then Majordomo reached out and closed his fingers over hers, with the Imperial Squid clasped between them.

"It did need a small Witch," he said. "And it still does. We'll figure out a way."

CHAPTER 40

"You'll never get Miss Handlebram melted," said Molly. "It's magic ice. It stays cold unless you've got magic fire to melt the outside bit. Once you're through that layer, it's ordinary ice and you could steam it away, I guess, but you have to get through the shell."

The eight of them—six minions, one goldfish, and Molly—sat around the kitchen table. Bugbane was posted as a lookout over the door, in case Eudaimonia or the bodyguards came downstairs.

When Majordomo had emerged from the boiler room, Molly beside him, everyone had been stunned—then delighted—then afraid. They cast nervous glances upward, in the direction of the Sorceress's bedroom.

There was a long, awkward moment when Molly looked from face to face, knowing that she'd lied to all of them. *A Witch takes responsibility for what she does.* She took a deep breath and said, "I'm sorry, everyone."

"Ah, well," said Edward, squeezing her shoulder with

one mailed hand. "It's not like you cut off anyone's *head.*"

All eyes turned to Majordomo.

He sat down at the table and said, "The real Master of Castle Hangnail has returned. It's time get rid of the imposter," and everything was okay again.

Molly pulled out the Tasks. There were lines through all of them, except for one.

"Take possession of the castle" was no longer marked out. It was underlined in pulsing red.

Molly frowned. "Oh, I wish it didn't keep changing!"

"It's the nature of magical stationery," said Majordomo. "We have to get Eudaimonia out of here, then perhaps it'll change back."

Molly shook her head. "First, we have to save Miss Handlebram."

"So how do we get magic fire?" asked Pins. "Can you . . . ?"

Molly shook her head. "I'm sorry. That's a different kind of magic."

Angus turned his teacup in his big hands. "What about dragon fire?" he asked.

"Dragon fire melts just about anything," said Molly.

"That's what that one Wizard chap said," added Edward. The Imperial Squid around his neck gleamed. "The one from a few hundred years ago—you remember him, Majordomo, tall old fellow, wanted that magic ring melted? We were fresh out of dragons, but I think he found a volcano or something."

"Well," said Pins, "where do we get a dragon?"

Molly grinned. "There's one on the south lawn," she said. "At least, there will be."

It is no easy thing to smuggle a donkey into a castle. Eudaimonia had retired for the night, after writing forty-three letters to various individuals announcing Clockwork Bees for sale. Majordomo had bowed and scraped and promised faithfully to deliver the letters, after which he chucked them into the fireplace and came downstairs.

"Is bringing this to bodyguard," said Cook, handing him a cup of hot milk. Brown flecks floated on the surface.

"What is it?"

"Is *useful*."

Majordomo did not inquire further. The bodyguard— not Gordon, but the other one, who didn't seem to have a name—sneered at him, but took a sip. A few minutes later, he was snoring gently against the wall.

They led the donkey in through the garden gate, through the kitchen, into the dining hall, and into the Great Hall. His hooves clattered on the stone floor and Majordomo cringed. "Can't we do something about the noise?"

"Yes!" said Pins, whipping a set of napkins off the table. A snip with the scissors and a few quick stitches, and the donkey had a bootie on each hoof, secured at the top with a string.

The donkey seemed puzzled by his new footgear, but when he walked on the flagstones, he went "thunk" instead of "CLOP!" and that was a vast improvement.

Angus led the donkey to the block of ice and pulled off the sheet.

Molly stroked the donkey's neck, came away with a hair, and recited:

"Accreus Illusus Equine Accompli-cia Margle Fandango!"

The donkey yawned hugely and stretched and somewhere in mid-stretch, the yawn got larger and his legs got shorter and his ears went somewhere else and wings arched over his back.

"Grrraww?" said the dragon.

"Marvelous!" cried Serenissima, applauding.

Edward pulled the sheet from Miss Handlebram's block of ice. A thin veil of frost had formed on the outside of the ice, and the sheet left complicated triangular marks where the folds had pressed against the frost.

"Now we just need him to breathe fire on the ice,"

said Molly. "Not a lot—not enough to roast Miss Handlebram!—but enough to melt a little hole in the magic. Then Serenissima ought to be able to steam it away."

"That'll be an awful lot of water, won't it?" said Majordomo. "Once the ice melts. Where will it go?"

"I think I've got that worked out. I hope." She hugged the Little Gray Book to her chest. "There's a spell for turning water into fog. I thought if I could turn the water into fog, then we could open all the doors and it'd drift outside."

Molly had hoped that someone would say "That's bound to work!" or "Great idea!" or "It can't fail!"

"Well, it'll probably be better than a foot of water on the floor," said Pins. "Now, how do we get him to breathe fire on the ice?"

". . . um," said Molly.

For the dragon showed no interest in breathing fire at all. He was quite a nice little dragon and everyone in the room had been kind to him, particularly Molly and Angus. He had no desire to set fire to any of them.

In fact, he was starting to show signs of turning into a donkey again. He was starting to get extremely shaggy.

"I've got it!" cried Angus, and dashed for the kitchen. The sounds of his hooves on the floor were a great deal louder than the donkey's had been, but there wasn't anything to be done about it.

Majordomo looked up the stairs nervously. How strong had Cook's potion been?

The Minotaur dashed back into the room, brandishing . . . a carrot.

The dragon sat up, suddenly alert. He loved carrots.

Angus held up the carrot—on the far side of the block of ice.

"Graaaaww?"

"It's over here, buddy," said the Minotaur, waving the carrot. Through the distorted lens of the ice, the carrot appeared even larger. "You just have to get through that nasty ice to get it . . ."

"Brilliant!" whispered Edward.

The dragon bobbed his head up and down, following the movement of the carrot. He seemed confused. He stretched his muzzle out, bonked the ice, and pulled back, looking surprised.

"Just melt that ice, buddy, and you can have the carrot . . ."

If the dragon had still been a donkey, it would never have worked. Donkeys are quite intelligent, and he would simply have walked around the block of ice to get to the carrot.

Dragons, however, are not terribly intelligent, and they do not go around things. Part of being a dragon is a bone-deep belief that you are the biggest thing in the world and everything else gets out of your way.

Dragons have been known to have staring contests with mountains. They usually win.

The dragon saw the carrot, saw something cold and unpleasant between himself and the carrot—and went "HUFFFF!"

Quite a large bit of the block of ice vanished.

"Careful!" cried Molly, diving toward the dragon. Angus had held the carrot as far from Miss Handlebram as he could, but the dragon had produced a very impressive flame. She wasn't burned, but the tip of her sun hat had turned to ash.

"Good dragon!" said Angus, coming around the edge of the ice. "You showed that ice who was boss! Have a carrot! Have all the carrots!"

The dragon munched a carrot, terribly pleased with himself.

An enormous puddle was forming under the block of ice. Much of the ice had turned into steam, but the rest poured over the floor and soaked the rugs and ran zigzags between the flagstones. Majordomo ran for towels.

Serenissima stepped up and put both hands on the remaining ice. It went *FSSsssssssssssssssss* . . .

The ice melted. Water dripped off Miss Handlebram's shears and her sleeves and the tip of her nose. The temperature in the Great Hall went up by twenty degrees until it felt like a greenhouse.

Molly's hair, always frizzy, looked like a dandelion gone to seed.

"This is going to mildew," said Pins, studying the upholstery with a professional eye.

"Let it," said Majordomo, surprising everyone.

Serenissima shoved the last of the ice away and put her arms around Miss Handlebram.

The embrace of a steam spirit would warm the heart of a glacier. Miss Handlebram blinked a few times, lowered her shears, and said, "Wh . . . what . . . Serenissima? My dear, what is going on?"

"We'll explain everything in just a minute," said Molly. "But I've got to do something about this water!"

For the floor of the Great Hall was now several inches deep in water. A rug floated by, tassels rippling. Edward had climbed laboriously halfway up the staircase, trying to keep his metal ankles dry.

Molly took a last look at the Little Gray Book, hoped she'd gotten the words right, dipped up a palmful of water, and recited:

"Mistus Horrengious Noseferatus!"

There was a brilliant flash of light . . . and nothing happened.

Molly looked back at the book, worried. Had she gotten all the ingredients right? It was a cupped palmful of water and a thyme leaf under your tongue, and she had the thyme—her mouth was puckered with the taste—so that was all right, and the words looked right, and it certainly *felt* magical . . .

The water sloshed gently along the floor. The dragon—now almost entirely donkey-shaped again—chomped a floating carrot.

"I'm not a good enough Witch," Molly said miserably. "It shouldn't be that hard a spell, but—"

"Look!" said Pins, pointing.

Across the surface of the water, almost imperceptibly, white mist was starting to form.

"It's turning to mist!"

"I think it's going to work!"

"It's starting to get foggy!"

". . . really foggy."

"Can anybody see me?"

Water was no longer sloshing over Molly's very impressive boots . . . at least, as far as she could tell. She couldn't actually see her feet. All she could see was a solid wall of white.

She could see her hand in front of her face, but only just.

"Can anybody hear me?"

Their voices echoed weirdly in the fog. Molly put out her hands and tried to walk toward one of the voices.

"Has anybody got the donkey?"

"Someone open a door!"

"I've got the donkey right here."

"HEE-HAW!"

"My dears, can you please explain what's going on? Are we having a blizzard?"

There was a crash of metal as Edward ran into something.

Creeeeeaaaaaaak . . . Someone had gotten to the front door. The mist began to swirl as the night air tugged at it.

And then, from overhead, came the one voice that none of them wanted to hear.

"What is going on down there?" shouted Eudaimonia.

CHAPTER 41

In the fog and the damp, Molly heard a *whoosh* beside her. From somewhere nearby, armor clattered, the voice of Miss Handlebram said "Oh my!" and then the dragon—who by now was probably a donkey again—said "Hee-haw?"

Hooves clicked on the flagstones. Molly saw a dark shape loom briefly out of the mist, then vanish.

"What's going on?" shouted Eudaimonia.

Light flared overhead, at the top of the stairs. The fog was thicker toward the floor and thinned as it climbed the staircase. Staring upward, Molly could see Eudaimonia on the landing, holding up her wand. Cold white light streamed from its tip.

Molly sank down on her heels. Several feet of water vapor seemed like the flimsiest possible protection. She held her breath, hoping it would take effect before she was spotted.

"Majordomo!" snapped the Sorceress.

"Err . . . yes . . . Mistress?" asked Majordomo. There was a noticeable pause before the word *Mistress*. Molly wondered if Eudaimonia would notice.

"What is the meaning of this? Why do I hear livestock? Why is my castle full of smoke? Is something on fire?"

"Errr . . . yes!" Majordomo seized on this explanation. Molly crept toward the wall, hoping to find a doorway she could duck into. "There was—ah—a small fire in the kitchens."

"Is being the quiche," said Cook from somewhere in the fog. "Is catching fire. Stupid quiche."

"The fire's out now," said Majordomo hurriedly. "Just—err—cleaning up. Nothing you need to concern yourself with, Mistress."

Eudaimonia made an exasperated noise. "I see that I shall have to do everything myself." The light moved as she swept the wand in a circle.

The fog began to roil and shift, then to fray apart at the edges. In a few seconds, Molly could see the stairs quite clearly, and the shapes of Majordomo and Edward. Cook, farther off, was dim and gray, but still visible.

No Angus. No donkey. Angus must have gotten him out the front door. Good old Angus!

At the top of the stairs, looking pale and regal and angry, stood Eudaimonia. Her hair was mussed from sleeping and stood out in wild white ringlets around her face.

At the moment, thankfully, she was looking at Major-domo. "Very—ah—impressive, Mistress. I assure you, though, it's under control . . ."

Molly looked hurriedly along the wall and saw the bathroom door. She opened it silently—Majordomo's love of creaking hinges did not extend to bathrooms, thankfully!—and slipped inside.

There is something about a bathroom that feels like a fortress. A closed bathroom door may only be about two inches of plywood, but it *feels* like an iron bar. Molly had to fight against a sudden sense of safety.

I'm not really safe. She's right out there. Not that I think she'd hurt me . . . probably . . . but . . . well . . .

Miss Handlebram might not be hurt in that block of ice, but I don't think she's having much fun either.

I'm going to have to face her eventually, if I want her to leave the castle.

And she has to leave. Castle Hangnail isn't big enough for both of us.

It was weird, she thought. Deep down, she and Eudaimonia weren't that different. They both wanted a place of their own, a place where they could do magic without someone coming along and stopping them. Eudaimonia's mother was just a lot meaner about it than Molly's family was.

She scowled at the mirror. The fog had left her wet and

clammy, and frizzed her hair out in all directions. Bugbane clung behind her ear and shivered in his sleep.

Well, she couldn't do much about the hair, but at least she could towel the worst of the wetness off.

She kept an ear to the door while she toweled off.

"Perhaps the Mistress would prefer to retire to her room, and I shall bring a full report in the morning?"

"I shall do no such thing! Where is my block of ice with that meddling old woman in it?"

"Ah . . . that is . . . the fire melted it."

"*Melted* it?"

"The quiche was . . . err . . . on fire. So Cook . . . err . . . ran it out this way to . . . err . . . get some ice . . . and threw the quiche on it . . . ."

Molly put a hand over her eyes.

"You are telling me"—Molly could almost hear Eudaimonia pulling herself up to her full height—"that a block of ice five feet thick was melted by a *burning quiche!?*"

"It was a very large quiche," said Majordomo.

"Is having lots of garlic in it," said Cook. "Also red peppers."

"And the old woman? Did she melt too?"

"Err . . ."

"*Lots* of garlic."

There was a pause, and Molly could hear footsteps on the flagstones.

"I don't wish to have to do this," said Eudaimonia, and Molly jumped back from the door, because it sounded like the Sorceress was right outside. "But you've left me no choice."

There was a noise that sounded like *Zzzzot!* Major-domo yelped.

"Now," said Eudaimonia coldly, "perhaps we could have a little less *lying*, dear Majordomo, and you could tell me what is really going on?"

She zapped him! She zapped Majordomo!

Molly was suddenly, instantly furious. It was like seeing those boys in school tormenting the bat all over again—somebody big and strong was kicking something little and weak that hadn't done them any harm.

Nobody zaps minions on my watch!

She yanked the bathroom door open.

CHAPTER 42

Majordomo was halfway on the floor, being held up by Cook, who had a murderous look in her eyes. Eudaimonia was looming over both of them, her wand raised, and there was a flicker of ice around the tip. It was clear that she wasn't going to stop at just one zap.

Molly caught a glimpse of Edward stock-still by the staircase, of Pins in the open doorway, one hand to his mouth—but none of them were close enough to help.

It was up to her.

Molly threw her shoulders back, marched up to Eudaimonia, and yelled, "Why don't you pick on someone your own size?!"

"I'd love to," said Eudaimonia. "Why don't you run along and find someone like that?"

This is the problem with Evil people. They are usually very, very good at snappy comebacks.

Being Wicked, about the best Molly could do was say "Yeah—yeah—well, you better stop or I'll turn you into an earwig!"

"*Dear* Molly," said Eudaimonia. She turned away from Cook and Majordomo. "I wondered where you had gone off to. I didn't think you'd leave—not when we're such good friends, after all." She paused. "And still talking about earwigs, I see . . ."

Molly scowled and folded her arms. She kept one eye on Eudaimonia's face, and the other on the sparkling wand.

Cook helped Majordomo to his feet. The old minion cleared his throat.

"I fear, Miss Eudaimonia," he said, "that there has been a misunderstanding. I take full responsibility, you understand. However, it seems that the post at Castle Hangnail has already been filled."

"Is belonging to Molly," rumbled Cook. "Molly is being Master here."

Eudaimonia raised one eyebrow. One corner of her mouth—on the same side as the eyebrow—went up in a crooked little smile.

Molly knew that look. If they had been back home, sitting in Eudaimonia's bedroom, Molly would have apologized immediately for whatever she'd done wrong—or right—and if it *wasn't* her fault, she would have agreed immediately that whoever Eudaimonia was mad at was completely in the wrong, totally, and she hoped they fell down the stairs and got splinters in their knees.

But we're not back home. And this is my castle, not hers!

"And where do you suggest I go?" asked Eudaimonia coldly. "There are no other castles going begging at the moment."

"Well," said Majordomo, clearing his throat. "That's very unfortunate, of course, but I'm sure there will be plenty of other invitations as other castles—or crags, or fortresses, or whatever you like—come open. Most Masters choose to retire in spring, when the new crop of magical folk are getting out of school, but there are always occasional vacancies. Meanwhile, however unorthodox the method, the Tasks have been performed and Castle Hangnail is taken."

He stood up as straight as he could when he said it, and Molly felt proud and frightened all at once.

"So it is," purred Eudaimonia. "So it is . . . and yet, I don't feel like waiting for someone to die or retire to the seaside." She tilted her chin toward Molly. "Do you know what happens, dear Molly, when a Sorceress wants another Sorceress's castle?"

Molly shot Majordomo a quick, worried look. He shook his head.

"They fight," said Eudaimonia. "And the more powerful of the two takes the castle for herself."

Molly had to lick her lips twice before she could speak. "I'm . . . I'm not a Sorceress."

"No," said Eudaimonia. "That should make it easier, don't you think?"

And she grinned a grin like a starving wolf and snapped her fingers. "Gordon! Andrew! Attend me!"

Gordon stumbled down the stairs. He was bleary eyed and looked as if he'd been sleeping in his clothes. "Sorry, Mistress. Can't wake Andy up. He's out cold."

"Hmm. Nicely done, dear Molly. Perhaps this will be more entertaining than I thought."

Molly braced herself—and Eudaimonia turned away. "Tomorrow at noon," she said. "Tonight I require my beauty sleep—and it wouldn't do you any harm either, dear."

She swept out of the Great Hall, toward the front door. Pins ducked hurriedly aside. Majordomo and Cook and Molly followed, crowding into the doorway—was she leaving? Would it really be that simple?

No.

She halted on the stone steps before the door, facing the moat with its single stubby tower. She pointed her wand, and spoke a single guttural word.

The moat rippled, then heaved itself upward. Frost formed on a causeway of sparkling ice, stretching to the door of the tower.

Eudaimonia turned back to the little knot of minions in the doorway. "Until tomorrow," she said.

 296

And then her hand darted out like a striking snake and she snatched Pins up by the back of the neck. The doll squeaked as her nails dug into the burlap.

"No!" said Molly.

"Pins!" said Majordomo.

Eudaimonia strode across the causeway. Gordon blocked the others from following, backing across himself.

"Give him back!" yelled Molly, hating how feeble her voice sounded—how thin and how useless and how *young*.

Eudaimonia laughed.

The edge of the causeway began to melt. Gordon waited

until the gap was too large for any of the minions to jump, then hurried after his Mistress.

The tower door slammed. The causeway lost its shape and slumped into the moat. Small icebergs bobbed in the murky water.

Eudaimonia was beyond their reach, and she had taken Pins with her.

CHAPTER 43

"I don't understand," said Molly miserably as Major-domo pulled the door shut. "Why did she want Pins?"

The old minion shook his head. "She was interested in him earlier. Wanted him to make her a wardrobe."

Molly sighed. She could believe it. Eudaimonia never could stand for anyone to be better dressed than she was. "Well, it doesn't matter now. We just have to get him back—and I'm not waiting until tomorrow! She could do horrible things to him!"

"Well, cloth is pretty resistant to ice, so I don't think she could do him any real harm . . ."

"Yes, but is he resistant to a pair of scissors?"

Majordomo went a bit gray. That was the problem with being around Sorceresses and Witches—you got in the habit of thinking of magic first and foremost and forgot that somebody could do all sorts of nasty things to you with ordinary objects lying around the house.

The fog had mostly cleared from the Great Hall. Cook

went up and knocked on Edward's armor. "Is being all right?"

"*Gaaaaah!*" said Edward, in a surprisingly feminine voice, and then the helmet flipped up and revealed the brown face of Miss Handlebram.

"Is that awful girl gone? I can't hear anything in here—it's like wearing metal earmuffs!"

"Miss Handlebram! You're okay!" Molly flung herself at the suit of armor and hugged it fiercely.

"Oh, yes. Sir Edward here very kindly . . . err . . . disguised me . . ."

"Mmmm-ffmmghff!" said Edward.

"And now I should like to get out, please."

"Mmmff!"

It took less time to get Miss Handlebram out than you might think. Armor is very unwieldy, but magic armor will help you get in and out, so in a very little time they had freed Miss Handlebram and she stood, panting and slightly damp, on the floor of the Great Hall.

"Forgive me, Sir Edward," she said, "it was very gallant of you, just—err—*stuffy.*"

"Honored to be of service, madam," said Edward, readjusting his helmet. "No offense taken. I always thought armor was hot and stuffy when I was inside it. It's different when you *are* the armor, if you understand."

Miss Handlebram did not remember anything of being frozen, and was quite perturbed to learn that she had been encased in ice for several days. "My cats!"

"Serenissima fed them," Molly assured her.

Serenissima peered out of the kitchen and curtsied. She had had to run from the Great Hall when the water turned to fog. To a steam spirit, it felt as if Molly's spell were tugging at her, trying to unmake her into fog as well. It had been a very unpleasant sensation.

They gathered in the kitchen. Cook put the kettle on and began vengefully baking scones.

Angus appeared, to tell them that the donkey was safely away at Berkeley's farm. "And he's given me a spare set of keys so that if we need a dragon for anything, I can go and fetch him."

Majordomo vanished for a few minutes. When he returned, he was cradling the goldfish bowl between his hands.

Molly inhaled sharply. Did the goldfish know that Pins was missing?

"It's all right," said the goldfish. "He already told me." She pushed up the sleeves of her tiny sweater. "So this is our council of war?"

Council of war sounded awfully grand for seven people and a goldfish gathered around a kitchen table, but—

"Yes," said Sir Edward. "When Lord Sevenshanks took the Tower of Otters from his ancient foe, he started with four men and a bushel basket of laundry. We already

300

have more men and more arms than he did." He banged the point of his sword on the floor.

"May we see the Tasks?" asked Majordomo.

Molly pulled it out.

All the Tasks had been crossed out.

"But—" Molly blinked.

Majordomo, though, was nodding. "You've thrown her out. She left. The tower is not, technically speaking, attached to the castle, and however . . . confused . . . the paperwork has gotten, the Board has acknowledged you as the ruler of the castle."

"But that's wonderful!" said Serenissima. "That means—"

Majordomo tapped the Tasks.

A note had appeared at the bottom, in elegant, flowing script.

Due to multiple irregularities, the Board has determined that a representative will be sent to investigate the situation in person.

"What will they do?" whispered Serenissima.

Majordomo shook his head. "Maybe nothing. Maybe they'll decide Molly's too young. Maybe they're just coming because I filled out the paperwork wrong. But if Eudaimonia's not gone by then . . ." He spread his hands.

"They may decide the Tasks weren't properly finished. They may even decide that the castle belongs to her by right."

The goldfish let out a low moan. Lord Edward clutched the Imperial Squid around his neck.

Molly took a deep breath and looked around the table.

Her friends. All her friends in the world, except for Pins, who was being held captive by someone who had never really been her friend at all.

What am I doing? I can't fight Eudaimonia! She was always better than me—stronger than me—she only let me hang out with her because she liked having someone to boss around—and now she's got that wand, and how am I supposed to stop her?

Molly listened to the little voice in her head. She acknowledged that what it was saying was probably the absolute truth.

And then she shut it up in a high tower inside her heart and threw away the key.

None of that matters. I have to try.

Across the table, Majordomo met her eyes. He nodded, very slightly.

"All right," said Molly. Her voice surprised her, because it sounded older and like it knew what it was doing. "We'll deal with the Board when they show up. Castle Hangnail is mine now—even if just for a few days. Our first priority is to get Pins back. Who can tell me about that tower?"

"The tower wasn't part of the original castle," said Majordomo. "The moat used to run around the entire thing. The builder wasn't good with drains, though, and it all settled around that one tower. A later Master built the causeway, and they've been falling down and getting rebuilt ever since."

"Between the sludge and the mud, it's between six and eight feet deep," said Angus. "Water on top of mud. You can't wade in it without getting stuck, so just walking across and trying to climb up is right out."

"I suppose we could build a raft," said Miss Handle-bram dubiously.

Molly tapped her fingers on the table. "If the moat is that deep, it must be covering up the bottom floor of the tower . . ."

Majordomo nodded. "The causeway runs to a second-story window. I think the bottom floor is full of water."

Molly turned and looked at the goldfish.

The goldfish nodded.

"It's going to be full of muck," said Molly. "Probably crawling with germs."

"Yes," said the goldfish. "I know." She removed her sweater and tore a tiny strip off with her fins. They watched as she tied it around her forehead (or what passes for a forehead on a goldfish) so that the ends trailed behind her. "I'm ready. Let's go now."

"Don't take any risks," Molly cautioned as they crept out to the moat. "We need information. It won't help Pins if you get caught too."

"You're a good Wicked Witch," said the goldfish. "Moles and bats and plants—yes, those things you're very good with. But you're not a fish. Leave water work to me."

Molly knelt down by the edge of moat, on the far side of the tower, where there were no windows. She set the goldfish bowl down at the edge of the moat and the fish gave a great leap over the rim and landed in the murky water with a splash.

She vanished with barely a ripple. Molly and the minions went back inside the castle, while Bugbane clung to the side of the castle and waited for the fish to return.

"What are you thinking?" asked Majordomo.

Molly rubbed the back of her neck. "Well . . . if the tower is open underwater, maybe we can drain the moat and just walk out to it."

"We'd need to put down boards over the mud," said Angus dubiously. "A *lot* of boards . . ."

"No, we wouldn't," said Miss Handlebram. "Molly, you've got that one spell, haven't you? The one that makes plants grow? You used it on my creeping thyme and filled it in so nicely."

"Well, yes . . ."

"So we'll plant our way to the tower and walk on those instead of the mud." Miss Handlebram grinned. "Something with a nice deep taproot to stabilize the mud, and then between those—mint, do you think? Or lemon balm?"

Molly clapped her hands together. "Yes! That's perfect! Although I hate to let mint run around loose—still, desperate times . . ."

"Will be making mint jelly," put in Cook. "Lots and lots of mint jelly."

"That's all well and good," said Majordomo, "but even assuming we drain the moat, what then? We still have to face Eudaimonia."

Molly exhaled. "Yeah."

There was a glum silence.

"I think it's mostly the wand," said Molly. "She just . . . just wasn't that powerful before. I mean, she could *do* things, but she couldn't have called up a block of ice and frozen somebody, or made an ice causeway. And she only had the one spellbook." She twisted her fingers together. "I think she must have gotten a better one. She couldn't have controlled her mother's mind when I knew her."

"Are you sure?" asked Serenissima.

Molly chewed on her lower lip. It sounded awful to say this about her friend (*But she's not my friend anymore! She*

never really was!), but—"Yeah. If she could have done that, she would have. She was always yelling that her mother wouldn't let her do stuff. Um . . ." She poked at the table. "We didn't do serious magic. Just, you know, little stuff. Changing the color of our hair, or getting the tangles out. Turning leaves into teacups. Starting a fire with your thumbnail. Shadows. You know."

"If it was a shadow that scared Freddy Wisteria," rumbled Angus, "it seemed like pretty big stuff to me."

Molly smiled faintly. "He wasn't magicky, though. Although Eudaimonia was surprised when I could summon one up, so maybe . . ." Cook slid a scone in front of her, and she stared down at it without seeing it.

She seemed scared, almost, but—no, surely nobody who knows magic would be scared of my shadow. For all I know, she can do the spell herself now.

"We have to assume, therefore, that she's found a better spellbook and is drawing on the wand," said Majordomo. "We can't do much about spells she already knows, but if we can find a way to get the wand away from her, that would help. Breaking it would be even better. A broken wand will recoil on its owner, and there's no telling what it might do."

It was Serenissima who said, rather sadly, "But how are we going to do that?"

CHAPTER 44

Now we must go back for a moment to our friend the goldfish, who was swimming through the dark water of the moat.

Goldfish are not brave creatures by nature. They aren't much of anything by nature. They are remarkably sturdy fish, capable of surviving dirty water, terrible food, and wretched conditions, and that's about all that you can say about them.

Pins's goldfish was, despite her fears, as sturdy as any of her kind. She felt the grimy water slide past her gills and muttered "Ewwww . . ." but that was all. An angelfish would have fallen over dead in the first five minutes, poisoned by the rancid liquid, but the goldfish didn't even cough.

Her big fear was turtles. There weren't any fish in the moat, but it was the sort of place that would attract turtles, and a turtle would love to make a snack of a goldfish.

"I must be quick," she told herself. "I must be brave.

There may be turtles, but there is definitely a Sorceress, and she has Pins!"

For the goldfish loved Pins as dearly as he loved her, and the two of them had been friends for a very long time, since he had carried her across a great desert in a plastic bag and had fought Djinn and Ifrits and Ghouls for her. She would have gone anywhere with him, but since he had chosen to settle at Castle Hangnail, she had been more than happy to swim in her bowl and look out over the countryside from the window.

(Which only goes to show that even minions have their own stories that may be long and heroic and have no bearing on the story at hand.)

The goldfish swam down, down, into the depths of the moat, where the light was brown and gritty and full of tiny wiggling things. A human would have found them disgusting, but the goldfish knew that they were mosquito larvae and good to eat if you're a goldfish.

When she reached the stones of the tower, she swam in a long circle around the outer edge. There was a barred window—easy enough for a fish to slip through, but much too small for a regular-sized person. She kept swimming.

The water was as dark as coffee and she veered away from black shapes in the mud. Probably they were rocks—probably—but what if they were turtles?

She came at last to a doorway and let out a tiny fishy cheer.

For the doorway was almost clear. The door had rotted away until it was only a few scraps of wood clinging to rusted hinges. Eudaimonia might be able to block the doorway with magic, but she could not block it with wood or iron.

The goldfish swam inside. The interior of the tower was very dark, lit only by pale squares at the door and window . . . and by an arched opening near the roof.

"It's the old staircase," said the goldfish to herself. "The humans must have needed a way up."

The archway gleamed. A shadow moved across it, as if someone were pacing back and forth in front of the light. Cool water pulsed across the goldfish's fins, spreading in tendrils from the archway. Whatever was up there, the air was very cold.

The goldfish knew that she should go back. She should go back, and report to Molly, and tell them everything. They needed to know so that they could plan their assault on the tower.

But it might be Pins up there, she thought, and swam upward, toward the cold water and the light.

Molly had just finished her third scone and was no closer to figuring out how to break Eudaimonia's wand, when Bugbane winged his way into the kitchen. He had been yawning all night and had nearly dozed off watching for the goldfish, but he was wide-awake now.

"She's back!" he chirped. "She's back—oh, come quick!"

Molly dropped her scone and ran out to the moat. Majordomo limped after her, carrying the goldfish bowl.

The goldfish was swimming in agitated circles at the meeting place. "Oh!" she said. "Oh-oh-oh! It's horrible! Oh!"

"Here!" Molly grabbed the bowl from Majordomo and dropped to her knees. The goldfish leaped into the bowl, but even then she didn't settle down. "Oh! Oh!"

"Come inside," said Majordomo. "Calm down."

They brought her back to the kitchen. She shuddered her fins.

"Okay," said Molly. "Tell us everything."

"Oh! Oh, it's horrible!"

"There, there," said Sir Edward. "Chin—err—gills up! Stiff upper lip! Start at the beginning!"

"We can't help Pins if you can't tell us what you saw," said Majordomo quietly.

That steadied the goldfish's nerves. She straightened. "Yes. Yes. Oh, it was terrible. The whole room, made of ice. The water's so cold, it's frozen all around the edges. And she's got Pins in a—a jar—like a b-b-bug—"

The goldfish burst into tears. Since you cannot give a handkerchief to a goldfish, they stood around helplessly, until Serenissima dipped a finger in the water and warmed it by two or three comforting degrees.

When the fish had calmed down a bit, Molly said, "We'll rescue him. I promise. But we have to know how to get in. Is there a door?"

The fish shook her head. "An empty doorway. The first floor is underwater. You can swim right through and up into the tower. The second floor is full of ice."

Majordomo nodded. "She's an ice Sorceress, we knew that. Her magic probably works better if she keeps the room cold."

"Her bedroom always was freezing," muttered Molly.

"Did she say anything?" asked Majordomo.

The goldfish nodded. "I couldn't stay long," she said. "It was too cold—I thought my fins would freeze—and it wouldn't help Pins if I froze before I got back to you—"

"You did exactly the right thing," said Molly.

"Well." The goldfish thought for a minute. "She said that she was keeping him. Even if she had to leave the castle, he was coming with her, to sew clothes for her."

"Now that's interesting . . ." murmured Angus.

They all looked at the Minotaur. Cook nodded.

"Yes. Is being very interesting."

"What?" asked Molly.

"Is assuming that she may have to leave. Is thinking she could *lose*."

Molly blinked.

Eudaimonia thought that she might *lose* to Molly? That there was a chance she wouldn't win?

Molly was aware that her mouth had fallen open.

"Well, when we defeat her, if she's made a jar out of ice, we'll just melt it," said Serenissima. "We wouldn't let her take Pins with her. She can get her wardrobe off the rack, like anybody else."

Molly knotted her fingers together. "Um," she said. And then, slowly, "I don't think we should rely on that. Defeating her, I mean."

"Never say die!" said Edward firmly.

"I'm not saying die, whatever that means! I'm just— look, if I win, great! But what if I don't? I'll have to leave and she'll still have Pins. We need to rescue him and get him away."

Cook nodded. "Is good," she said. "Is hoping for best, but planning for worst."

"If you lose," said Majordomo, "we must all plan to leave. Angus especially." And he told them about Eudaimonia's plan to sell the Minotaur.

Angus stood up and walked to the edge of the garden. Molly started to go after him, but Majordomo caught her shoulder and shook his head. They watched the powerful line of the Minotaur's muscles tense until they looked like steel cables, then slowly ease.

He came back to the table and sat down. "I'll go to Farmer Berkeley," he said. "Mother—"

Cook nodded. "Will take knives. And cutting board. Have only just been getting proper seasoning on cutting board, is not going to leave it."

"What about you?" asked Edward, looking at Major-domo.

"I shall inform the Minion's Guild that this castle is no longer a place of safe employment," said Majordomo. "You may experiment on your minions or kick them or even eat them when the pantry runs low—but you do not *sell* them." He drew a deep breath. "And then I shall leave. If Molly has need of me, I shall serve her. Otherwise I shall present my resume to the Minion's Guild and see if they can find a place for me."

There was a great silence in the room. All the minions knew what it cost Majordomo to say that he would leave Castle Hangnail; Molly did not know, but she could guess.

"You can come stay with me," said Miss Handlebram firmly. "I'll fix up the back bedroom until you've got a place of your own. And Sir Edward too."

The enchanted armor rattled in embarrassed gratifica-tion. Majordomo blinked back tears.

"I'd rather it wasn't necessary," Molly said. "Let's fig-ure out how to get Pins out, shall we?"

CHAPTER 45

The plan in the end was straightforward. "Because," Sir Edward said, "the fewer parts of a battle plan, the less parts can go wrong."

Bugbane—very tired now, as the early-morning light started to creep over the hills—zipped by the tower windows. "She's in bed," he reported. "And Gordon is watching the causeway out the second-story window, in case we try to build a bridge or something. I think the first floor is unguarded."

Molly fidgeted. She knew that Eudaimonia knew an alarm spell, like the rosemary one she'd used on the barn. Would she have put alarms around Pins?

If she has, there's nothing to be done about it. We'll simply have to be very fast.

"Dragonfire and steam melt enchanted ice," she said. She looked down at the goldfish. "Are you sure you want to do this?"

"For Pins," said the goldfish, "I'll do anything."

Serenissima waded into the moat. The water around her began to steam gently, but she was trying very hard not to make the water uninhabitably hot.

"All right," said Molly. "The spell is only supposed to last a minute—it lasts longer on the donkey, but I don't know how much time you'll have—"

She took a deep breath. Balanced on the tip of her finger was a scale the size of a sequin.

"*Accreus Illusus Piscene Accomplicia Margle Fandango!*"

(*Piscene* is the equivalent of *Bovine* or *Equine*, only for fish. Molly wasn't sure if the spell would even work on a fish.)

The goldfish blinked. She blinked several times, and then she belched and a tongue of flame shot out of her mouth and set the surface of the water boiling.

"Excuse m—eee!" said the fish. Her voice cracked, went several octaves deeper, and then she wasn't a fish at all, but a beautiful golden sea serpent not much bigger than a garter snake. "Oh my . . ."

Molly would have loved to stop and admire the tiny sea serpent, but she knew they didn't have time. "Go!" she whispered. "Hurry!"

They went. Serenissima dove into the moat and the sea serpent went wiggling downward. Bubbles of steam boiled up from their passage and burst on the surface of the water.

The seconds ticked by. Molly tried to imagine where they were—had they reached the sunken doorway? Were they inside? Oh, surely they must be inside by now! Serenissima could breathe water, sort of, being a water spirit, so she wouldn't drown, anyway. And once they were inside, as long as the goldfish was still a dragon, they only needed a little fire, only a tiny bit, and Serenissima could melt the ice and free Pins—

She looked at her watch. A minute and a half.

"They've got to be at the top by now," she whispered to Majordomo.

He nodded. "If there's an alarm spell, it would have gone off by now, wouldn't—"

There was a roar from the tower, like a falling avalanche. Light flashed in the windows. Molly let out a squeak of horror.

Bugbane zipped past the windows and dove into her hair. "She's awake!"

"There *was* an alarm spell . . ."

The surface of the moat went as flat as a sheet of paper, and ice crackled and zigzagged across it, until it was frozen solid.

Majordomo and Molly clutched each other's forearms. There was nothing they could do.

"Turn *me* into a dragon!" said Majordomo. "I'll melt the ice—"

"I can't! It only works on animals! You can't turn people into dragons! You'd get stuck or explode!"

Bugbane fell out of her hair. "Me!" he squeaked.

"I don't know the magic word for bats!"

(Should you ever find yourself in this situation, by the way, the word is *Chiropteran.* Molly looked it up as soon as they got back to the castle and learned it by heart.)

The voice of Eudaimonia rang over the icy moat. "Very well! You may have gotten your precious doll back—but he won't do you much good locked under the ice!"

"They got him," whispered Molly. "They *got* him! He doesn't need to breathe, does he?"

Majordomo shook his head slowly. "No . . . but the goldfish . . . she'll *freeze.*"

They clung together by the side of the moat. Molly felt tears prickle her eyes.

And then, a few feet away, the surface of the moat seemed to sink a little, as if an invisible foot had stepped in it. The ice turned to slush and the slush fell away.

Serenissima rose out of the hole.

Pins clung to her hair. Steam rose off her.

Cupped in the minion's hands, fins barely moving, lay the goldfish.

"Oh *no*," said Molly. She and Majordomo grabbed Serenissima by the arms and pulled her up. Her normally scalding skin was barely lukewarm and her teeth were chattering together.

Molly held out the bowl, and Serenissima gently dropped the fish in. She did not swim, but drifted toward the bottom.

Pins leaped to her shoulder. Molly ran for the kitchen, one hand over the top of the bowl to keep the water from splashing out. The fish sloshed back and forth.

She threw herself past Cook and set the fishbowl on the counter next to the stove, where the heat could warm the water.

"Fish," moaned Pins. "Oh fish, fish, love, you saved me, you were glorious, please be okay . . ." He reached into the bowl and pulled the sweater around her with agonizing tenderness.

The minions held their breath.

For a long, long moment, the goldfish simply lay there. Molly put a hand on Pins's burlap shoulder.

Then the fish opened one eye and whispered, "I shall get ich . . . and fin rot . . . and moat fever . . . and sarcoptic mange . . ."

Her voice trailed off into a tiny goldfish snore.

The kitchen erupted into cheers.

They had saved Pins, and their tiny aquatic hero had survived.

CHAPTER 46

"When the alarm went off, I thought we were done for," said Serenissima. "Ice grew over *everything*. Fortunately the goldfish was still a dragon, and we managed to melt a hole in the ice over the opening to the moat. She was hopping mad when she saw that Pins was in that jar, and she was breathing fire on *everything*."

The steam spirit was bundled up by the stove with her feet in a bucket of hot water. Cook dumped a boiling kettleful into the bucket and Serenissima sighed in relief. "It was so cold," she said. "I knew we had to get back out of the tower, and it was getting light enough that I could just see the door—but I've never been so cold."

"We'd better start on the moat now," said Molly. "The less time she has to prepare, the better."

Angus and Miss Handlebram tramped out to the donkey pasture with her. The basilisk glared at them balefully over the stable door.

"If we win, I hope we can do something for him," said

Angus. "Send her to a nice home for orphaned basilisks, perhaps. She's not a bad monster, but she hasn't been treated well at all."

It didn't take Molly long to find what she was looking for. The early-morning light was gray and faded as the sun crept over the hills, and in the first rays, she saw a little mound of dirt and a hole.

She knelt and put her mouth near the hole. "Excuse me? Can anyone hear me? I need to speak to Stonebreaker, please. It's urgent."

She sat back on her heels.

A few minutes passed, and then a fuzzy head popped up. "Eh? Eh?"

Molly repeated herself.

"Stonebreaker," said the mole. "Witch. Eh?" He considered for a moment. "Eh!"

He dove back into the earth.

"Not much for conversation, are they?" said Angus.

"And to think of all the trouble I've gone to keeping the little devils out of my garden," said Miss Handlebram. "I had no idea they were so smart. I'm a little embarrassed now."

The ground rumbled. Molly stepped hurriedly aside, and a white snout broke out of the earth.

"Witch," said Stonebreaker, clasping his claws together.

"Stonebreaker," said Molly respectfully.

He smiled. "You need a mole?"

"Very much," said Molly. "You know the moat around the tower? I need it drained."

Stonebreaker listened carefully. His whiskers twitched occasionally as she described the mud and the moat and the empty tower.

"But you have to be careful," said Molly. "There's a very bad Sorceress in the tower. I don't want anybody to get hurt."

Stonebreaker waved his claws. "Sorceress won't see us. For Witch of Wormrise—yes. Moles will do this. Be ready."

He dove back into the earth.

"Not much on long good-byes, are they?" asked Angus.

Molly and the minions tromped up to the belfry. It was the best place in the castle to watch the tower from, although at first, there wasn't anything much to watch.

Cook handed around hot chocolate. From overhead, the bats snored quietly. (The Eldest opened one eye, said "Oh, it's you," and went back to sleep.)

Then—"Look!" said Pins.

They all crowded to the window.

From all directions, like the points of a strange and wobbly star, mole tunnels were converging on the moat.

They zigzagged back and forth, avoiding boulders and fence posts, coming in from all directions.

"Ten—" said Pins. "Twenty—thirty-five—look at them all!"

Moles began popping up out of the ground all over, scurrying over the grass and diving back into the dirt. Molly held her breath.

"Is it some kind of magic?" asked Miss Handlebram.

"No," said Pins, quicker to catch on. "They can't burrow right into the moat—they'd get washed away. They went right up to the edge, though, and now—"

A large molehill formed. Stonebreaker came up out of it. He was a tiny white shape from this far up, but Molly saw him lift up his claws.

The ground began to shake.

Stones fell off the tower—*all* the towers. The floor rocked. The Eldest grumbled and pulled her wing over her head. Majordomo grabbed for Pins to keep him from falling out the window.

From down below, the voice of Eudaimonia floated over the moat. *"What is going on?!"*

"He's breaking the end of the tunnels!" said Molly. "It's a little tiny earthquake! Now the water's going to drain into the tunnels!"

And so it was. The ice in the moat teetered and split apart into chunks, like a river breaking up in spring. The water level was clearly sinking. There was a sharp crackling noise.

A bolt of cold fire snaked out of the tower window at Stonebreaker.

Before the minions could do more than gasp, the mole shaman had thrown his claws in the air in front of him. The magical attack sprayed in all directions, like cold sparks, and then Stonebreaker himself dove into the earth.

The damage was done. The moat was already half drained.

"We've got to move, before she figures out how to refill it!" said Angus.

"Seeds!" said Miss Handlebram.

"Spells!" said Molly.

"Keep it down . . ." grumbled the Eldest.

A few minutes later, Molly and the minions came out the front door, carrying bags of seeds. Angus had an enormous planter full of mint.

Molly had wanted to go alone, but the minions wouldn't hear of it. "If it's just you, she'll have one target," said Angus. "If it's all of us, she'll have to think about who to freeze, and there's more chance we'll all get away."

He smiled. "And anyway, even if that's rubbish, we're not letting you go alone."

"For the Master!" said Edward.

"For the Master!" cried the other minions and Miss Handlebram.

Majordomo met her eyes. Molly held her breath—

"For the Master," he said.

She blushed.

The moat was completely gone now, leaving an expanse of mud. The empty doorway to the tower gaped open.

Molly picked up a handful of seeds, whispered the words of a spell to them, and threw them down in the mud.

The seeds sat for a moment or two, then put out two little green leaves apiece. They added a second set of leaves, then a third.

Then they seemed to stall for a minute. Majordomo frowned, but Miss Handlebram nodded. "They're building roots," she said. "That's starry rosinweed, that is— roots can go ten feet deep. That's what we need here, to stabilize all that mud." She smiled. "Butterflies like it too."

Apparently she was correct. After a moment or two, the leaves suddenly erupted. They were as high as Molly's head in five minutes, and higher than Angus's in six.

Bright yellow flowers popped open, a cloud of golden daisies swaying eight feet off the ground. Molly threw out another handful of seed.

Angus scooped up a handful of mud and popped a

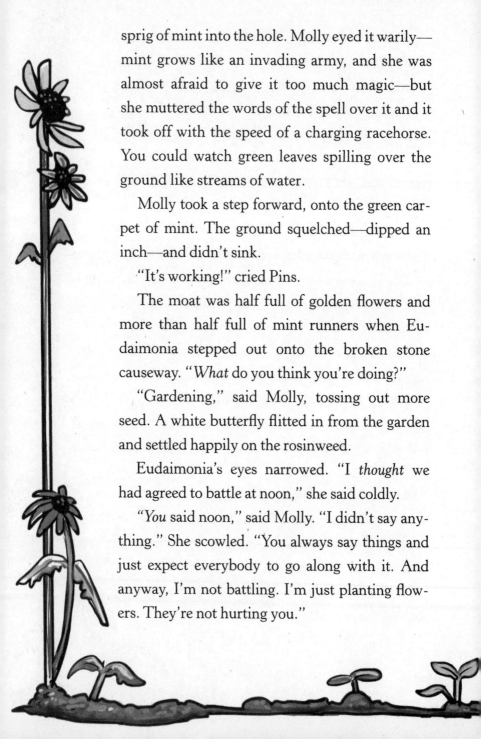

sprig of mint into the hole. Molly eyed it warily—mint grows like an invading army, and she was almost afraid to give it too much magic—but she muttered the words of the spell over it and it took off with the speed of a charging racehorse. You could watch green leaves spilling over the ground like streams of water.

Molly took a step forward, onto the green carpet of mint. The ground squelched—dipped an inch—and didn't sink.

"It's working!" cried Pins.

The moat was half full of golden flowers and more than half full of mint runners when Eudaimonia stepped out onto the broken stone causeway. "*What* do you think you're doing?"

"Gardening," said Molly, tossing out more seed. A white butterfly flitted in from the garden and settled happily on the rosinweed.

Eudaimonia's eyes narrowed. "I *thought* we had agreed to battle at noon," she said coldly.

"*You* said noon," said Molly. "I didn't say anything." She scowled. "You always say things and just expect everybody to go along with it. And anyway, I'm not battling. I'm just planting flowers. They're not hurting you."

Eudaimonia whipped out her wand and froze a stand of rosinweed in ice. "Then I'm just weeding."

Molly shrugged. She knew—and Eudaimonia didn't—that you can't kill a plant with deep roots merely by freezing the green bits. The rosinweed would grow back twice as big once the ice melted.

The mint was even less impressed. When the Sorceress blasted a hole in the carpet of green, the mint overgrew it in five minutes flat.

"You always did like playing in the dirt," said Eudaimonia. "I suppose I shouldn't be surprised you're still at it. It's all the magic you can do, I guess."

Molly threw another handful of seed. She knew that the Sorceress couldn't see underneath the causeway, but the rosinweed was growing right up to the door now, and the mint had already crept inside.

With a bass drone, the Clockwork Bees arrived. They settled on the flowers, mechanical legs working busily.

Eudaimonia shot a quick look at the position of the sun. Her lips twisted together.

That's odd.

That's very odd.

She looks . . . scared.

Why would she be scared of the sun? She isn't a Vampire. I'd have noticed. And Vampires don't eat quiche.

Eudaimonia scowled and blasted another set of flowers. A Clockwork Bee fell off, encased in ice, and crashed to the ground.

"Hey!" said Molly. "What did you do that for?"

"Oh come on," said Eudaimonia. "It's a stupid little wind-up toy. You might as well get upset over a broken toaster." She zapped another one.

"Those are my Bees!" Molly gritted her teeth. "They belong to the castle! Leave them alone!"

One of the working Clockwork Bees landed beside a frozen one and tapped it gingerly. Its little metal antennae swiveled as it examined its fallen comrade.

"It's not your castle yet," said Eudaimonia pleasantly.

She stole another glance at the sun, which was just coming over the top of the castle.

"Yes, it is! The Board of Magic said so!" Molly had an urge to add "Well, mostly," but squelched it.

Angus set a hoof on the mint. The mud held up under his weight. He nodded to Molly.

All right. The moat's clear. We can attack and she can't hole up inside the tower.

I guess it's time.

"It *is* my castle," said Molly. She took a deep breath. "And we're not waiting 'til noon. We're doing this now. This is my place. And I want you to leave."

A second Clockwork Bee landed beside the first. It repeated the tap-tap-tap inspection of the frozen Bee.

Eudaimonia rolled her eyes. *"That's* your idea of a formal challenge? 'I want you to leave'? Molly, dear, you're throwing an enemy out of your territory, not trying to get that stupid sister of yours to stay on her side of the room."

Hey! She called my twin stupid!

Nobody calls my twin stupid but me!

"Fine!" yelled Molly. "You're a mean person and I don't like you and I want you to leave right now and *never come back!"*

The older girl sighed. "It'll have to do."

She lifted her wand.

Battle was joined.

CHAPTER 47

If you have never seen a battle between a Wicked Witch and an Evil Sorceress, then you have likely missed a great and terrible sight. For while a battle between a Purple Djinn and a Diabolical Mentalist will consist of two people clutching their temples and glaring at each other, and the fight between a Haggischarmer and a Cursed Beastlord will be too gruesome to bear, a Witch and a Sorceress is the sort of battle that people make up songs about.

For Witches are tough and fierce and stubborn—and no Sorceress anywhere ever did anything quietly.

A bolt of ice shot from the end of Eudaimonia's wand and Molly flung herself flat. The bolt shot over her head and froze ten feet of flowers. Another Clockwork Bee dropped to the ground, to be investigated by an increasingly large group of its fellows.

There were not very many offensive spells in the Little Gray Book. Witches do not go in for zapping people with pure power. Instead they make use of the objects at hand.

When Molly had been hiding by the boiler, she spent every waking moment reading and rereading the book. Now she just had to put the spells to use.

She yanked up a handful of mint leaves, waved at the stones under Eudaimonia's feet and yelled *"Grappa Electroi Caseus Formatus!"* The mint leaves caught fire in her fingers and vanished into smoke.

The stones at the front of the tower went pale and wobbly. Eudaimonia fired off another shot, but missed as she started to sink.

"What—?" She yanked one foot free with a sucking sound.

A peculiar aroma drifted from the tower.

Molly got to her knees.

"Cheese?" said Eudaimonia. "You've turned stones into *cheese?*"

The minions, who were mostly hiding behind the door, snickered at this. Miss Handlebram leaned around Majordomo and called, "Good for you, Molly!"

Eudaimonia was now waist deep in a rather runny brie and Gordon had to pull her free. Molly took advantage of the distraction to set up another spell.

"Ready, Bugbane?" she whispered.

"Oh! Oh! Yes! Yes!" The little bat did a pirouette in midair in excitement. "Oh, I've been wanting to try this!"

Molly balanced one of his hairs on her fingertip.

"*Accreus Illusus Chiropteran Accomplicia Margle Fandango!*"

"HRRAWWWW!" cried Bugbane, and turned into a dragon.

He was . . . well, he was a very *small* dragon. The mass of a bat isn't even a thousandth of the mass of a donkey. His wings looked just the same and his scales were fuzzy and he had a wrinkly little snout.

But he took in a deep breath and shot out a little tongue of flame, like a cigarette lighter, and took off toward Eudaimonia.

She had just gotten one leg free of the cheese. Gordon was pulling like anything.

Bugbane let out a great huff and set the bodyguard's hair on fire.

"*Auuugh!*"

He dropped Eudaimonia back into the cheese. She cursed and struggled free, leaving her left shoe buried in the cheese.

Bugbane did another bombing run, breathing fire. The smell of burned hair and grilled cheese sandwiches drifted over the meadow.

Eudaimonia whipped her wand around and fired a shot at the dragon-bat. It clipped one of his wings and he went into a spiral.

332

"Bugbane!" Molly clutched her hands to her mouth.

He pulled up almost immediately. "I'm fine, I'm fine, I'm fine!"

The next shot got nowhere near him. For acrobatic flying, there is nothing in the world that can equal a bat. Bugbane danced across the sky while Eudaimonia fired bolt after bolt and frost splattered across the stones of the castle.

Molly reached into her pocket. There was another spell she should do now—another one—to use the time that Bugbane was buying her—but she was suddenly tired. Why was she so tired?

Another bolt of ice shot out of the tip of Eudaimonia's wand, narrowly missing Bugbane, and a wave of exhaustion hit Molly, radiating out from the center of her chest.

Hey!

Hey, wait a minute!

She's not—she can't be—

She is!

She's taking my energy! Just like she used to! She's fighting me with my own magic!

All those times I let her—she must be really good at stealing it by now!

"Hey!" yelled Molly. "Stop that! I didn't give you permission to do that!"

A startling emotion passed across the Sorceress's face. Molly had never seen it there before.

Guilt.

Any doubt that Eudaimonia knew exactly what she was doing vanished instantly.

"But Molly, *dear*," began Eudaimonia.

Bugbane did a last run at her. He was mostly breathing smoke now, and his scales were getting hairier. Eudaimonia swatted at him and Molly felt another tug from the center of her chest.

"Stop that!"

"You never used to mind," said Eudaimonia. "And I let you be my friend. It was a fair trade."

"You're not my friend!" said Molly. "You never were! And you can't use my magic anymore!"

She tried to picture the cord—and Eudaimonia zapped

334

at her again. Molly had to throw herself sideways and her concentration slipped.

I need a minute—I can't do this if I can't picture it— she's going to keep zapping me—

Molly saw a hundred dark specks suddenly diving toward the tower.

With a furious buzz, like a hive of hornets, the Clockwork Bees struck.

They had *not* enjoyed being frozen.

Gordon took the brunt of it, slapping the Bees away, his heavy leather jacket proof against their stings. Eudaimonia shrieked and waved her hands. A small localized hailstorm formed over the tower, battering at the Bees and driving them away.

Molly knew she couldn't waste the moment that the Bees had bought her. She closed her eyes, bit her lower lip, and concentrated fiercely.

She pictured the silver cord coming out of her chest— and sliced her hand down across it like a sword.

Her whole body felt as it had gone *twang.*

Eudaimonia staggered. The small hailstorm dissipated, and the Clockwork Bees were left crawling through the mint, looking confused.

"How dare you?" yelled Eudaimonia.

"It's my magic!" Molly yelled back.

Eudaimonia no longer looked like the most elegant

girl in Molly's hometown. Her hair was disheveled and as frizzy as Molly's, and her long robes were covered in cheese. Molly climbed to her feet, feeling suddenly energized.

I can do this. She's not that powerful. She's just been stealing my magic all along!

She'd been mad before. Now she was furious.

All this time—and all those times I tried to do magic and she laughed at me for not doing it right! I wasn't doing it wrong! She was taking my magic away and using it herself!

She wanted to make me fail!

Molly remembered all the times she'd done something right, and Eudaimonia had said "Oh, very good, dear Molly," in that tone that made you think it wasn't very good at all.

Every time! Every time—except when I summoned the shadow—

Now that was an interesting thought. Unfortunately, Molly didn't get very long to think about it.

The Sorceress leveled the wand.

Uh-oh—

Angus dove between Molly and the blast of ice. Molly gasped.

The Minotaur fell heavily, frost riming the edges of his horns . . . and then shook himself off, and stood up. He snorted.

"Angus!"

"M'okay," he rumbled. "Just—just—cold. Won't kill me."

"No," called Eudaimonia, "but *he* might! *Gordon!*"

Gordon stepped out of the tower. He was missing most of his hair and he had to fight his way through the plants choking the doorway, but he was still twice as big as Molly.

"I'll hold him," Angus told her. His big teeth were chattering. Molly cringed.

And now the other minions were coming forward. Molly wanted to yell at them to stay back, stay safe—but they clearly weren't going to listen.

"Is being your minions," growled Cook. "Is fighting for you."

"And for Castle Hangnail," said Serenissima. She stepped past Molly and grabbed Angus's shoulder. The last bits of ice steamed off him, and his teeth stopped chattering.

Eudaimonia flung another bolt of ice. Sir Edward froze in place. "My joints!" he said, sounding more annoyed than hurt. "Oooh, that tingles!"

Angus and Gordon circled each other. Eudaimonia tilted her head back, glanced at the sun again, and gave a loud, imperious whistle. A distant, furious clucking indicated that the basilisk had heard her.

337

"But—" said Molly.

"We'll deal with her minions," said Majordomo. "It's what we do. You stop *her*." And he gave her a little push toward the tower.

CHAPTER
48

Eudaimonia shot another bolt of ice and Serenissima slapped it out of the air. They were definitely getting weaker.

Gordon leaped for the Minotaur.

Now, you may be thinking that a fight between man and Minotaur would be very one-sided, and you'd be right—but not in the way you're thinking. Angus was huge and muscular and fierce, but he was also a farmer. He delivered calves and milked cows and threshed grain. He could lift an entire bale of hay with one hand, but he spent his time farming, not fighting.

Gordon was smaller in every way, but he had the look of a man who had spent his life fighting. When the two of them came to blows at last, Angus was the one who staggered back, looking surprised.

"I'll give him vinegar!" yelled Sir Edward. "Just let me get my joints unfrozen . . ."

Three things happened more or less simultaneously.

The basilisk arrived.

Gordon pulled a knife.

Molly realized why Eudaimonia kept looking at the sun.

The basilisk looked like an enormous scaly chicken, with dark goggles and a mouth full of sharp teeth. Like a chicken, it didn't fly very well. It wobbled, lost height, flapped furiously, gained a little more, and then tried to glide.

That didn't go well.

As it careened in for a landing, the shadow of its wings passed over Eudaimonia—and the Sorceress cringed back as if she'd been struck.

It's not the sun she's scared of . . . it's the shadows.

That's why she wanted to fight at high noon!

She's afraid of the shadows!

Someone must have told her about Freddy and my shadow!

A shadow at noon is a small puddle of darkness. But a shadow at seven thirty in the morning streams off to the west. The tower's shadow was a long black bar and Molly's own shadow was twelve feet tall and capering at her heels.

She never could do the shadow spell, but she knows I can. She only had me try it because she thought I'd fail at it. And I thought it was a stupid little spell and just for dancing— but Freddy Wisteria didn't think so.

And I have to do something.

Gordon charged for Angus, slashing with the knife. It might have gone very badly for the Minotaur, except that Pins was underfoot and jabbed him in the ankle with a sewing needle. The bodyguard howled, his charge interrupted, and hopped on one foot.

The basilisk aimed a kick at Majordomo, hissing and clucking, and the old minion ducked out of the way. Molly caught a glimpse of Miss Handlebram approach-

ing it from behind, carrying her hat and a determined expression.

Eudaimonia lifted her wand again.

Molly squeezed her eyes shut and recited:

"Shanks and shadows—

up and down—

inner and outer *and magic unbound!*"

Her shadow yawned and stood up.

It was very tall in the stretching morning light. It
flexed its long hands and slipped into the tower's shadow,
and then it was taller yet.

Molly's chest fizzed again.

If I looked for the silver cord now, what would I see?
Would it be going to the shadow?

Eudaimonia took a step back. The expression on her
face was suddenly much less confident and a lot more
scared.

"You can't have remembered that spell! You weren't
supposed to be able to do it! It's too dangerous!"

"You never told me it was dangerous," said Molly.
"You just wanted to see me fail."

The shadow slithered past Molly's feet. Her heart was
hammering in her chest.

I have to command it. I have to tell it what to do.

"Break her wand," croaked Molly.

The shadow nodded.

It went up the side of the tower as slow and sinuous as a snake. Eudaimonia took a step back, turned as if to run—and realized that the *inside* of the tower lay completely in shadow.

She fired three bolts of ice into the shadow in rapid succession. They didn't pass through. They didn't freeze. They just vanished, as if swallowed up by nothing.

The shadow arched itself up like a cobra and reached out its hands.

Eudaimonia's face was white as ice, white as china, white as bone. Terror made her look young, as young as Molly, a teenage girl and barely a Sorceress at all.

"No!" cried Eudaimonia. "No! *Molly, don't let it get me!*"

The shadow's impossibly long fingers closed over the wand, and the shadow snapped it in two.

There was a shattering, clattering noise, like dropped crockery, and the wand blew up. Cold air exploded outward, and there was a brief, unseasonable snow flurry.

The shadow chuckled.

Everyone immediately clapped their hands over their ears. The basilisk was lying on the ground, with Miss Handlebram's hat over its eyes and Miss Handlebram herself sitting on its neck, but it moaned and tried to fit its entire body under the hat.

"That's enough," said Molly. "You're done. Go home."

The shadow picked Eudaimonia up in long tongues of darkness and slithered down the wall of the tower. Eudaimonia began to cry.

"Go *home,*" said Molly. Her voice was shaking terribly. "The spell's over. Go."

The shadow started to fade.

So did Eudaimonia.

It was really quite horrible. Molly could see right through the older girl, as if she were made of gauze. The tower was stark and visible behind her.

"It's taking me with it!" shrieked the Sorceress. "Molly! Stop it! I'm sorry I ever tried to take your castle—I'm sorry I wasn't a good friend—please, don't let it take me!"

"Stop!" yelled Molly. "Stop, shadow! You can't take her along."

The shadow had no face, but Molly had a sudden feeling that she had its attention.

What had the Little Gray Book said about shadows? There had been a spell, hadn't there? She could see the words of the Little Gray Book as if it was open before her.

A spell to feed the hunger of shadows.

Use only in the direst emergencies.

Molly took a deep breath. Her chest ached as if she'd been kicked in the heart.

She could let the shadow take Eudaimonia. Castle Hangnail would be hers, really and truly, and no one would say otherwise.

They hadn't *really* been friends.

Eudaimonia twisted in the shadow's clutches and wept silently.

It doesn't matter. I wouldn't let a shadow eat my worst enemy. That's . . . worse than Wicked.

That's wrong.

Molly took a pin out of her hat and jabbed her forefinger with it.

It was a very simple spell. The simplest spells are often the most powerful.

She held out her hand. A single drop of blood fell onto the mint leaves.

"Here," she said. "For you."

The shadow crept toward her. It didn't look like a person now, but like some dark liquid pouring along the ground. The tower's shadow bent in her direction, against the light. The shadows of the minions crawled across the grass.

Let it work, let it work, let this be enough to satisfy it—I don't know what I'll do if it's not enough—I don't think it'll be content to just dance now, it's gotten so big . . .

Her shadow reached the drop of blood.

"Now go," said Molly. "And leave Eudaimonia here."

There was a vast roaring in her ears. Her heart pounded, skipping beats, as if she were asking too much of it. She thought perhaps she might die, or at least faint, if the shadow didn't leave soon.

It reared up. For a moment, in Molly's eyes, it blotted out the sun.

She stared through it, into the Kingdom of Shadows, and learned what some Witches live and die without learning—that every shadow everywhere is a portal to that dark kingdom. That the Kingdom of Shadows is vast and terrible and hungry, and yet there is an awful beauty to it, the kind of beauty that can stop a heart.

Rivers of ink flowed past obsidian stones. Great black mountains stretched toward the black sky, backlit by a dark, un-shining sun.

If I step forward, just one step, I'll be inside it.

I could learn things. I could be more powerful than any Wicked Witch has ever been. I could be ten times as powerful as Eudaimonia.

From the other side, her shadow beckoned. In the light of the shadow sun, it was no longer just a blot—it was her, down to the last detail, a shadow-Molly the color of jet.

I could do anything. No one could ever make me stay

home or tell me not to do magic. I'd never have to share a room with somebody or go to school or anything.

It wouldn't matter what anybody thought of me.

She leaned forward. The shadow-Molly stretched out a hand.

The other Molly's eyes were dark and black and deep . . .

Something streaked across her field of vision—something small and silvery bright, wildly out of place against the shadow. Molly's eyes followed it, involuntarily, and her gaze broke from her shadow-twin.

She dragged her eyes away, turned her head—and saw her minions. Saw Cook, who was standing over the fallen Gordon, holding a frying pan. Saw Angus and Serenissima and Pins. Saw Majordomo, who was helping Miss Handlebram hold down the basilisk, and Edward—who had just thrown the Imperial Squid and broken the gaze of her shadow.

Saw her friends, who loved her, and who wanted her to stay.

She looked back at the shadow-Molly and almost, almost laughed—because she'd spent her whole life being the bad twin, and here was a twin of her own, dark and terrible as the shadow-world itself.

No. I'm the bad twin. And I'm just bad enough to do it right—but I'm not like that.

And I don't want to be.

I will never cast this spell again.

She pulled back, and away from the Kingdom of Shadow.

The shadow vanished.

Eudaimonia let out a sob of gratitude and Molly fainted.

CHAPTER 49

The Lugnasadh party was, everyone agreed, the finest that Castle Hangnail had ever held.

The halls were hung with streamers sewn by Pins, and the table in the dining hall groaned with the weight of canapés and baklava and bowls of strawberries with whipped cream and little squares of fudge and pastries stuffed with sweet and savory fillings. There was even a chocolate fountain that sprayed molten chocolate high in the air. (Bugbane could not resist flying through it, and was now hanging in the corner licking chocolate off his wings.)

A huge bowl of honeyed punch glistened under the lights. The Clockwork Bees had worked around the clock making honey for the occasion. The frozen Bees had all recovered once they were thawed out in warm water and the rosinweed honey was the finest that they had ever produced.

"These are lovely deviled eggs," said Postmistress Jane. "So large!"

"They're basilisk eggs," said Majordomo. "Angus said

the poor creature just needed a flock of its own, so Cook put it in the henhouse. It's never been happier."

All the village had come up for the party. Harry Rumplethorn the plumber looked uncomfortable in his suit, but it did cover all the relevant parts of him.

His wife beamed at him, and his two apprentices took turns flirting with Serenissima. Farmer Berkeley and Angus were discussing the finer points of modern threshing machines and the waitress from the café was swooning over Cook's famous shortbread scones.

Postmistress Jane had even brought two very small black kittens up with her. "Not a white hair on them," she said stoutly. "I knew they must be for you." They were curled up in a basket under the refreshment table, with Edward standing guard over them. "Will you look at their little toes?" he whispered to passersby. "And their little whiskers?"

Majordomo saw Molly in conversation with Stonebreaker the mole and made his way toward them. The moles had their very own tray of hors d'oeuvres, including cookies in the shape of earthworms. Their little gray shapes trundled between the taller human guests.

The white mole smiled at Majordomo's approach and bowed his head. "Witch and minion," he said. "Leave you to talk." He patted Molly's boot and went off for another canapé.

Molly smiled as she looked after him, but her smile was rather sad.

"I've had a letter from Andrew," said Majordomo. "The second bodyguard. He's out of the hospital, and we've all been invited to the wedding."

Andrew had slept through the battle, and indeed, clear through until the next day. What with one thing and another, everyone had quite forgotten about him, until Serenissima had tripped over him while cleaning the hallway. He'd let out a yell, jumped up, and chased her.

Unfortunately for him, he chased her into the room with the hole in the floor. Majordomo never had gotten around to putting up a warning note, and Andrew had fallen through the carpet that was over the tarp that was over the hole that was over nine feet of empty air. Andrew had broken his leg and they'd had to take him down to the village and send him off to the hospital. While there, he had fallen madly in love with his nurse and become quite a reformed character. The same could not be said of Gordon, who was recovering from his frying-pan-related injuries in the county jail.

"That's nice," said Molly. She sighed. "I won't be here for the wedding, you know. My parents are going to be here tomorrow to pick me up."

"I know." Majordomo took her hand and squeezed. "I've got some ideas."

She tried to dredge up a smile. He could see that she was worried.

"I'll come back next summer," she said. "Will that be enough for the Board?"

"It would be," he said. "But it might not yet come to that. As for the Board . . . well, you could ask him." He nodded his head toward the foot of the table.

The representative from the Board stood there, holding a glass of punch.

After all their fears, all the Tasks, all the nerves, Molly had half expected the man from the Board to be nine feet tall and breathe fire.

Instead, he was a little rabbity fellow, not all that much taller than Molly, with thick glasses and a hairline that had not so much *receded* as gone into headlong flight.

His expression, however, was fierce.

"*Miss Utterback,*" said the representative of the Board. "I must have a word with you at once!"

Molly gulped.

"*Do you know how old this is?!*"

"I'll be thirteen in three months!" said Molly. "And I read at a tenth-grade level!"

They stared at each other.

"Wait—" said Molly, finally realizing what he had said. "*This?* Not me?"

"This!" he said, and pointed dramatically at—

—the Complicated Metal Thing.

They had run out of vases early on in the party, and the Thing had been pressed into service as a bouquet holder. A sprig of rosinweed stuck out at a jaunty angle.

"Do you know what it is?" asked Molly cautiously.

"Of course! I have three! Lesser ones, to be sure, only good for voles and perhaps very small bats—one is for walnuts, and of course you can imagine how much use *that* is—"

"Oh, naturally," said Molly, who hadn't the faintest idea what he was talking about.

"But to see one so old, and in such perfect condition . . ." The representative of the Board paused. "Why are there flowers in it? Does it work on flowers?"

"Like a charm," said Molly firmly.

"Amazing! And do they bite afterward? The walnuts try, poor devils, but of course they haven't the teeth for it . . ."

"We're still working out all the details," said Molly. "It's at the top of my list for research, but what with completing the Tasks, it's been difficult to find the time."

She paused. The representative gazed at the Thing and waved a hand vaguely when she mentioned the Tasks. "Yes, yes . . . of course . . . quite right . . ."

"In fact, if you have any books you can suggest that might give us a clue to this *particular* one, Majordomo would be happy to compile a list—I'd like to make sure we don't overlook anything."

"Certainly!" said the representative. "There's the definitive monograph by Sonney the Alchemist, but of course you have that already—"

Molly tried to look like someone who was *of course* already in possession of a definitive monograph.

"I'm afraid it wouldn't be appropriate to demonstrate in front of the other guests," she said cautiously.

"Oh, certainly not! There are children present!"

Molly paused. "Err . . . "

"Present company excluded, of course," said the representative. "Obviously you're a Wicked Witch, so that's a different matter. Oh dear, wait, we haven't done the thing yet, have we?" He began patting his pockets.

"The thing?" said Molly, who was now cautiously optimistic but would have preferred a specific noun.

"The thing! The thing! Oh dear, where did I put it . . ."

Majordomo appeared at his left elbow with an envelope and said, "Sir, I believe you have left this in your jacket."

"*There* it is," said the Board representative happily. He took the envelope. "Had a few doubts," he confessed, opening it up. "Power's no indication that you know how to run a castle. There are terribly powerful magic folk out there that I wouldn't wish on my worst enemy. But you've done the Tasks and your minions speak highly of you." His gaze strayed to the Complicated Metal Thing again. "And of course, if you've got one of those working . . ."

Majordomo looked at Molly, who shook her head imperceptibly and shrugged.

"Ah, there we are." The representative adjusted his glasses. "A few questions, Miss Utterback—purely a formality, you understand."

"Sure," said Molly. Majordomo gave her an encouraging smile.

"Do you promise to protect and defend Castle Hangnail and those within it, up to and possibly including with your last dying breath, assuming you're not a Vampire or otherwise undead?"

"No. Err . . . yes? I mean, yes, I will. No, I'm not undead."

"Do you promise to cherish the minions who serve you?" He looked over his glasses. "They don't have to serve you, you know. They can always leave. Most of them won't, because it looks bad if a minion leaves, but that means that it's twice as important for the Master to make sure they don't *want* to leave."

"I understand," said Molly. "I promise." Her gaze slid to Majordomo again. The old minion looked solemn.

"You understand that the Castle Hangnail is given to you, not as property you own, but as a sacred trust to protect and pass down to the next generation of magicians?" He paused, and added, "Well, in your case, probably the generation after that. Which is all advantage, believe me—turnover in castles is a dreadful amount of paperwork."

"I do," said Molly, thinking briefly of Freddy Wisteria and people who wouldn't understand that a place can own *you* far more than you own it.

"Wonderful! Now, if you'll sign here, my dear, and here . . . and here . . . and initial here . . ."

He laid a complicated document down on the table. Majordomo hurried to shift a plate of baklava.

Molly signed the paper with a flourish. (She was a bit relieved to see that it read "Ms. Utterback, Wicked Witch" with no mention of first names. She still didn't know if the Board thought she was named Eudaimonia, and it was nice to see that it wouldn't be an issue.)

"There we are, then," said the representative. He cleared his throat and clapped his hands loudly. "Ladies and gentlemen—esteemed minions—if I may have your attention please?"

The room quieted and everyone looked over at Molly

and the man from the Board. Molly concentrated on standing up very straight and trying not to look scared.

"By the authority vested in me as a representative of the Board of Magic, I hereby declare Miss Utterback the Master of Castle Hangnail, Wicked Witch in Residence!"

He began to applaud. Everyone else joined in. Bugbane did acrobatic loops and swoops overhead, cheering in a tiny, high-pitched voice.

Molly's throat was tight. She could feel the tips of her ears getting hot.

Majordomo reached out and took her hand. "You did it," he whispered.

"*We* did it," said Molly.

The little man from the Board dusted his hands off. "Well, that's that, then. Good job." He went back to gazing raptly at the Complicated Metal Thing.

"If you leave your address, we'd be happy to send you any information we turn up on this particular device, if you like," said Molly.

The representative babbled a few words that seemed to indicate that he would like this very much.

"Nicely done," whispered Majordomo, drawing her aside. "I imagine he'll give us quite a glowing review. Not that it matters now, but it never hurts to be on good terms with the Board."

"The Thing gives walnuts teeth!" Molly whispered back. "We've got to figure out what it does!"

"I'll order the definitive monograph tomorrow."

Molly sighed, deflated. She wouldn't be around tomorrow to read it.

Majordomo gripped her shoulder briefly. "It'll be okay."

Molly laughed softly. "Hey, you're my minion. Aren't I supposed to be cheering you up?"

Majordomo smiled. "Sometimes you cheer up the Master, sometimes the Master cheers you up. Sometimes the Master hooks you to a lightning rod. It's a complicated job, minioning."

"I'm fresh out of lightning rods," said Molly.

"I never really enjoyed that part of the job anyway."

Sir Edward clomped over to them. His freshly oiled armor gleamed, and the Imperial Squid around his neck glinted in the light. "You're supposed to be mingling!" he said. "The kittens are asleep. Miss Handlebram was just looking for you."

Majordomo cleared his throat and looked at Edward meaningfully.

"Oh! Yes! Right!" He patted his breast plate. "Ah . . . where did I put that . . ."

The minions drifted toward them. Serenissima left a damp silvery path. Angus and Cook loomed up on either side of her.

"We got you a present," said Majordomo.

"You didn't have to get me anything," said Molly. "I mean, you put together this whole party—"

And I'm leaving tomorrow! she cried out internally. *Don't make it harder than it is!*

"Nevertheless," said Majordomo, "I will not have it be said that the minions of Castle Hangnail did not treat your investiture as Master with proper ceremony!" He sniffed.

"It was here a moment ago . . ." muttered Edward. "I know it was—oh, there it is!" He pulled off one of his gauntlets and pulled a tightly rolled scroll out of it. He offered it to Molly with a flourish.

The scroll was sealed in dark bronze wax, which Molly recognized as coming from the Clockwork Hive. There was a lovely black ribbon embroidered with a tiny silver bat. Molly opened the scroll, holding her breath.

In a clear, strong hand, at the top, it read "An Infallible Spell for the Temporary Turning of Humans into Earwigs."

Molly sucked in her breath.

"You're always muttering about it," said Pins, grinning up at her. "We had to scour the place for it. The author was named Quentin, so Cook had dumped it in the dungeon, but Serenissima saw it when she was cleaning and Angus copied it out for us—"

"Oh—oh, everybody!" Molly didn't know who to hug

first. She threw her arms around Serenissima and Angus. Pins put an arm around her knee. "Cook—Majordomo—" She had to wipe away a tear. "You're the best minions anybody ever had."

"It was Edward's idea," said Majordomo. "Now go on, Miss Handlebram's waiting."

Molly stood on her tiptoes and kissed Edward's metal cheek. "Thanks, Edward." She clomped off toward Miss Handlebram, her boots thudding on the floor.

"Well!" said Edward, gratified. "The old Vampire Lord never did *that!*"

· Miss Handlebram was in conversation with Postmistress Jane. "Molly, my dear! I was just telling Jane how you dealt with that awful young Sorceress who was here."

Molly gave an embarrassed cough. "Oh . . . well . . . it was nothing . . ." She dipped up a cup of punch, and flicked a droplet into the goldfish bowl. The goldfish waved a fin. Other than a dreadful cold, she had come through her adventure just fine, and Pins had knitted her a tiny party dress for the occasion.

"Nothing!" Miss Handlebram snorted. "She froze me in a block of ice for two days! I shan't forget that in a hurry!"

"You're sure she won't come back?" asked Jane.

"Positive," said Molly. "All her spells broke and her mother came and got her. She's gone to a reform school for incorrigible girls."

"Well, I should hope so," said Miss Handlebram. "Nasty girl. Just goes to show that being powerful's not worth much if you haven't got heart to go with it."

"A magical battle, right in our own town," said Jane. "And we all missed it!"

"You're happier having missed it," said Miss Handlebram. "She was a nasty piece of work. Is it a good reform school, Molly?"

Molly shrugged. From her point of view, reform school was never very good. "It's supposed to have classes on ethics for magical people. I guess that's good?"

It couldn't hurt Eudaimonia to have some classes on ethics. I guess she'll be happier being away from home, anyway. Although wearing a school uniform will drive her crazy . . .

She stared into her punch. If her parents found out that Castle Hangnail wasn't a summer camp, she'd probably be in the reform school alongside Eudaimonia.

What were they going to say?

Would they even notice?

She rubbed her thumb over the side of her glass, making a track in the condensation on the side. In fact, there was a great deal more condensation than usual, which meant—

"Hi, Serenissima," she said, turning around.

The steam spirit smiled at her and squeezed her shoulder. "Cheer up!" she said. "This is *your* party." And then

361

she leaned down and whispered, in an echo of Major-domo, "It *will* work out."

She excused herself, and took Postmistress Jane off to talk to the Widow Carrboro.

Miss Handlebram caught Molly's eye. "Worried, my dear?"

"I might have to leave tomorrow," said Molly. "Err. I *will* have to leave tomorrow. My parents are coming to get me. They . . ." She took a deep breath. "They think I've been at summer camp."

To her surprise, Miss Handlebram laughed out loud. "Camp? Oh, Molly!"

Molly didn't think it was all that funny.

"How novel," said Miss Handlebram. "So they think you've been—oh, making lanyards and singing around a campfire, and instead you've been saving a castle and running off Evil real-estate developers and defeating Evil Sorceresses? Oh my . . ."

One corner of Molly's mouth crooked up. "Well . . . I guess . . ."

Miss Handlebram grinned down at her. "You just leave everything to me and Majordomo."

And the last thing Molly saw, as Miss Handlebram swept away to find the chief minion, was that extraordinary grin.

CHAPTER 50

The car chugged up the long approach to Castle Hangnail with a maximum amount of complaint. It was a road better suited to mountain goats than to elderly family sedans, particularly when the trunk and the luggage rack were already overflowing with suitcases. The car sounded as if it were about to expire.

Draped across the front of the castle was an enormous, hastily sewn banner that read "Camp Hangnail Welcomes Parents." Pins had been up half the night with it, and it looked very good, if you ignored the fact that the letters were mostly made out of old dishtowels.

The car ground to a halt. Doors slammed. Molly stood on tiptoe, looking out the window.

"That's them," she said gloomily. Not that there had ever been any doubt.

Molly's mother had sensible hair and sensible shoes. Molly's father had round glasses and a vague, cheerful expression.

CAMP WELCOMES

Molly's twin sister . . . well . . .

"Hecate's ghost!" said Majordomo. "She *is* the good twin, isn't she?"

"That's Sarah," said Molly.

Sarah was exactly the same height as Molly and had exactly the same slightly frizzy hair, but she wore it in a ponytail with a pink scrunchie. Her shirt had a comical kitten on it and her shoes were covered in sequins. Her expression was one of saintly good temper, and Majordomo wondered how anyone lived with her for more than five minutes without going barking mad.

Majordomo waited until they were a few feet from the door and then threw it open. "Hello!" he said heartily. "You must be Molly's family!"

(He had practiced saying this in the mirror for over an hour. Heartiness was not in his nature.)

"Oh, you poor man," said Sarah. "Does it hurt much?"

"Does what hurt?" asked Majordomo.

"Err—you've got all those stitches—"

HANGNAIL PARENTS

"Oh!" said Majordomo. "Yes. Um. Accident. With a . . . um . . . lanyard. Looks worse than it is. All part of running a summer camp, you understand."

He extended his hand, and Molly's father shook it, then her mother. They looked around the castle.

"Goodness," said Molly's mother. "You've . . . err . . . got a lot of space here . . ."

"We need it," said Miss Handlebram, sailing into view.

She was dressed in a neat gray suit, with an old-fashioned wax flower pinned to the lapel. The creases in her pants legs were sharp enough to slice through cheese. She looked like an elderly businesswoman.

"It's not just the camp, although of course that takes a lot of room," Miss Handlebram continued. "It's the facilities for the school." She smiled warmly at Molly's parents. "And I am so glad that all the other campers have left, for it gives me a chance to speak with you personally without distraction."

365

"Speak with us?" asked Molly's father. "She hasn't done anything bad, has she?"

Miss Handlebram laughed. "Not at all! In fact—Molly, my dear, are you ready?"

Molly had been waiting for her cue. She hurried down the intact staircase. (The other staircase had several saw-horses on either side of the gap, and a large sign that said "Renovations in Progress—Please Forgive Our Dust.")

"Mom! Dad!"

She ran down the stairs, jumped the last few, and flew toward her parents. She hadn't realized how much she missed them. Even though she wished, more than anything, that she could stay at Castle Hangnail—well, it was her *mom and dad.*

Unfortunately Sarah stepped in her way and flung her arms around Molly's neck. "Oh, Molly! Sister! I missed you so!"

"Ugh," said Molly, prying at her sister's arms. "Get off."

"It felt like forever!"

"I was at *camp*," said Molly, "not *dead.*"

"Part of me felt dead without you!" declaimed Sarah.

"That's enough . . ." said Molly's mother. Molly managed to wriggle free, while Sarah blinked back tears of joy and Majordomo tried not to gag.

"Hey, squirt!" Molly's dad picked her up, said "Oof!" and set her back down, the way he always had since she was five years old. Her Mom held her at arm's length and said, "Molly! Goodness! You look wonderful—and that *coat!*"

"Sewing is one of the many things we teach here at Castle Hangnail," said Miss Handlebram. "We have a truly excellent instructor, and Molly was kind enough to volunteer as a practice model."

"It's very dark," said Sarah dubiously.

"Now, then," said Miss Handelbram. "If you would be so kind as to step into my office . . . ?"

The office she stepped into was actually the old armory. It was the only room on the ground floor that could be made presentable in a hurry. There were picture frames hung up over arrow slits in the wall, and a large area rug covered places where old swords had rusted to the floor.

Angus had dragged an old desk in and they had leveled it hurriedly with an old brick. While Molly had been sleeping, the minions had been steaming chairs and mending upholstery, and there were very convincing stacks of papers scattered about the desk.

"If you'll have a seat, Mr. and Mrs. Utterback?"

Her parents sat. Molly and Sarah engaged in that time-honored tradition of sisters everywhere, nudging each other in the ribs and then looking immediately innocent whenever anybody looked in their direction. (Good twin or not, some things are universal.)

"Now then." Miss Handlebram looked over her glasses at them. "I'm sure you don't need me to tell you that your daughter Molly is *extremely* bright for her age."

"Oh, well . . ." began her father.

"We're aware," said her mother firmly.

Miss Handlebram nodded. "Very bright. In the ninety-ninth percentile, in fact."

(Phrases like "ninety-ninth percentile," as Witches and advertising executives know, sound very impressive and don't have to mean anything at all.)

"That high?" asked Molly's father.

"Perhaps higher." Miss Handlebram folded her hands together. "She is, I can honestly say, one of the brightest students to ever attend our camp, and I would like to extend an offer to her to attend our boarding school."

"Boarding school?" asked Molly's mother, raising her eyebrows.

"Indeed," said Miss Handlebram. "Castle Hangnail is not merely a summer camp, you understand—dear me, no! We also offer a very exclusive boarding school for young ladies, particularly those who have displayed an . . . ah . . . magical disposition."

Molly held her breath. She knew perfectly well that her mother didn't really approve of magic, and Miss Handlebram would have to proceed carefully.

"So often," said her neighbor, "*so* often—as you undoubtedly know—young women with magic in their blood go untrained and it comes out in the most unfortunate ways." She waved a hand, as if dispelling an unpleasant smell. "Here at Castle Hangnail, we believe in channeling that energy into constructive and socially acceptable ways. Otherwise—well, I'm sure we all know the stories, don't we?"

Molly didn't know the stories. Apparently her parents did, however, for they both murmured agreement.

"This sounds expensive . . ." her father began.

"Absolutely," said Miss Handlebram. "It is. We are very choosy about our students."

Molly winced. Sarah elbowed her in the ribs again and Molly scowled.

"Girls . . ." muttered her mother.

Molly moved a few inches away and tried to look innocent.

"Girls will be girls, yes? Although I believe that's quite enough, Molly."

"Yes, Miss Handlebram," said Molly dutifully, and was rewarded with a twinkle from Miss Handlebram's eye. Molly's mother looked impressed.

"As we were saying," the gardener continued, "this is quite an expensive school." And she named a figure that made her father turn gray and which would have fixed the boiler several times over.

"Per year," she added.

"Well—that's—very flattering, of course, but I'm afraid—" stammered Molly's father, while Molly gaped at Miss Handlebram.

"*However,*" Miss Handlebram continued, "as I was saying, Molly is extremely bright. And I do have some discretion in these cases, as Headmistress.

"We can, I believe, offer Molly a full scholarship against the school fees. Perhaps with a small stipend to cover incidentals, though I shall have to consult with the Board. Majordomo!"

Majordomo shuffled in, laid some papers on the desk, and winked at Molly.

"Here are our credentials," said Miss Handlebram, handing the papers to Molly's parents. "My contact information, should you have any questions. As you can see on page three, one hundred percent of our students place in institutions of higher learning, and over seventy percent go on to extremely exclusive colleges."

The murmurs this time were surprised and appreciative. Molly craned her neck over her dad's shoulder and got a look at the papers. They had elegant letterhead and did not look at all as if Majordomo had been up until the small hours of the morning typing them.

"At any rate," said Miss Handlebram, rising from her chair, "I hope that you will think about it. We very much enjoy having Molly here and we would like to see her return in the fall. If money is an object—well, it shall *not* be an object, I'll see to that."

Molly's parents rose too, shaking hands with Miss Handlebram. They had thoughtful looks on their faces.

Molly had already said her good-byes to most of the minions. As they went to the door, though, she threw her arms around Majordomo and whispered, "I'll come back! I swear!"

"Yes, Master," said Majordomo, and smiled.

Miss Handlebram gave her a brisk embrace. "Very good, Molly. Now, behave well, remember all that we have taught you about deportment, and we shall hope to see you in the fall. Mr. and Mrs. Utterback, if you have any questions at all, please contact me at once. We are all very impressed with Molly's potential, and hope to see her in the future." She squeezed Molly's hand.

"Yes, Headmistress," said Molly demurely. "I hope to see you again." And she dropped a very small curtsy.

Sarah gaped at her. Molly's mother lifted an eyebrow, surprised and approving.

They got into the car. "Mom," said Molly as she buckled her seat belt, "can I come back to boarding school? I'd really like to go. They're really nice." She thought for a minute about the things that her mother approved of, then added, "Strict, though. You have to make your bed *every* morning."

"We'll talk," said her mother firmly.

"There's no doing magic outside of class, though," added Molly. "That's kind of annoying. But they say it's important."

"We'll talk," said her mother again, but Molly thought her tone of voice boded very well indeed.

"A full scholarship . . ." muttered her father, almost to himself. "Wouldn't that be a thing?"

Molly watched Castle Hangnail shrink in the distance. She waved until the towers were out of sight, then slumped back in her seat.

The car chugged down the long road, toward Molly's house.

But not home, thought Molly fiercely. Home was behind her. And sometime very soon, with a little luck, she'd be coming back.

Bugbane moved against her neck and poked his face out under her ear.

"Ew!" said Sarah, "Gross! What's that in your hair? It looks almost like a bat . . ."

"Don't be silly," said Molly, pushing Bugbane back into her hair. "A bat in your hair? That'd be *Wicked* . . ."

ackNOWLeðgmeNts

I sat down at the Cafe Diem coffee shop one day and hammered out the first thousand words of this story, so the staff there is probably at least partly to blame. But it wouldn't have gone much farther if my agent, Helen Breitwieser, hadn't said "YES!" and then my editor, Kate Harrison said "YES!" I owe them a great debt of gratitude for shepherding Molly along, and to my art director, Jenny Kelly, who was patient when I announced my desire, somewhere around page thirty-five, to never draw humans again and to write all future books about talking hamsters.

Thanks go also to my husband, Kevin, who is always patient and always reads the first draft to reassure me that it will not bring shame to my ancestors, to all my awesome blog readers who make encouraging noises whenever I have decided to quit writing and become a medical test subject, and to my cats, because they have not yet eaten me in my sleep.

Finally, to the late, great Eva Ibbotson, who wrote children's books that made me want to try writing them too, and who I still kinda want to be when I grow up.

aBOUT THE aUTHOR

Ursula Vernon (www.ursulavernon.com) is the creator of the books in the popular Dragonbreath series, which have been Indie Next Picks, *Kirkus* Best Books of the year, and received an IRA/CBC Choice Award. She has also won a Hugo award for her comic *Digger*. Ursula has always had a great fondness for moles and bats. She lives in a castle (okay, maybe it's more like a house) with her husband in Pittsboro, North Carolina.